CARNAL RISK

A Club Altura Romance Novel

Kym Grosso

Copyright © 2015 by Kym Grosso
All rights reserved. No part of this publication may be reproduced, distributed, or transmitted in any form or by any means, including photocopying, recording, or other electronic or mechanical methods, without the prior written permission of the publisher, except in the case of brief quotations embodied in critical reviews and certain other noncommercial uses permitted by copyright law.

MT Carvin Publishing, LLC
West Chester, Pennsylvania

Editor: Julie Roberts
Formatting: Polgarus Studio
Cover Design: LM Creations
Cover Model: Stuart Reardon
Photographer: Peda Rochelle

DISCLAIMER

This book is a work of fiction. The names, characters, locations and events portrayed in this book are a work of fiction or are used fictitiously. Any similarity to actual events, locales, or real persons, living or dead, is coincidental and not intended by the author.

NOTICE

This is an adult erotic paranormal romance book with love scenes and mature situations. It is only intended for adult readers over the age of 18.

ACKNOWLEDGMENTS

My books aren't released without the assistance of many wonderful people, and I'm very grateful to everyone who helped me:

~My husband, Keith, for encouraging me to write and supporting me in everything I do.

~Julie Roberts, editor, who spent hours reading, editing and proofreading Carnal Risk. You've done so much to help and encourage me over the past two years. As with every book, I could not have done this without you!

~My alpha readers, Maria and Rochelle, who give me such important feedback and insight during the editing process. You both are awesome!

~My dedicated beta readers, Brandy, Elena, Gayle, Denise, Janet, Jessica, Jerri, Julie, Kelly, Leah, Laurie, Stephanie and Rose for beta reading. I really appreciate all the valuable feedback you provide.

~LM Creations, cover artist, for designing Carnal Risk's sexy cover.

~Stuart Reardon, cover model, for the amazing images on Carnal Risk's cover.

~Love N. Books, for image acquisition.

~Peda Rochelle, for image photography.

~Polgarus Studio, Jason, for formatting Carnal Risk. You do terrific work, presenting my books so they look their best digitally and in print.

~Nicole, Indie Sage PR, for helping me with promotion and supporting my books.

~Denise and Jennifer, for subject matter expertise.

~Gayle, my admin, who is one of my biggest supporters and helps to run my street team. I'm so thankful for all of your help!

~My awesome street team, for helping spread the word about the Immortals of New Orleans series and my new romance series, Club Altura. I appreciate your support more than you could know! You guys are the best. You rock!

Chapter One

Plummeting eighteen thousand feet brought the same rush it always did. Death was ever close, yet Garrett had never felt more alive. The deafening roar of the air cut into his mind. Not a cell of his body was left untouched by the adrenaline that pumped through his veins. Every single jump brought forth the clarity of not only his mortality, but his vitality.

As he passed through the clouds, Garrett spread his arms wide and pointed to his friend, Evan, who gave him a thumbs up. He glanced to his altimeter. *Twenty more seconds.* He let out a celebratory scream, exhilaration slamming through his limbs. *Ten seconds.* Spiraling recklessly through the air, the best part of the dive was coming to an end. *Five seconds.* Garrett smiled up at Evan, still holding out for one last moment. *One second.* He reached for the pull and with a pop, Garrett's chute exploded. The harness jerked him as the canvas ballooned open into the sky. Closing his eyes, he took a deep breath, descending like a feather from the sky. As he opened them, the breathtaking horizon of the beach came into view.

As he drifted through the wind, his heart seized as he glanced down to the field. A turbulent form whizzed past him through the air, and Garrett swore, his heart pounding as he watched his best friend plummet to his death. The chances of survival were infinitesimal. Hundreds of successful jumps and he'd never witnessed a fatal dive. He gasped for breath, aware that barring a miracle, Evan had already died.

Garrett's mind stormed with anger and grief. Like he'd been impaled by a knife, the reality of the accident speared through his chest. He was helpless, his descent stretching for what seemed like hours, and when his friend's body came into view, he fought the nausea. Tears came to his eyes as a gut-wrenching sob tore through his throat. *Evan, my friend. He's gone.* He couldn't comprehend how this could have happened, yet as grim faces below came into focus, he knew it could not be undone.

For years they had cheated death, victorious in achieving the ultimate high. Today, however, Garrett's world would come crashing down around him. As his feet touched the earth, he ran to embrace Evan. Tragedy rained down upon them and he cried up into the sky, devastated that his friend was forever gone.

Chapter Two

Garrett stared into the bottom of his scotch, its burn still fresh on his lips. Darkness crept into his soul, the grief consuming him. Fear wasn't a word in his vocabulary, yet he couldn't scrub the sight of his friend's lifeless body from his mind. *Unlucky.* That's what first responders had called it. Words like 'accident' and 'casualty' were tossed about, but he refused to accept their initial findings. Garrett had pressed the prosecutor's office for a special investigation, suspecting foul play.

As far as he was concerned, there was no such thing as luck. Strategy? Yes. Hard work? Most definitely. Accidents happened to other people, not Evan. Every single jump, he'd been meticulous when checking his rig. Some might even go so far as to call him obsessive compulsive, but Garrett knew it was what made him the very best. There was no fucking way he'd concede that his friend, the one who'd first taught him how to skydive, had simply succumbed to human error.

Garrett slammed his glass on the copper bar and slid it

toward the bartender, nodding at her. The perky blonde barkeep promptly brought the Macallan, poured two fingers and set the bottle in front of him. She gave him a sympathetic smile. As she turned around and bent over to give him an unobstructed view of her assets, he swore. Not even that perfect heart-shaped ass was enough to stir his dick. Garrett shook his head in disgust, aware he needed to get his shit together. As he ran his forefinger along the edge of his drink, a familiar voice caught his attention.

"Hey."

"You're late," Garrett responded, giving his friend a glare.

"Yeah fuck you too, G." Lars smiled at the bartender.

"Hi, baby. What can I get ya?" she asked.

Lars glanced to the whiskey that sat in front of Garrett. "A glass. We're taking the bottle."

"You sure about that now?" She raised a judgmental eyebrow at him.

"Yep, it's that kind of night." He shrugged. "Looks like you've started before me. You driving?"

"Nope. I've got a driver tonight." Garrett glanced to Lars, whose not so subtle eye roll told him he'd gone too far. "Is there a problem? No, don't answer."

The last thing he needed was a fucking lecture. Sensing one was coming, Garrett shoved out of his seat and snatched the decanter, gesturing to a secluded table in the corner. He sighed, settling into a well-worn leather chair and caught Lars' shadow flying by him, right before he took another swig of the amber liquid.

"Nice club," Garrett commented.

"Best jazz in the city. Got a special surprise I think you'll like."

"Oh yeah?" Garrett swirled the glass, never taking his eyes off the golden vortex.

"I thought you could use a distraction." Lars smirked, pouring himself a drink.

"That right, huh?"

"Listen, G, I know it's been a few weeks since…"

"Evan…"

"You and I both know this was no accident, but we've both got contracts to fulfill. Business goes on. It sucks, but if you don't start looking for his replacement, we can't…"

"What do you think I've been doing? I'm in the office. Day in. Day out. Even though Evan's not here, the world keeps spinning." Garrett gave Lars a sideways glance. "But I'm sure as hell not going to let it go. Something happened up there."

Over the years, Garrett had taken Emerson Industries from a garage start-up into a billion dollar corporation. Not only did Emerson's civilian suppliers count on timely shipments, government contracts needed to be fulfilled. Ongoing research and development took place on campus, ensuring the most advanced equipment in the world, and Evan had been a critical player in its success. Finding a suitable replacement for him was imperative, but it wouldn't be an easy task. Since the accident, Garrett had been operating in a daze, attending to small matters, but had neglected the critical infrastructure projects that needed intensive attention from a chief technology officer.

"Maybe, but you have to let the authorities handle it," Lars commented, his eyes falling onto the singer who'd stepped up on stage and picked up the microphone.

"I can't let it go. I've got to find out what happened. You know as well as I do that Evan used to be in the military – Airborne Division. He taught us all our shit. There's just no way he made a mistake. It's almost as if it's…" Garrett's words trailed off as he followed Lars' train of vision, the gorgeous creature capturing his attention.

The bar went silent as her golden voice resonated throughout the room. The jazz band transitioned into a sultry version of *You Put a Spell on Me,* and the seductive beauty stepped down from her perch, passing by a couple who sipped martinis. Garrett noted how she effortlessly weaved her way through the crowd of patrons, not allowing anyone to touch her. With a tantalizing flair, she turned her head toward Garrett and flipped her long blonde hair. The playful glint in her eyes told him she'd come for him next, a glimpse of desire hidden behind the violet contacts she wore. She stopped mid-song and slowly peeled away her gloves, tossing them into the crowd.

Lars laughed, and it was at that moment that Garrett realized he'd brought him here not just to distract him, but for a purpose. Momentary anger was promptly quelled as the blonde stepped out of a shadow. Her pale blue corset hugged her curves. Again she caught his gaze, slowly lowering the side zipper on her black pencil skirt. A drum solo began and the garment dropped to the floor, revealing ruffled panties. A cream-colored garter belt secured black thigh-high stockings. His cock jerked as she trailed her fingertips over her thighs, blowing a kiss to the quiet sophisticated crowd that continued to order drinks from passing waitresses.

Garrett wanted to be pissed at Lars, but he knew that his friend cared about him, how profoundly he'd been affected by Evan's death. It'd been months since he'd indulged in the fairer sex. Despite the temptation, he had no intention of initiating contact with the sultry performer.

The fragrance of her perfume drew him out of his contemplation, and through his peripheral vision, he spied his stealth singer. Tendrils of her hair brushed the back of his neck as she descended. Having given up on his resolve to show no interest, he glanced at Lars, whose eyes flashed to the entertainment. Delicate hands clutched his shoulders and Garrett slid his chair from the table to get a better view of her. His temptress ran her fingertips down his cotton shirt, causing his nipples to pebble in response. *Shit, I'm not here to fuck anyone*, he thought to himself as the blood rushed to his cock.

His eyes locked on hers as she straddled him, trailing her hands over his pecs. When her palms slid over his bare forearms, he fought the searing arousal that threatened his control. Garrett sucked a breath as she sat firmly on his lap, and her eyes snapped to his as they both registered his erection pressing through his jeans onto the thin fabric of her panties. It was in that moment that she gave him a small knowing smile. Rather than standing, she slowly tilted her hips, dragging her groin down the length of him. From a distance, no one would have seen. He resisted the urge to grab onto her waist. The fantasy of flipping her onto the table, tearing off the wet strip of nothing she called underwear and fucking her in front of the entire audience flittered through his mind, and he wondered if she'd like a little public action. The mere idea of it turned his dick into concrete, and he attempted to shift in his seat to relieve the growing ache.

If control was an Olympic sport, Garrett would hold a gold medal. Whether plunging out of a plane from eighteen thousand feet or plunging into a woman, his blood pressure never rose a single point. But despite his cool demeanor, Garrett failed to will his erection into submission. He took a slow breath, irked that a burlesque singer had cracked a sliver in his composure. He caught a glimpse of Lars, whose smile had faded. *Fuck me, he knows. Why the hell does it matter to him? Is he dating her? Yes, that's it. He knows her. Serves him the hell right for bringing me to this place.*

The lovely creature rose gracefully off him. Presenting her posterior like a meal on a plate, she arched her back and gestured to the black ribbons laced up the back of her corset. When he didn't respond, she abruptly sat on his thighs, jolting him back into his aroused state. She glanced back to him and grinned, tugging one of the strings. Her soft fingers met his, bringing them to the laces.

"I think that's good enough," Lars commented.

"What?" After this was over Garrett was going to kill Lars for fucking with him like this. He shook his head, confused as to what the hell was happening.

"A little help," she whispered, ignoring Lars.

Garrett noted that she'd turned her face away so he couldn't read her expression. He broke his resolve and began to pull open the tight threading, loosening the corset. He despised his body's lack of response to his demand to cease the arousal. His cock was harder than piling and the only relief he'd be getting tonight was from the palm of his hand.

The soft silky fabric brushed his hand as she pushed off him and made her way back to the stage. Holding her arms across her breasts, she stopped to wriggle her bottom, allowing the fabric to fall to her feet. As she turned for the big reveal, a velvet bra covered what the audience had expected to be bare. She wrapped both palms around the microphone, setting it back into the stand, and resumed her song. Like an angel, her alluring voice filled the room, and not a soul appeared disappointed that she hadn't bared more skin.

Garrett struggled to conceal his interest, aware that he should leave, but he sat captivated until the last note. A small chuckle drew his attention to Lars, who wore a broad grin.

"What's so funny?"

"You like her?"

"And? So what? She's beautiful. Moves well. Smells nice. Assertive…wasn't going to take no for an answer with that corset. What's not to like?"

"I'm glad you like her, I really am, but you might not want to sport that hard-on around her in the office," Lars said, nervously flexing his fingers.

"What the fuck is this about?"

"I'm about to help you is all."

"I saw the way she looked at you. What's going on between you and her?" Garrett asked, his voice tense. "And why exactly would I be seeing her in my office?"

"Just hear me out, bro."

"What did you do?"

"I didn't do anything. Just chill a second."

"Yet?"

"I know you, G. You're stuck on this thing with Evan," Lars noted.

"Thing? He's fucking dead," Garrett stated coldly.

"I hear you haven't even tried to replace him."

"What the hell did Chase say to you? You know what? I don't care what he said. The last time I checked, I ran Emerson. I don't need a babysitter." Garrett picked up his whiskey and glared at Lars. Of course he hadn't replaced Evan. No one could ever replace him. "You need to mind your own business. Seriously. Besides, whoever takes that position has to be one of us…someone I can trust implicitly. That's not gonna happen overnight."

"Exactly. And this is where she comes in."

"You're joking, right? The stripper?"

"Singer."

"Singer," he conceded. Garrett took a swig of his drink

and set it forcefully down on the table.

"MBA. Wharton."

"Her?" His eyes darted to the stage. He watched with curiosity as she quickly wrapped herself up in a robe, concealing her costume. "So she's smart. So what? It's not enough. This isn't just some tech job. Evan had his hands in all sorts of shit. He was working on several major projects. There are so many requirements for whoever comes into his position it isn't even fucking funny. I'm not going to rush this."

"She's got clearances."

"Not enough." He glanced up and caught her staring at Lars. The flare in her eyes told Garrett that she wasn't happy with him.

"Listen. I've known her for ten years. She's the real deal. She's brilliant. Has rocked all my top accounts."

"What did she do for the government?" Garrett immediately wished he hadn't asked. There was no way this would work.

"Hacker. White Hat. She's in tune with problems our clients don't even know exist."

"Okay, great, well, we're very specialized. You know this. Does she jump?" He held up his hands to Lars as his friend glanced away. "No? Okay, great. What does she do? Does she do anything?"

"She's not so adventurous, but she can help you get the outsourcing project back on track, recruit for a permanent replacement," Lars responded, ignoring Garrett's question.

"What kind of a burlesque dancer doesn't actually take

her clothes off?" Garrett paused, putting together the pieces of the puzzle. "Don't get me wrong, she was sexy, but it wasn't lost on me that the ending was a little anticlimactic."

"Give her a break. I just told you that she's a singer, not a dancer. This is just kind of a hobby, anyway. It takes guts to get up and perform like that. She may be a little more cautious than most people, but she's working on it."

"Working on it?" He laughed.

"So she's a little repressed, okay? What the hell difference does it make, if she can do the job?" Lars asked with a sigh. "Listen, I promise you that she is what you need now. Yeah, you'll find someone to take Evan's position eventually but it's not going to be anytime soon. At least this way, you can keep things moving forward with our deal. Listen, you know I would not fuck with you. I'm telling you that she's the best. And she's tough. In fact, she's probably going to kick my ass for bringing you here."

"Why would she do that?" Garrett found it amusing that he'd misread the situation. Perhaps it hadn't been lust in her eyes; she'd been pissed at Lars. Whatever this meant to her, apparently it had been a secret and she wasn't at all pleased he'd mixed her worlds.

"She, uh, doesn't really want people to know she does this."

"Why did you bring me here then?"

"Because you need to get out and do something other than wallow in the office. And besides, if I'd told you about her without you actually seeing her sing, you'd have shot me down. This is the only thing she does that, you know, is risky."

"Risky? Are you high? I'd hardly call singing a song risky." Garrett laughed and rolled his eyes.

"You get up there, then, if you think it's so easy." Lars' smile fell away as he grew angry with his friend's resistance. "Look, this is the deal. I can loan her to you. We just ended the Elkinson account. I moved a few people around. She may not be Evan, but she knows her shit. I know you're going to vet the hell out of her anyway, even though she already technically works in your network. Evan's death has been hard on all of us, but you've got to keep these deals moving. You need help, and I'm offering it to you. *She* is what you need."

"I need you to mind your own damn business." Garrett blew out a breath, staring at the bottom of his glass.

What Lars had said about her already being in the network was somewhat accurate. All the subsidiary corporations were independently owned, yet Garrett had a minority share within each, ensuring the viability of Emerson Industries. But clearances to work in the corporate building were a stricter, higher level, having access to covert government contracts.

Regardless of his opposition to Lars' suggestion, Garrett was aware that it could take months to find a suitable replacement for his chief technology officer. In the meantime, he'd been given a gift. A nice shiny one…very attractive and hard to resist. How he'd like to see what was underneath the wrapping she'd failed to peel away. Fuck it all, he knew he was thinking with his dick, but the temptation remained. It wasn't as if she'd really be his employee anyway.

"Two weeks. That's all she's got. If she doesn't add value, she's gone." Garrett shoved the chair out from the table and stood. "But if she screws up, she's out. I'm not in the business of taking on interns. If she doesn't hit the ground running, she's done. I'm not messing around."

"Good...because I don't want you messing around. We should, uh, maybe have some rules."

"You're kidding, right?"

"Come on, G. I know she's attractive but this is business. She's not like us."

"Yeah, I get that."

"She shouldn't come to our events."

"We haven't had any events since the accident."

"True, but she's not into jumps or any of our other extracurricular activities." Lars wiped his mouth with a cocktail napkin.

"I saw her looking at you. Are you fucking her?"

"Oh, no. Come on, man."

"Don't give me that shit. What's going on between you two?"

Lars shook his head.

"Spill it or we're done here." Garrett wasn't sure why it irritated him to think Lars had been intimate with her.

"We met in college. That's it."

"Anything else?"

"No, we didn't click that way. But we stayed friends over the years. She came on board five years ago."

"And you never brought her around? Ever?"

"No, she's not like us. Besides, you saw the look she gave me. Nothing's lost on you."

"She's pissed."

"Yeah, I just told you. I knew she did this, but I don't usually come to watch. So she's probably wondering why the hell I'm here."

"I'm sure she's going to love that she basically just had an interview with her new boss."

"Let's not get crazy now. I'm her boss. You have her on loan."

"This isn't going to work…"

"She's the best you're going to get, considering the circumstances."

Garrett just shook his head. *Yeah, I just undressed her while she ground on my cock. Great way to start a business relationship. Awesome.*

"What? She's not going to care that you were here."

"You're delusional. No wonder you can't keep a woman."

"Glass houses, bro." Lars shrugged. "There is one tiny thing…"

"What?"

"You can't fuck her. And before you go all CEO on my ass, this is a deal breaker."

"You're a dick, you know that. Why bring me here to see her like this?" Garrett raked his fingers through his hair in frustration.

"I told you. I brought you here so you could see her in her element, doing something that pushes her a little outside of her comfort zone. She's no jumper, but she's brave. If I hadn't done this, you wouldn't have ever considered her. You are sinking fast, my friend, and desperate times call for desperate measures. It worked. I got you to say yes." Lars set his palms on the table, his expression serious. "For years I've kept her away from that side of my life, away from you. She's my golden goose. I'm proud of her. There's nothing she does half-assed, including what she just did. I love you, Garrett, and because I love you, I'm not going to let you fuck up business. This thing with Evan…I can see how this is affecting you and I don't like it a damn bit. So I'm letting you borrow one of my finest assets. But I care about her, and because of that, she's off limits. Got it?"

"Fine. Whatever. Bring her to the office and we'll talk. I've gotta go. She stays two weeks, that's it."

"Two weeks," Lars repeated.

Garrett wasn't sure if he believed the words he was speaking but they sounded good. He caught the raised eyebrow Lars gave him, but ignored it. With a slap to his friend's shoulder, he saluted goodbye and headed toward the door. He hated that Lars sometimes knew him better than he knew himself. For the first time since Evan had died, he'd been distracted by something else, someone else.

Granted, he couldn't be sure whether or not she was going to be as good for his business as Lars promised. But considering his depression, he had to admit that for those few seconds she'd brushed against him, she'd taken his mind off of his grief. Despite his attraction, he'd promised Lars he wouldn't touch her. Garrett told himself it would be easy to ignore his feelings, and rationalized his arousal as temporary lust. A couple of weeks was all he needed to get the search for Evan's replacement on track. He'd put her in charge of the outsourcing deal, and she'd be in and out. Hopefully, he'd be able to stick to his word and not be in her.

Chapter Three

"What were you thinking?" Selby shouted.

"I was thinking that there was no way I could help him without bringing him to see you."

"Garrett Emerson?" Selby turned to the window, mindlessly shuffling folders.

She'd been surprised when Lars had showed up to hear her sing. It wasn't as if she'd kept it a secret. Far from it. She'd been performing for two years now. At first it'd been more of a dare from a friend, something to distract her from reality. But the moment she'd started singing again, the performances became a therapeutic remedy, both to stress and her fears, alleviating the anxiety that threatened to choke her.

She considered how different her upbringing had been from Lars'. While other kids partied in college on Mommy and Daddy's dime, Selby had scraped by on loans. Keeping her nose to the grindstone, she'd graduated summa cum laude and landed a graduate assistantship at Wharton, where she'd first met Lars. He'd been dashing and charismatic. She'd been awkward and quiet. They'd gone on a few dates, but rather than discovering romantic sparks, they'd ignited a long-lasting friendship. After graduation, they'd stayed in touch. He'd started his own company and she'd gone to work for the government. It was there where she'd utilized the coding skills she'd learned in undergraduate school. Hacking had come naturally for her, helping companies identify weaknesses. She excelled within the confines of her endeavors.

After working her way up the corporate ladder, Lars had approached her with the opportunity at his corporation, DLar-Tech. Five years later, she routinely worked high profile clients, incorporating business solutions with complex data issues. Along with outsourcing, she specialized in turning around fledgling IT departments. Whether the corporation was large or small, she had the ability to successfully analyze operations, recruiting human resources into the system like fitting pieces into a puzzle. No matter the assignment Lars gave her, Selby had never blinked an eye at any request....until now.

Garrett Emerson. Billionaire playboy. He'd been reputedly ruthless in business as well as the bedroom, leaving a trail of broken hearts in his wake. She cursed herself for not recognizing him in the club. She'd seen several photos of the clean-shaven mogul, but last night, his scruffy beard had disguised his face. It wasn't as if she hadn't studied him in business school. They'd spent an entire semester dissecting the case study, discussing how he'd built his empire from the bottom up, focusing on extreme sports, patenting innovative technologies and snaring top secret government projects. With secretive alliances, he'd cast his net, virtually creating a monopoly.

Selby's thoughts refocused on Lars, who sat at her desk, playing with a pencil. She couldn't believe he'd gone behind her back and brought Garrett to her club. As her anger surfaced, she sifted through the papers on her desk, searching for the stapler she didn't need. *Where's my fucking stapler?* She located the metal weapon and began to look for something she could bang together

"It's not what you think," she heard Lars say.

"How exactly isn't it what I think? I mean, for real, Lars. You brought him to see me sing and then…" She laughed and rolled her eyes, recalling how she'd sat on his lap. It had all been part of the show, but now she regretted every second of the encounter. "You have the nerve to ask me to take him on as a client. No. Just no."

"I'll owe you." He smiled and crossed his legs.

Selby glanced into his baby-blue eyes, the same ones that had won him a first date with her. God, the man was beautiful. Blond hair, tanned skin. And he could sweet talk the panties off of a vestal virgin. As his friend, she'd watched him work his magic on the ladies, but had never fallen under his spell.

"Owe me. That's rich." She swept her fingers through her long blonde hair, nervously twisting the end. With a sign of defeat, she fell back into her leather office chair. "It's not that I have a philosophical issue about going to work for him, but Lars, you're killin' me here. You saw what I did to him last night…what I did to *Garrett Emerson.*"

"It's not like he's the President of the United States, for Christ's sakes. Besides, I saw what you did, and he seemed to enjoy it." Lars gave a laugh.

"It's not even funny. You should have stopped me."

"Hey, you wanted me to come see you perform."

"It might have been nice if you'd told me you were coming, you know? Look, I've taken every job you've ever given me…even the shitty ones. But take him on as a client? After last night? Seriously? I'm supposed to waltz into his office and say, what? 'Hi, I'd like to look at your hard drive?' You and I both know what happened." Selby certainly had felt his erection. Heat flushed her neck and face as the thought popped into her head.

"You go in like you always do. Why were you dancing last night, anyway? I thought you were a singer. Not that I minded the show."

"I don't dance. I was working the room, that's all." Selby wished she'd had the guts to take it all off, but she kept her sexuality and emotions well concealed. "Look, it would be one thing if he'd met me prior to last night, you know, as a professional."

"You are a professional. The best. And the fact of the matter is that he needs us…you."

Selby gave him a hard stare, sensing Lars' change of tone.

"You remember last week…the funeral I had to go to,"

he began.

"Yeah."

"It was for a friend of mine, Evan Tredioux. Evan worked for Garrett. Was an advisor of sorts. He was a really good friend of Garrett's." Lars rimmed his coffee cup with the tip of his finger.

"I'm sorry." Selby's voice softened.

"You know I skydive sometimes, right?"

"I didn't think you did that anymore. In college but you don't still..." Selby's heart sank as she realized there was more to the story than Lars was revealing.

"Garrett and I have been friends for a long time. I know you don't like," he paused, "heights."

"Yeah, me and a million other people."

"Confidential time, got it?" Lars gave her a hard stare, his expression serious.

"Of course." Selby moved to close the door, returned and sat on the edge of her desk.

"You've done special projects for me over the years but I haven't disclosed everything. You need to know that there are parts of DLar-Tech that are intimately tied to Emerson Industries."

"What are you saying? Your business is in trouble?"

"No, not at all. What I'm saying is that what affects Garrett affects me. Evan's death is hitting all of us hard but he was Garrett's right hand man. It's not like he can fill the position right away. He needs the kind of expertise you offer."

"I don't know," she hedged. *Expertise?* She pretty much

gave him an eyeful of it last night. She didn't want to say yes to the assignment, but already felt herself caving to his request.

"Please. I'll owe you. If you do this for me, I'll give you an extra bonus."

"Does he know that you want me to do this? Did you already tell him you were sending a consultant? Me?" Selby's resolve cracked, the water pushing through the tiny hole that held back the dam. Looking at the mess on her desk, she shook her head. This was a bad idea. A really bad idea.

"Now that you bring it up...um, yes he does."

"This isn't going to work." Her eyes flashed to his.

"Trust me, he'll be grateful for the help. I've already been working on getting the outsourcing contract in place, but I need you to sell it to his board. It's short term. Do the deal, work on finding recruits for the CTO position. This is easy for you. A no brainer."

"Maybe." She sighed.

"Consider the business. Wrapping up the contract is no problem. The hardest part will be recruiting Evan's replacement. That resource needs to be top notch. An expert in some facet of the extreme sports business. One who walks the walk. But they'll also need to know IT."

"Sounds routine." Selby took a deep breath, forcing the muscles in her chest to relax.

"You need to know something." Lars averted his gaze to the pencil he twirled in his fingers. "Garrett can be, how should I put this? He's very concerned about the way our friend died."

"Didn't you say it was an accident?"

"I don't want to get too much into it, but Garrett isn't fully on board with replacing Evan."

"What are you saying?"

"He's a bit reluctant."

"He doesn't want me there, does he?"

"He's expecting you tomorrow."

"If anyone else was asking me to do this, you know I'd just say no." In the past, she'd faced the same kind of situation but she'd made the client pay extra for time spent on the job. "Am I working for him or you?"

"You'll work for me. I'm just loaning you out."

"I'm not doing it without a contract. Time on the job will be predetermined. Two weeks. A month. You call it. Every extra day spent working for him attracts a bonus fee. I also want a nondisclosure out clause."

"If he fucks this up, you want to leave free and clear?"

"With no repercussions or lawsuits. There's got to be a gag clause should we decide to part ways. He keeps quiet about me and I do the same for him. I'm not going to let him screw up my reputation because he's having some kind of a CEO tantrum if we can't agree on a replacement. I'll take on the special projects while I'm recruiting candidates. Also, I want your name on the contract. If he wanted me to help him, it would be his ass sitting in that chair, not yours. So because it's yours, you both have to agree. That's the deal. Terms aren't negotiable."

Lars' lips tightened in a fine line. He set the pencil

onto her desk and blew out a breath.

"Okay," he reluctantly agreed.

"Okay." A familiar sense of accomplishment washed over her despite the fact that she'd given in to his request. The agreement would give her the control she needed in order to be able to face Garrett. "And Lars?"

"Yeah?"

"No funny business. This is my career here. I don't want to see either of your faces in my club. When the contract is over, I'd love to have you back, but until then…"

"Fair enough. But for the record, since you're in the city at night, you might want to consider some protection."

"I'm careful. Besides, I'm not there that often." Selby had always feared going out at night by herself but she refused to feed the dark monster inside her.

"Done on the contract. I'll text you the address of the complex. Expect some hits on a background check today. Even though I vouched for you, Garrett's going to vet you like you were going into the FBI. He doesn't mess around," Lars warned.

"Not a problem. It's business." Selby tried to act nonchalant about his prediction. She didn't like clients going too far back. Years had gone by but the mere thought of her childhood caused her pulse to race.

Selby wore her most conservative suit, the antithesis of the form-fitting corset she'd had on the last time she'd seen Garrett. As she pulled her car through the heavily guarded gate, she regarded the sprawling location of Emerson's headquarters. Set in a suburban area, the gated facility sat on several hundred acres of private property. Although she'd worked at similar sized government facilities, this one radiated an aura of wealth with its slick reflective windows and well-manicured landscaping.

"You've got this," Selby told herself, parking her car. She glanced in the rearview mirror and took a deep breath.

The image of Garrett Emerson flashed through her mind. When they'd first met, he'd looked dangerous, his wavy brown hair tousled as if he'd just had sex. Despite his evident arousal, he hadn't touched her. Cool and collected, he'd resisted, only tugging her corset open after she'd insisted.

Selby smoothed her hand down her blouse, her ripe tips begging to escape the confines of the fabric. She cursed under her breath, aware that she had to get her sophomoric urges under control and focus on business. Developing a crush on Garrett Emerson would cause nothing but trouble. She had no future with someone like him. She reasoned that his reaction to her the other night had been nothing more than a chemical one. She'd tuck the memory away, pretending that it had never happened.

She contemplated what Lars had told her about Garrett's reluctance to accept help. Whatever had happened to Evan, she considered that Garrett must have relented somewhat about needing assistance. After all, they'd let her in the gate. Still, a nagging worry flittered in her stomach. She hadn't received the contract she'd been promised. After texting Lars, he'd responded saying he'd meet her at Garrett's office.

The idea of working with a disgruntled client squelched any excitement she may have been feeling about working with the tycoon. She was confident that she had the experience to deal with the situation, but this was Garrett fucking Emerson. Regardless of any nondisclosure he signed, the man could make or break her, and she'd have to be on her game.

She wore a mask of business competence, deliberately slowing her pace as she approached the building. Two well-dressed men stood watch outside, giving her a warm smile. Ushered inside by the guards, Selby attempted to conceal her amazement as she took in the sight of the enormous atrium. Despite its modern architecture, the potted Majesty palm trees in the lobby brought a sense of warmth to the otherwise stark décor. As Selby attempted to acclimate, her thoughts were interrupted by a male voice.

"Excuse me?" Selby gave a polite smile to a tall well-dressed man who looked as if he'd stepped off a Milan runway. From his impeccable Italian suit to his fine leather shoes, he exuded wealth. A glass elevator sped upward, and she swore she saw Lars staring down at her.

"Hello, Miss Reynolds. I'm Norm, Mr. Emerson's secretary. He's expecting you. Please, this way." He gestured to her to follow him down a long hallway, its black marble floors reflecting up into the stainless steel walls.

"Do you know if Mr. Davenport has arrived?" *Lars better have his ass in that office by the time I get up there*, she thought. While Selby was impressed by the state-of-the-art building, intimidation never factored into her thoughts. She'd worked hundreds of companies in all kinds of corporate cultures, and this was just one more.

"I'm sorry, I'm not permitted to disclose which guests are in the building. I'm sure that Mr. Emerson will assist you with your inquiry," he stated, pointing to a silver elevator door.

Selby watched with interest as her escort pecked at the security pad and leaned his face into the iris scanner. As they entered the private elevator, she caught a glimpse of the armed guard patrolling the corridor. His ice-cold glare didn't falter as she gave him a small smile. The doors zipped shut, and with lightning speed, they ascended. Selby consciously counted to ten, taking slow breaths, keeping her eyes on the numbers that ticked by overhead.

She despised heights and supposed she should be grateful that she'd avoided the glass box in which she'd watched others ride upward. A sheen of perspiration broke out on her forehead as it lurched to a stop. Closing her eyes, she regained her composure, clutching her leather briefcase. Long ago, she'd learned to recognize symptoms of the impending panic attacks. Racing pulse. Certainty of death. She'd cough a few times before the invisible throttle around her throat commenced. *Breathe. Meditate. No fear, no fear, no fear.* As the metal door slid open, Selby forced herself to relax, trying not to appear as if she'd just been chased by a serial killer. Her foot landed on the other side of the grate and her body and mind calmed.

Selby took in her surroundings as they walked onto the executive floor. Every corporation was different. Some were old school with mahogany walled offices for the C-level employees. Others were more egalitarian, with dividers, open cubicles, leaving little privacy for any employee. This, however, was contemporary, sleek. The bright office space was countered with colorful abstract art. Ficus trees grew in the corners, sprouting from ornate in-floor wrought iron planters. Asiatic lilies sat perched on decorative side tables, their sweet aroma permeating the air. Crown molding adorned the walls, with heavy wooden doors leading into individual offices. Selby wondered if Garrett had discovered the secret to productivity via workplace décor or if some designer had simply created the peaceful aura within his corporation's secretive walls.

Selby eyed a platter of ornate chocolates that had been set out in a small waiting room, but her focus was soon drawn to Lars' booming voice which sounded from the end of the long hallway. Without asking, she sped past her chaperone. She barely gave notice to his order not to enter the office and didn't waste time contemplating whether or not to go through the door that was already slightly ajar. As it flew open, she observed Lars standing with his hands on his hips, and his angry eyes met hers. As if she'd slapped them both, silence befell the room. Selby's attention immediately went to Garrett, whose commanding presence sent a shiver down her spine. Frozen in place, she reached for the courage she knew she possessed on any other given day.

"Do we have a problem?" she asked, feigning confidence.

"Miss Reynolds, please have a seat."

Selby stood firm as he ordered her to sit. She shook off the fleeting urge to submit to his wish and instead glared at him. His blue eyes flickered in amusement, but the tight line drawn across his supple lips gave no indication of acquiescence. She braced her nerves, anticipating his next command. It wasn't as if she hadn't been subject to demanding executives in the past. But she'd never felt the hardness of their body against hers, the electric desire that sparked between a man and a woman.

"Are we *all* sitting?" she challenged.

"Play nice, Selby," Lars warned.

"Doesn't sound like you were playing nice? Or do you two like it rough?" Her expression flared with sarcasm.

"Hey now." Lars laughed.

"Sometimes," Garrett answered with a small knowing smile, "but I assure you, Miss Reynolds, this is a gentleman's disagreement. Nothing to worry about."

"Selby," she corrected. *I bet he does like it rough*, she thought. Was he flirting? Determined not to let him shake her, she glossed over his comment and addressed Lars. "Did you bring the contract?"

"We were just discussing the terms." Garrett approached Selby, closing the space between them. "But before we continue, perhaps it's best that we get off on the right foot. You can hardly expect me to engage with a stranger."

At his statement, Selby resisted the urge to give a nervous laugh. He knew damn well that they'd met. But in the interest of client relations, she stepped forward, extending her hand to him as if it was the very first time they'd met.

"Selby Reynolds. Executive recruiter and information systems expert. I work for Lars." As he took her palm in his, her skin sizzled with sexual awareness.

"Garrett Emerson. CEO and owner of Emerson Industries."

"Nice to meet you…I, um…Lars said," she stammered. Flustered, she lost her words as he stared deep into her eyes as if he was trying to read her thoughts. She unsuccessfully fought the heat that rose in her cheeks as the memory from the club flashed in her mind.

"A pleasure," he replied, releasing her. As if a switch had gone off, his demeanor changed as he turned to the window.

"I understand you're in need of my services. Lars explained that you have a critical position that is currently unoccupied," she continued, attempting to regain her composure.

"I'm well aware of the impact the recent loss of personnel has had on my business." Garrett gestured to the chair and walked behind his desk. "Please. Take a seat."

"I'm sorry for your loss." Selby did as he asked, but inwardly cringed as hardness washed over his face, his eyes darting from Lars back to her.

"As I was saying…a loss of staff." Garrett fell back into his chair, ignoring her comment, and held up several pieces of paper. "This contract…I'm not sure the terms are clear."

"The terms are both standard and non-negotiable. This is what I can promise you. Whatever sensitive projects your staff member was responsible for, I can handle as long as they are technology related. I'm not an accountant. I'm not a lawyer. Nor am I a scientist. So if your CTO was involved in these matters, I do need to be aware when I recruit; however I cannot provide those services. I do, however, have a proven track record of inserting myself within organizations as interim CIO or CTO, depending on the situation, and managing current work flow within the organization. I can help with your outsourcing discussions, and present to your board. I will also recruit and help you acquire talent who can permanently fill the position." Selby's back straightened as she fell into her comfort zone, discussing what she could easily provide to not just Garrett but any client who required her services. "As I've explained to Lars, the contract must be in place for me to begin. Please don't take offense. I have utilized it for other clients as well. I understand he's doing this as a personal favor to you, but I prefer to treat this as any other transaction. I assume you've checked my clearances, but I want to personally assure you of my confidentiality with regards to all aspects of Emerson Industries' business matters. If there's anything you need to ask me in order to proceed, please feel free."

Every word of what she'd said was true, but she'd never worked for anyone as powerful and influential as Garrett Emerson. Despite the risk, working for Emerson Industries was a huge opportunity, and as she sat before the mogul, she hoped she'd successfully presented her case.

As silence filled the room, Selby flattened her hands along her skirt, willing them not to tremble. Unable to read Garrett's expression, she waited on the momentous verdict.

Chapter Four

Garrett fought the urge to throttle Lars. *Why did I ever entertain the idea of listening to him?* Goddamn it, he'd brought a fucking contract to his office. Contracts were par for the course, but a nondisclosure? Garrett swore that he must have been out of his damn mind, because he'd already signed it. *Selby Reynolds.* She'd switched roles as if she'd been an actress in a play. Gone was the burlesque performer. She'd been replaced by an educated business persona, one who clearly had no intention of acknowledging their previous encounter. As if they'd never met, she'd met him with a cool smile, her palm soft as he took her hand in his.

Garrett eyed Selby, concealing his feelings. She'd stormed into his office and challenged him in a spirited banter, one that'd turned his dick to steel. Despite her fiery words, she'd eventually submitted quite nicely. A coil of regret tightened in his belly as he realized he'd have to keep his hands off the lovely Miss Reynolds. He knew it was wrong but he couldn't help wondering what she smelled like today, her perfume she'd worn at the club ingrained in his memory. He recalled how she'd sat on his lap, whispering for him to unlace her. It had only lasted seconds, but that brief interaction had been enough to intrigue him. He'd tucked away that little tidbit of her personality, guessing that Lars had been correct. With the way she sat prim and proper before him, the knowledge that she had the capability to push herself outside her comfort zone was an unexpected delight.

He found it curious that she could stand up to him, acting as if she could have cared less about the position. Despite her apparent indifference, all positions at Emerson, temporary or not, were highly coveted. Yet as he studied her, he came to the conclusion that perhaps she didn't really want to work for him. *Lars. This is all his doing.*

In truth, he'd been tempted to hire her from the second Lars had thrown him the lifeline. But he knew damn well from the background check that Selby Reynolds wasn't capable of assuming all of Evan's projects. No one could. From technology to secret projects, his knowledge had been ubiquitous across the business. Garrett noted that despite her confident speech, her eyes darted over to Lars for support.

He understood why she'd be nervous, but when it came to her technical expertise, there was no question about her qualifications. Garrett noticed that her breathing was unusually quiet, as if she was purposely controlling her reaction to him. A small smile broke across his face as the realization hit. Perhaps his little singer was attracted to him as well.

Garrett blew out a breath. *Well, fuck.* That would make it all the more difficult for him to resist her. Her eyes caught his and his small grin widened.

"You start today. You'll have to go down to HR to get your ID and biometrics processed for security."

"I'll need access to Evan's files," she began.

"I've arranged an office for you on this floor. My secretary will show you." *Not Evan's.* Garrett had had one cleared for her at the end of the hallway. If he was going to survive working with her, he'd keep her far enough away that she wouldn't distract him but close enough that he could make sure she wasn't causing trouble.

"I'll need the files. Do you have his laptop? Or if he used shared files here on the network, I could use that. But it's probably best if I can see his laptop too, just to make sure I don't miss anything," she persisted. Her eyes twinkled in irritation.

"About the contract." Garrett picked it up off his desk and leaned back in his chair. "I've signed it, but I plan to insert one of my own terms."

"Excuse me?" Selby asked.

"My business isn't nine to five. We work twenty-four-seven."

"That shouldn't be an issue."

"That means when I need you, you're there. If we don't need you on weekends or nights, you're on your own, but my orders come first. Am I clear, Miss

Reynolds?"

"I completely understand your concerns. It's not unusual for corporations to need my services on weekends, but I hardly think it's necessary to put that in the contract. It's implied."

"Perhaps, but I like to make sure my ducks are in order. In my business, there's no room for mistakes. Everything must be checked and double checked. Speaking of which, I do expect you to learn the aspects of my business. You do not need to participate in, uh," Garrett looked to Lars and smiled, "some of the more intensive aspects of research. But you do need to be ready and willing to learn. Are you, Miss Reynolds?"

"Yes, sir."

Garrett sucked a breath as the two little words from her soft lips caused his cock to jerk. His pants tightened around his groin, and he discreetly tugged on the fabric.

"I suppose we have a deal then. You help me get Evan's project back on track and start recruiting."

Selby gave him a hesitant smile. She didn't trust him, he knew. Shit, he didn't trust himself around her either. Lars grinned as well, but Garrett recognized the cautionary tick in his jaw. He shoved out of his chair and rounded the desk. He extended his right hand to her, still holding the contract in his left.

Selby stood to meet him, and her warm hand firmly locked onto his. He sensed that she was determined to exert her dominance, attempting to draw attention from the sexual tension that flared in their touch. He heard a deliberate cough from Lars, and caught his pointed glare. Releasing her fingers, he turned to the window, determined to resume control.

"When you come up from HR, please go directly to your office. Expect to find your laptop, tablet, and phone. We have standard security procedures. No equipment is allowed in or out of the office. You need to leave your personal electronics at home or check them in with security at the door. If you need anything else, please let my secretary know. He'll set up an appointment for us tomorrow to review the projects Evan was working on as well as an in detail review of the company. This includes getting to know what we do here. Not just reading about it either. Your participation will be required."

"I'm not sure why that's necessary. I can assure you I've worked at many companies and can attend to my projects without any sort of special orientation. I don't need to make a video game to know how it's used," she argued.

"It's the only way for you to comprehend even a fraction of what occurs behind these walls. You're going to be leading and interacting with people here who expect you to walk the walk. They may give you some leeway given your temporary status, but if you're responsible for bringing in Evan's replacement, you're going to have to learn more than just the surface of what's expected."

"I understand," she conceded.

"Since you and Lars know how the managed services contracts work, I want you at the board meeting tomorrow. I know it's short notice but between your expertise at DLar-Tech and Evan's notes, you should be able to handle it."

"Certainly. Not a problem."

"And Selby." Garrett loosened his tie and turned to address her as she went to exit his office.

"Yes, Mr. Emerson."

"Tomorrow, after the board meeting...you'll need to bring a bathing suit."

"What? I'm sorry?"

"A bathing suit. You own one, right?"

"Yes, but..."

Garrett smiled as Selby attempted to remain professional, but was unable to hide the flicker of shock in her eyes.

"I thought we'd start with aquatics, polymers...things like that. That is unless you prefer our skydiving division. If the weather's nice we could take the plane and..."

"Aquatics it is," she answered curtly. Her face went pale and she reached for her neck as if to try to get more air. She braced her palm on the doorjamb.

Garrett immediately recognized her change in disposition at his mention of skydiving. He rushed over to her side. Cupping her cheek, he tipped her chin so her eyes met his.

"Hey, I was just kidding. Take a deep breath, sweetheart."

"I'm sorry...no, I'm okay." She coughed. Her fingers reached for Garrett's forearm, clutching it for balance.

"Selby, you okay?" Lars asked.

Garrett held a hand out to his friend, who seemed intent on comforting Selby. While Lars certainly knew her better than he did, she was his responsibility now. Whatever was going on with her was something he'd need to address.

"Sure she is. Look, you're breathing's better already," Garrett assured her. He inadvertently put a comforting hand on her back and gently rubbed it.

"I'm sorry," she gasped. "Yes, I'm fine."

Garrett didn't resist as she broke away from him, releasing his arm. She thanked him once again before leaving, and he made no attempt to stop her. His eyes went to Lars, whose expression had gone serious, disapproving of how he'd handled the situation. Letting Selby go was something Garrett would have to learn how to do, he knew, but knowing and doing were two different things. He prayed he could get his shit together before his next meeting with Miss Selby Reynolds.

Chapter Five

Selby sat behind her desk and sighed, embarrassed that she'd nearly fallen into a panic attack at the mention of skydiving. Taken off guard by her fervid interaction with Garrett, she'd lost focus. At one time she would have jumped at the chance to work at Emerson Industries; now she regretted letting Lars talk her into helping him. She was well aware that it was the opportunity of a lifetime to learn from the maverick himself, one not bestowed on many professionals. The knowledge she'd gain, even in a few short weeks, would be of immeasurable benefit to her career.

But the sexual tension had been palpable, and setting aside the distraction would prove difficult. Although there'd been a few clients who she'd been attracted to over the years, she'd never given her feelings serious consideration, unwilling to compromise propriety. On past assignments, when she'd been approached for a date, she'd politely turned down the suitor. If he'd pursued her further, she'd resorted to her contract terms, which specifically allowed her to leave for any reason. All business, Selby had been successful in rebuking interest.

Garrett Emerson, however, had ignited her every nerve; her willpower was precariously close to disintegrating. Their fiery interaction had been nearly as satisfying as foreplay, and her thoughts had immediately gone to sex. When he'd shaken her hand, holding onto her just a second longer than what would be considered normal for a casual interaction, her arousal had flared, and she'd struggled to articulate the reason she was even standing in his office.

Selby put her head into her hands, recalling what she'd done to him at the club, the smell of his leather jacket and his erection prodding her bottom fresh in her mind. She closed her eyes and laughed, mortified at both her girlish reaction and the fantasies swirling about in her thoughts.

It was crazy to think he'd ever be with someone like her anyway. She could barely make it up the elevator without losing her shit. Meanwhile, his idea of fun was free time base jumping off a skyscraper in Dubai.

Over the years, she'd followed him in business magazines. Although he was undoubtedly known for his charisma, it was perhaps his Cinderella story that intrigued her more than anything else. Unlike others in whose circles he moved, he hadn't been born with a silver spoon in his mouth. On the contrary, he'd come from a blue collar background. He'd worked his way through Stanford, where he'd studied business. It was there he'd first experienced the joy of falling thousands of feet from a plane. He turned his hobby into a business, and Emerson Industries exploded into a Fortune 500 company within two years. He'd cornered the niche market on equipment for extreme sports and snared several high profile government contracts.

Wall Street loved him, but behind closed doors, they feared him. Respected for his cunning and innovative strategies, he'd decimated his competition. Men wanted to be him and women simply wanted him. While he reportedly lived a lavish lifestyle, he was well known for his philanthropic ways.

Selby shook her head, realizing how ridiculous she'd been for considering indulging in her fantasy. Once he found out about her panic attacks, the extent of her fears, there was no way he'd be interested in her. What he'd seen in the club was a façade. The real Selby wanted to be that fearless singer. Maybe someday she'd be that person, but today she was only confident in what she did best, working within the confines of cubicles with her nose rooted into a computer screen.

She prayed Garrett would ignore her. She couldn't afford to slip up, to compromise her reputation for an adolescent crush. After her epic fail at keeping her cool in a fifteen minute meeting, she wondered if she'd survive an entire day in his presence. As she churned it through in her mind, she hoped that he'd pawn her off to one of his executives. If she wasn't in close proximity to Garrett, she'd have an easier time dousing the flame inside her.

Selby glanced around her newly appointed office,

noting that it seemed to fit Garrett's avant-garde taste. She ran her fingertips over the smooth black Basalt desk surface. Its cool texture sat in stark contrast to the white walls and leather furniture. A tall bamboo plant sat in the corner, its stalks braided upward into a blossom of green leaves.

She looked to the laptop docked in its station, her name labeled on its cover, which told her that Garrett had known of and prepared for her arrival despite any misgivings he held. She opened it, and performed a cursory review of the Emerson policies and procedures. Within thirty minutes, she received a personal message from Garrett, complete with links granting her access to Evan's projects.

Immersed in the files, Selby lost track of time. From change requests to software upgrades, the existing IT initiative appeared to be nothing out of the ordinary. From what she'd discovered, Evan had laid the groundwork to ensure the successful outcome of outsourcing negotiations between DLar-Tech and Emerson. While the decision to take operations offsite wasn't always supported by all C level executives, the financials of doing so spoke for themselves.

As she pored through the information, it became evident that her predecessor had also worked on several key product initiatives. She jotted down her thoughts about who she could recruit to fill the position long term. Oversight of information technology and security needs was a given. But finding a resource with knowledge regarding materials related to skydiving and other extreme sports would certainly make her job more difficult.

As she delved further into the data, she saw several references to the PFx Prototype project. Unable to find any specific folders or projects relating to it, she ran a search on all drives, but found nothing. Selby guessed that if she backended the system, she might be able to worm her way into where she suspected the file had been hidden. But she was certain that Garrett wouldn't be thrilled if she hacked into his files. What she really needed was Evan Tredioux's laptop, access to all his files, not just the ones Garrett wanted her to see.

Selby rubbed her eyes, deciding how to handle the situation. As part of their contract, Garrett had agreed to give her access to everything she needed to do her job. She considered asking a secretary, but when she looked at her watch, it was already ten o'clock. If she could just take a quick look around Evan's office, she might be able to get his notebook and continue working.

Garrett's email had confirmed the morning board meeting where she was expected to discuss her transition and plan for recruitment. Whatever this PFx Prototype was, she wanted details. There was nothing worse than being blindsided by executives, who possibly already doubted the credibility of an interim consultant. And there was no way she was making a fool out of herself in front of Garrett Emerson again.

Selby smoothed down her now wrinkled shirt, straightened her skirt and slipped on her pumps, cursing the damn nylons she'd worn. She wrapped her hand around the cool metal doorknob and set off to find Garrett. She peeked her head into the darkened hallway and the motion activated lights flashed on. Her heels clicked along the dark cherry floors, cutting through the deafening silence. With not a soul in the office, it was eerily quiet, but she hoped she'd catch Garrett working late.

She stopped at a break alcove and took a bottle of water out of the staff refrigerator. As she continued toward his office, she found herself looking over her shoulder. She knew it was silly but she felt as if she was in a B movie, except this was no basement. It was a perfectly safe corporate building, one that was heavily guarded. She glanced up to a small black dome in the ceiling, recognizing it as a security camera. Taking a deep breath, she advanced toward her destination.

His door was closed. She knocked, once, twice, but no one answered. Disappointed, she rubbed her eyes and sighed. *Decision time.* Garrett hadn't given her his cell number, so she could either go searching for answers in Evan's office or attempt to catch Garrett in the morning.

Hacking once again crossed her mind, but she knew doing so would set him off worse than the other two options. It had been her experience that backdooring computer systems always made people uncomfortable. She knew that he knew she could do it, but going full on hack on day one in his company didn't seem like such a good idea.

As she walked back toward her office, she caught sight of the shiny nameplate outside Evan's door. Her feet came to a standstill, and her eyes darted to the camera, aware her activities were being watched. *It's not like I'm breaking and entering*, she told herself. *I'm this man's replacement after all, at least for the next couple of weeks.*

"Fuck it," Selby grumbled under her breath. "I'm not making an ass out of myself tomorrow because he didn't give me access to the files. I'll beg for forgiveness later."

She didn't look back as she tried the handle. As it clicked open, she breathed a sigh of relief. She flicked on the lights and shut the door behind her.

Selby slowly put one foot in front of the other, scanning the room. Unlike the décor of the rest of the building, Evan's office was traditional. Within its mahogany paneled walls, brown leather chairs and a matching desk sat to the rear of the office. Aside from a few magazines, not so much as a pen sat atop its surface. The dock for the laptop was empty.

As she passed a bookshelf, her eyes were drawn to a photograph of Garrett. Selby's heart thumped in her chest, recognizing the familiar face of the man standing next to him. Her fingers shook as she reached for the frame. She clutched the picture, brushing the dust away from the surface. *Patrick. Patrick Moretti.* Her head swiveled to the desk, where Evan's nameplate was, praying she was in the wrong office. *Evan was Patrick? No, no, no...it can't be*, she thought to herself in a panic.

A month ago she'd been approached by a handsome

stranger in the club. He'd flirted shamelessly, buying her a cocktail after her first set. Intoxicated from the encounter, she'd kissed him and agreed to a date. The next night, he'd taken her to dinner. But as conversation turned to work, he'd expressed an unusual interest in her career and knowledge of information systems. By the end of the evening, she grew uncomfortable when he'd probed her abilities to hack systems. She knew what he was asking for without him saying the words directly. Breaking off contact with him, she hadn't seen him since that night.

She bit her lip, trying to remember the details of their conversation. *Where had he said he worked? What information had he wanted?* It occurred to her that he hadn't given her specifics. As she studied the photo, she noticed Garrett's arm around him. They were standing at the top of a mountain. *Patrick. Evan. Who was he?* Had he deliberately approached her, knowing of her capabilities? Had he wanted her to do something illegal with regard to Emerson Industries? It had been clear to her that he'd been asking for her to hack into files. But why would he do that to Garrett? She could tell they were close by the way they were hugging. And now he was dead.

She heard the door creak open and her hands trembled as she attempted to place the frame back onto the shelf.

"What the hell do you think you're doing?" Garrett's voice boomed.

The picture slipped from her fingers and tumbled onto the ground, its glass shattering all over the floor.

Chapter Six

Garrett had been in the gym lifting when his phone alerted him to her presence. Aside from security cameras that were installed in every square inch of his facilities, he utilized sensors which notified him if anyone entered his office. At first, the image of Selby had brought a smile to his face. He'd watched with great interest as she knocked on his door, but when he saw her travel down the hallway and then enter Evan's office, he threw down his towel, taking off in search of her. *What the hell is she doing?*

As splinters of the frame crashed all over the hardwood, he took a deep breath, attempting to rein in his anger.

"Don't move," he ordered.

"I…I was just looking for," she stammered and bent over to pick up a shard of glass. "I'm so sorry. It's just that I…I needed information and you weren't…"

"I sent you the files," Garrett began. As he approached, he felt a crunch under his heel.

"I'll clean this up." Her eyes went wide.

"Don't. Just leave it."

"No, it will only take a second," Selby insisted. Crouched over, she carefully placed a jagged remnant into her palm.

"Selby, just stop."

As she lifted her eyes to meet his, his anger turned to sympathy. Instinct drove him as much as facts. Soon enough, he'd question her, and she'd either be fired or still working for him. His eyes flickered to the soft cleavage peeking through her blouse, and he struggled to stay on task. Unsure of whether she'd detected his momentary lapse of focus, he forced an impassive mask across his face.

"I'm sorry. It's just...the meeting tomorrow...I was..." She reached down, shifting her focus from his eyes to the floor and back again. Her lips trembled as her hand touched the picture frame.

"Just leave it."

"I'll clean it up." A small smudge of blood stained the dark wood.

"Do. Not. Move," Garrett commanded, taking sight of what she'd done to her hand. Surprised she hadn't flinched, he surmised the slice of the glass hadn't registered. He'd cut himself enough times to know that the pain didn't always set in until you saw the injury.

"But I...oh my God," Selby said as she realized what she'd done. The broken fragment fell to the ground as she gripped her wrist.

Without asking, Garrett scooped Selby up into his arms, and kicked open the door. He tried not to allow her citrus-scented hair to distract him as he made his way to his office. It was difficult to tame the twitch of his dick as her soft body brushed against his. He knew it was off limits to go there. Not only were they in the office, she was injured. *Get it the fuck together*, he thought.

Garrett eyed his bathroom. Squeezing through the entrance, he gently placed her on the counter, taking note of the small pieces of glass that sparkled from her shoes and stockings. Without giving a thought to what to do next, he stripped off his t-shirt and knelt down, his eyes meeting hers. Although she wasn't crying, he could see the tears readying to fall.

"You're going to be all right, sweetheart. Just give me your hand."

"I'll be fine. Please, no."

"We need to get it under some water, stop the bleeding. We have to make sure we get all the glass out." She extended her hand to him, and licked her lips, tensing as if expecting more pain. He took a quick look at the cut. He tested the water temperature before running both their hands under the stream. "This might sting a little."

"Ow. Dammit, I can't believe I just did that." She attempted to tear her hand away, but he held her firm.

"You're not going anywhere, now. I warned you it was going to sting." He raised an eyebrow at her until she stopped moving. Hearing her speak frankly was surprising but refreshing. Cursing could make even the worst agony seem tolerable. He'd known there was fire underneath the woman who'd negotiated the contract in his office.

"I'm sorry." She gave a small laugh, a rosy hue flushing

her cheeks.

"Almost done. Now listen, Miss Reynolds. You don't seem to take directions very well so far, so I'm going to remind you that while you're here, I'm the boss. That means, when I talk, you listen."

"But..." she began.

"No talking. This is my company, my office." He shushed firmly. "This is serious. The things we do here, which I'll get to in a moment, are sometimes dangerous. Confidential. Deadly, even, if they get into the wrong hands."

Garrett saw the flicker of fear in her eyes. He'd never intentionally set out to intimidate her, but the reality of his life was paramount to protecting every last soul who worked for him.

With her free hand, she wiped a tear, looking away from him. She took a deep breath, and returned his gaze.

The emotion he saw inside her caused a stir of arousal. Goddammit, of all the times to meet someone, this was not it. Even though she feigned confidence, he knew for a fact that she'd never taken on such a big account. He'd promised Lars that he wouldn't get involved with her, yet as he studied her face, he knew it would be a lost cause. Confused by his attraction, he focused his effort on cleaning her hand.

"It looks like the bleeding has slowed. Just keep it under the water a second while I get a towel." As he slowly released her wrist, he noted that she never took her eyes off him. Yet she submitted to his request...this time. No fighting or arguing. He couldn't be certain if she was acquiescing because he'd scolded her or if she truly understood he'd meant what he'd said.

Garrett slid open a cabinet drawer and retrieved a clean washcloth. After turning off the spigot, he wrapped the fabric around her hand, keeping pressure on the wound. He opened the bathroom closet door, and began to rummage through, in search of a Band-Aid. As he glanced back toward Selby, he noticed the look of shock on her face.

"You have a lot of injuries around here?" she asked, her eyes wide.

"Yes. No. Oh hell, okay, yeah, sometimes. Look, Selby, we really need to talk," he hedged. He knew his bathroom supplies made it look as if he was stocking an ambulance. Accidents happened. Granted, usually not on the executive floor, but he liked to be prepared. And out in the field, he was more likely to play down an injury than run to get first aid in front of co-workers.

Selby diverted her eyes, bringing her hand to her chest. The bright red stain on her shirt had begun to crust over into a deep shade of brown.

"Your hand should be all right." Garrett smiled as he set the butterfly bandage into place. "The patient will live. This time."

"Thank you," she said, shifting on the counter.

"Where do you think you're going?" he asked, placing his palms onto her knees.

"Um, out of the bathroom, I guess."

"No."

"No?"

"Nylons in California?" he asked.

"I'm sorry, what?"

"You may be a transplant but I didn't think these," he tugged at her stockings, "were very comfortable. But you know what's even more troubling?"

"What? No wait, how come you know so much about what women wear on their legs?"

"Many reasons." He smiled. "But I think I'll go with business. Yeah, that sounds good."

"Business?"

"Fabrics. Plastics. Metals. Some materials, you want them hard, impenetrable. Others," Garrett brushed the back of his fingers softly against her cheek, catching a stray hair that had come loose from her bun. His eyes fell to her soft lips and then met hers. "They're designed to be soft but strong."

She smiled, silently watching him.

"And these," he pinched a stretchy section off her thigh and let it snap back into place, "hold particles. Like glass."

"Oh," she replied softly. "I don't think...well, I don't feel a cut or anything."

"Let me have your shoes." Before she could protest, Garrett inspected her pumps. He carefully removed each one and shook it over the trash bin. A ping resounded as pellets rained into the tin container. He set them on the toilet seat and then evaluated his next move.

With her soft pink lips within inches, Garrett yearned

to touch Selby, and not just a little bit. He briefly closed his eyes, and his recurrent fantasy flashed through his mind, of her bent over, while he slammed inside of her. He fought a smile.

"Is something funny?" he heard her ask and his gaze beamed up to hers.

"No, not funny. Something to look forward to, perhaps."

"What?"

"About these." He ignored her question and glanced to her legs. "They need to come off."

"What did you say?"

"I think you heard me quite clearly. And since you aren't going to be able to get them off without the tiny bits of glass digging into your skin, the question is, 'How should we get these torturous things off of you?'"

"Do you really think that's necessary? Maybe if I lift up you could help me pull them off?" She raised her legs, and several tiny fragments reflected under the light. "Well, fuck. What am I supposed to do?"

"Fuck? Hmm, that may be an option later but let's get these off first, shall we?"

"No, I just was saying..." she stammered.

"I'm teasing you." He paused. "Maybe. Let me ask you a question, Selby."

"Yes?"

"Do you trust me?" He smiled as the idea came to him. She couldn't possibly trust him yet, but oh, how she would learn.

"I'm not sure. Lars trusts you."

"I'm not Lars."

"No you're not," she stated flatly.

"Do you want to close your eyes or open them?"

"What are you talking about?"

"Now don't shoot down this idea because I actually think it may be the best solution…all things considered."

"What is it? Just get them off."

Garrett turned his back and selected his instrument. Holding it up, he gave her a smile, hoping it'd take the sting out of his suggestion.

"Scissors? Are you kidding me?"

"Not in the least."

"No way."

"Way. They're bandage scissors. We can start at your waist and slide straight down to your toes. They'll peel right off without scratching your skin."

"Oh my God. I seriously don't believe this."

"Think of it as penance for going into Evan's office."

"About that…"

"Yes, about that." Figuring it was as good a time as any, he pressed her for answers. "Why were you in his office?"

"In my defense, I told you I needed his laptop. There was something in the files you sent me. Tomorrow's the board meeting and I didn't want to be unprepared."

"So you broke into his office…the first day you come to work for me?"

"I was going to ask you if I could have it, but you

didn't give me your cell phone number. I knocked on your door. You weren't there."

"I saw you," he replied, toying with the shiny metal instrument.

"You saw me?" She rolled her eyes and set them back on him. "The cameras?"

"Yes, the cameras. I see everything. You want to tell me why it couldn't wait until tomorrow?"

"There was no guarantee I'd see you before the meeting. You may not mind walking in cold to a board meeting, but that's not how I roll," she challenged.

"I see," he laughed. "Not how you roll, you say. I'm going to be setting some ground rules before you end up out the door."

"Ground rules?"

"See, you do listen." He smiled and held up the scissors. "Let's table this, shall we? It appears we have more pressing business at hand."

"Do you know what you're doing with those things? I probably could just scoot up." She tugged her shirt out of her skirt and wriggled on the counter.

"Hey, if you want to take off your clothes, then well, who am I to stop you, but I think if you just let me reach up..."

"Okay." She sighed. "I'll hold out the waistband and you snip it. Agreed?"

"It'll be painless." *For you.* As soon as he put his hands on her, it would be a race in time to control his growing erection.

"Promise?" She gave him a small smile and lifted the side of her skirt so he could reach underneath.

"You must learn to trust me, Miss Reynolds. Easy now," he instructed. His fingers worked quickly as he felt his way up her thigh to where she held the band taut. With a snip, he worked backward, cutting a line down to her toe. "Now the other side. Don't move. When I'm finished, I'm going to lift you out of here, get you away from all this glass."

Garrett's cock jerked as his wrist brushed over her leg. Clipping away, it only took him seconds to make his way down to her other foot. When he was finished, he placed the scissors on the counter. A pause of silence passed between them as his eyes met hers. Never shifting his gaze, he slipped his hands under her skirt. The warmth of her pussy heated his palms as he gripped the band, pulling it toward the ground. Sating his need to touch her, the tips of his fingers met her skin, carefully brushing the fabric aside.

She willingly spread her legs, allowing him to drape the nylon away from her skin. Freeing her toes, he stood up, the sides of his abdomen grazing her inner thighs.

"Put your arms around my neck," he instructed. Without questioning him, she did as told, and he shivered in anticipation of what he could do with her once they were out of the bathroom.

"You ready?" he asked, his voice low. He wasn't sure whether or not he was asking to move her, kiss her, or fuck her. His balls tightened and damn, if his brain didn't kick him right back in the nuts. *Get her to the sofa and stop fooling around, G.* Jesus Christ, Lars was going to fucking kill him.

"Yes," she breathed. She licked her lips. "Wait. Ready for what?"

"This," he responded, picking her up off the counter in one smooth action. He reached under her skirt, cupping her bottom, and plucked the offending stockings off, throwing them to the ground. He grunted as she wrapped her legs around him, the warmth of her core skimming against his abs.

Garrett wasted no time getting out of the bathroom, depositing her gently onto his sofa. The sound of her soft gasp took him by surprise and he forced himself to remove his hands from her waist. Not wanting her to see the expression of desire on his face, he turned back toward the bathroom, kicking his sneakers off. A glutton for punishment, he returned to her side. Kneeling down on the floor, he checked her legs for abrasions.

"Let me see." As he ran his palms down her thighs, inspecting her calves and feet, she squeezed her legs tight together. He glanced up to her flushed face and knew instantly she was every bit as aroused as he was. She nervously tugged at her shirt.

"You look good. I mean," he coughed, "no cuts. Do you feel any pain? Anything?"

"No, I'm fine, thanks. I feel like an idiot for making such a God-awful mess, but I think my ego will survive. Thank you, Mr...."

"Garrett. I think we're beyond formalities now, don't you?" He shoved up and went to the bar. Opening a cabinet, he retrieved a bottle of cognac and two tumblers.

"Garrett, I'm sorry about tonight. I'm really sorry about your friend," she paused, "Evan."

"Yes. Evan." He hesitated, his back toward Selby, and took a deep breath.

As he poured the amber liquid into the glasses, he tried to clear his head. Garrett had always been a rock for everyone around him. Nothing had shaken him. Painful memories from his teen years, the impetus for his penchant for extreme sports, came rushing back to him as if he was seventeen again. Brain surgeries, tumors, nearly dying. The brush with death had taught him that life was fleeting. The only way to live was to embrace life. Not just the soft fluffy parts, but the nitty-gritty in your face, near death experiences that brought euphoria to the surface, reminding you of why you were put here.

Over the past fifteen years, he hadn't given a thought as to whether or not to participate in high risk activities. Emotions weren't a factor. Strategy and safety planning were integral to the sport. Evan had taught him that. But now, Evan was dead. A swirl of emotions had built inside of him. Grief. Anger. Confusion. None of it made sense. Any day, the prosecutor's office would call, a determination of death announced.

As he glanced to Selby, he couldn't put his finger on what it was about her that had made him lose focus altogether. He'd been with many women, but he'd never been so attracted to a woman that he'd have stripped their nylons off with scissors. Shit, he knew damn well the entire scenario could have been avoided. He could have called up Rita from security to help Selby. But he hadn't. Ever since that night in the club, fantasies had danced in his head.

Catching her in Evan's office had been unexpected. If she really wanted access to the files as she claimed, there was no security clearance that would afford her that information. The only people in his life who he'd given that top priority information to had been long time, trusted employees. Selby would have to earn her clearance with him and it would involve a helluva lot more than simply asking.

As he turned to bring her a drink, he caught her staring at him. His eyes locked on hers. There was no way in hell he was going to be able to not have her. It was a matter of when, not if. But first he needed answers.

"Selby." He handed her a drink and eyed her with interest as she took a sip and coughed. "I think it's time we had a talk."

Shaking his head, he purposefully sat on the chair across from her and took a swig. As her pink tongue darted over her lips and she ran a fingertip over the rim of the glass, one thought blew through his mind. He was so fucked.

Chapter Seven

Selby attempted to catch her breath as Garrett slowly poured their drinks. She wrapped her arms around herself, willing her hardened nipples to relax. She'd just experienced the hottest twenty minutes of her life. Unfortunately, they'd also been the most awkward. Her thoughts drifted to the shattered photograph, and she couldn't help but wonder what the deal was with Evan. From the looks of the photo, he appeared to have been good friends with Garrett Emerson. Under any other circumstances, that alone would have given him credibility. But he'd used an alias, lied to her. Aside from his dubious motives, he'd had no long term plans of seeing her. He'd been a user looking to use.

Why he'd done it was another question. Had he succeeded in stealing data? Found another hacker to do his bidding? The itch of curiosity in her belly wouldn't be scratched until she unearthed every skeleton rattling in Evan's closet. Selby considered telling Garrett about what his friend had done, but was reluctant to do so. Even though he'd almost kissed her, attraction wasn't enough to shake the foundation of friendship. If Evan had perpetrated a crime, had sought Emerson Industries harm, she couldn't make an accusation without evidence.

Selby's contemplation was broken by the sound of glass clinking. She lifted her lids, and studied the corded contours of Garrett's muscular back. When he'd ripped off his shirt to stop her bleeding, she'd barely noticed the blood. Holy hell, the man must spend a lot of time in the gym. She'd had to resist the temptation to reach for his tanned abs, ones that looked as hard as granite. Licking definitely seemed a viable option, given how close her lips had been, but she'd behaved. As his fingers glided over her thighs in the bathroom, she'd grown wet with desire. She hoped he hadn't noticed how she'd stopped breathing as the scruff of his beard had scraped her neck. When he'd picked her up, continuing to caress her legs, she'd tightened them, the throbbing pain of arousal rushing through every vein in her body.

But now, the moment was gone. She sat alone, waiting to face the music. His silence told her that his lust had cooled. He'd been drawn into thought and when he turned to her, his eyes had grown weary. Garrett handed her a glass, and while she didn't ever drink on the job, this seemed as good a time as any to break precedent. She suspected that by the time she was done with her assignment, she'd have shattered every last carefully constructed rule she'd ever put in place.

As he sat back into his chair, demanding they have a

talk, her stomach dropped. His voice brought her back into focus.

"Ground rules," he growled.

Selby took a small sip and coughed. *Ah yes, ground rules.* She couldn't suppress the small smile that crossed her face, and she shook her head.

"We can discuss whatever you'd like. But I'd like to remind you that I have a contract."

"Yes, I know what I signed. Correction, what we signed." Garrett plowed his fingers through his hair and set his eyes on hers. "Confidentiality. Clearances. There's a reason for all of this."

"As there is in every assignment I take," she responded. "I'm sorry I went in his office, but I assure you I was just looking for the information I'm already supposed to have. I'm really sorry about Evan's accident, but…"

"What happened to Evan…if it was an accident…"

"I know. Skydiving. But Garrett, I mean it's kind of high risk," she interrupted.

"It's none of your concern, Selby." Garrett set his glass down onto the coffee table, hard enough that it caused her to jump.

Without apology, he stood and walked over to the wall, which had built in shelves. He opened a drawer and retrieved a white cotton t-shirt. Mesmerized by his intensity, Selby stared as he dressed. She was almost relieved when his chiseled physique was covered, no longer distracting her.

"Duly noted, Mr. Emerson," she replied, slipping back

into her work demeanor.

"Rule number one. I decide what access you have and when. Until we know what happened, you will most definitely not have physical access to Evan's office or any of his physical belongings, including his laptop." Garrett didn't miss a beat as he turned to her and continued, "I'm well aware of your, how should I say, ability to acquire his files by other means. So while I appreciate you attempting to get them in a legitimate way, you will not have access to all the files until I'm comfortable that you have a solid understanding of what we do here. Clearances only tell me that you can be trusted with information. They don't tell me that you grasp why we are doing the things we are doing here. So for now, I need you to focus on infrastructure. Convince the board that the outsourcing is mutually beneficial for both our companies."

"Outsourcing information systems at Emerson Industries to DLar-Tech? I can do that in my sleep. But in the files you gave me, they referenced something called a PFx Prototype. Now I don't know what that is, but if it's in his files, they may ask…"

"They won't ask you."

"But…"

"Rule number two. I make the rules. If it comes up, I'll stop the discussion. Tomorrow's about introducing you to the board, establishing credibility. Your résumé speaks for itself, but Lars is responsible for bringing you in."

"So I'm interviewing?" She smiled.

"Something like that. Decision's already been made. I

know it. They know it. But it's essential they feel comfortable with you."

"I'll do my best to sell them on the outsource plan. I can do this."

"Rule number three." As Garrett considered his next words, he lifted his eyes to hers, attempting not to stare as she toyed with the hem of her skirt. She shifted on the couch, and he swore he saw the faintest hint of a small tattoo on her inner thigh. *Interesting.* Miss Reynolds was a dichotomy of personalities. Her business woman persona was rigid in many ways, yet she bent rules when needed. Perhaps part of her yearned to rebel?

"Here's the thing, Selby. My company isn't just about technologies. I've built this by taking risks."

"Don't you mean danger?"

"To some but not us. Nor our customers either. We do this to experience life in a way that most people never see. The exhilaration of dropping from the sky."

"Exhilaration?"

"Yes. The kind that takes your breath away. Like the best fucking sex you've ever had in your life. Do you know what that feels like?" he asked, never moving to touch her. He watched as she struggled to keep an impassive expression.

"Um, I don't think that's something you really need to know."

"Oh but I do, Selby. And do you want to know why?"

She nodded, her fingers moving to her bloodstained blouse, where she fidgeted with a button.

"Because these are things that remind us we're alive. Sex. Fear. Anticipation." Garrett had had enough of pretending. *Fuck it. I'll apologize to Lars later.* He stood and walked behind the sofa. Placing his palms on her shoulders, he steadied her before she had a chance to move. He knelt, bringing his lips to her ear. "Here at Emerson Industries we strive to bring customers face-to-face with the mind-blowing rush they want. Sometimes it's a high-tech operation that requires calculated strategy. Sometimes it's as easy as ramping up technology in a way to let Mother Nature provide the high. Stratospheric skydiving suits and helmets, to experimental polymer surfboards. We understand needs, enabling that rush. We push boundaries."

"I've read about your company, how you built it," she challenged.

"But you haven't felt it, have you, Selby?" he pressed, his lips brushing against her ear. The subtle scent of her perfume teased his nostrils. Her fingers glided up over his and he knew he had her. He would make her understand, teach her. She'd breathe in the rush of the high, and never be the same.

"Mr. Emer…Garrett," she began. "I can't…I don't do the things you do. I just can't."

"But you want to feel it. That rush from base jumping or from riding a wave. We all have our own threshold of how much is enough, how far we'd go. Tell me, Miss Reynolds, do you really want to learn about our culture?"

"But of course I do," she quickly responded.

"What's enough for you? Where're your limits? How do you get your rush? Hacking into places you shouldn't be? No, no, no, that's much too easy," he breathed. "Singing in front of a live audience? Is that where you come alive? Grinding your ass into my cock the other night? Did that do it?"

"I didn't mean to…we need to talk about that."

"Yes, I think we do, because I know you're capable of pushing the envelope, too, sweetheart. I want to feel you tremble, Selby." Garrett placed his lips on her neck and heard her sigh. He dragged the tip of his tongue behind her ear, tasting her skin. His dick was hard as rock, but he'd take her only after she trusted him, after she learned why this company was so damn important to him. "That rush you feel right now. That's what I'm going to teach you. In the bedroom and out."

"Who said we're going to…?"

"Limits. Boundaries. They're all meant to be bent, sometimes even broken. And I suspect we're going to break a few together." Garrett slipped his fingers over her lapel, gliding his hands across her collarbone. Her head lolled back against him, her eyes closed. He smiled at her acquiescence. Jesus, it shouldn't matter what she did, but there was something about her. "Tomorrow, we're going to rock the shit out of this board meeting. You'll do this for me and then we're going on a personalized tour. Participation isn't optional."

"Participation?" Her head snapped up and he laughed. Refusing to let her go, he brought his lips to her neck once again and spoke softly against her skin.

"Ah, ah, ah, Miss Reynolds. Rule number two. I make the rules. Just consider this employee training. I promise," he paused, "to keep you safe. You can trust me."

"I don't know if I can…"

"You can and you will. After the meeting, you're all mine." Garrett stood, removing his hands from her shoulders. As he made his way to his desk, he observed her blink in disbelief. He picked up his cell and texted security to come to his office.

"I think I should get going so I can come in early tomorrow," Selby said. Standing, her eyes fell to her bare feet. She glanced to the bathroom and then to Garrett. "Um, can you bring me my shoes?"

"Leave them. You shouldn't risk getting glass in your feet. Here." Garrett went to his cabinet, and took out a clean pair of socks and slip-on sandals. "They're a little big but safer than getting a chunk of glass in your foot. Not sure I'm up for surgery this late at night."

"Really, I think I'll be fine."

"Rule number two," Garrett said with a smile. "I promise to get you your shoes back after I have housekeeping clean up the mess."

Selby sat down on the couch and slipped on the socks. He reached for her feet, gently placing them into his sandals.

"You're right. They are a little big." She laughed. "That and I don't want you doing surgery. No offense, but I don't think my heart will take another episode with the scissors."

"How's your hand feel?" He reached for her hand and carefully lifted it, inspecting the bandage.

"I'm fine. Thank you again. I'm sorry."

"Just remember the rules and we'll get along fine." Garrett brought her palm to his lips and kissed it. "Until tomorrow."

"Tomorrow," Selby repeated, unable to take her eyes off him.

"Hey, Chloe." Garrett's gaze moved toward the door. Selby tugged her hand out of his as the security guard approached. "Selby, this is Chloe. She's going to help see you to your car. She may even have a pair of sandals downstairs that will fit you."

Garrett gave a sly smile as Selby jumped to her feet, the flush on her cheeks caused by the sudden intrusion. Aware that she was capable of taking over some of Evan's responsibilities, Garrett had to admit that he needed her. With Evan gone and an investigation to come, he couldn't afford to lose sight of his company's interests.

Chapter Eight

Selby had barely slept, replaying the scene over and over again in her mind. The sound of his commanding, sensual voice soothing her as he took care to clean up the shattered glass. His masculine scent entrenched in her senses. The memory of Garrett's body heating her skin was both erotic and terrifying all at once.

A night of restless sleep hadn't hampered Selby's professional routine. She'd woken early, gone to the office and had Garrett's secretary prepare dossiers. Impeccably dressed, she checked her face in her compact mirror and dabbed at the circles under her eyes. Aside from the light gloss on her lips, she wore little make-up. Closing her eyes, she breathed out the nerves that threatened her control.

The board meeting was an audition, a test of sorts. She anticipated they'd scrutinize her, but aimed to gain their trust. She was well-prepared, had studied all the players that were expected to attend. The proposal was solid. Numbers and facts had been memorized and reviewed with Lars during her drive to Emerson Industries. Lars would stoically sit as she presented her case, watching his protégée cinch the deal. She'd done it many times, yet she knew this was different. Garrett would expect nothing less than perfection and she planned on giving it to him.

The ultra-sleek conference room hummed with the power of the twelve executives who waited on the presentation. They ignored Selby as she handed the portfolios to Garrett's admin, and loaded her presentation on her laptop. As it flared onto the big screen, Selby lifted her gaze and met Garrett's eyes. His lips were drawn in a tight line, the heat of his gaze reminding her of the night before. Retraining her vision on the projection, she cleared her throat, drawing everyone's attention.

Within fifteen minutes, she'd presented her case to outsource to DLar-Tech. She'd caught the condescending look directed her way by Ryder Tremblay, Head Legal Counsel. Nate Killian, Chief Financial Officer, scribbled on his notepad and darted his eyes over toward Garrett. Chase Abbott, who headed up the scientific division, appeared uninterested, flipping through a journal. Lars gave her a small nod as she prepared to open it up for questions.

"So as you can see, the move to DLar-Tech will conservatively save Emerson Industries approximately ten million dollars a year," she concluded. "I'd be happy to review any of the processes with you in more detail if needed. The breakdowns on the financials are in the spreadsheet."

"Garrett, I think we need to reconsider this move. With Evan gone, you can't expect us to seriously vote on this based on the presentation of his temp." Nate gave a small condescending laugh. "She's only been here a day."

"True, Mr. Killian. However, at least ninety percent of the data for the proposal was collected by Evan. It's clear that everyone in this room knew managed services were being considered." She tapped the end of her stylus against the table in a deliberate attempt to keep herself calm. "I won't make the assumption you reviewed the financials but you can confirm the feasibility study that was done."

"What happens to staff? You know this is one of my main concerns. We've built up talent to specifically serve our needs," Ryder asked Garrett.

Selby swore they could hear her heart pounding as the void of silence widened. Garrett never took his eyes off her as he waited on her to speak. She'd never been one to expect rescue, confident in her merit. If she sank or she swam, it would be her charge.

"Consideration has been given to human resources," she began, reminding them she was still leading the discussion. "If you wish to retrain staff to stay on in other positions, repurpose if you will, that's your choice. However, as we proceed, we'll be taking on those positions, and remaining employees will become part of DLar-Tech. I can assure you that we'll be utilizing excess staff in other key positions within our company."

"How's that possible?" Nate pressed Lars.

Selby flashed back to the slide, discussing resources. "We do full disclosure before taking on accounts…"

"I was asking Lars, not you," he challenged, a hard expression crossing his face.

"I see, but I'm the one giving the presentation and currently the chief technology officer, not Lars. So if you want answers, I'll be happy to provide them." She glanced down to her friend, whose face told her he was about five seconds away from bursting out laughing. He knew better than anyone that she wasn't the type to take shit. Still, she couldn't figure out Garrett's game. He continued to allow his team to go hard, never intervening, despite the fact that they were edging on unprofessionalism.

"Garrett, I don't think…" Ryder interrupted.

"Mr. Emerson isn't giving this presentation either. Up here." She clicked on her laser and pointed to the screen. If these good ole boys wanted to play rough, she'd be happy to go a round. "This," she pointed to the graphic displaying the process for transitioning employees, and resisting the urge to use her kindergarten teacher voice, continued, "is the slide I reviewed previously that came directly from Evan's notes. Of course, I'm quite familiar with this process because, I, in conjunction with Lars, developed it. It's my understanding that this process, as well as the initial contracts, were reviewed with both Garrett and Evan."

She waited on Garrett to confirm her findings but he

merely gave her a small smile. Before she had a chance to ask him to elaborate, Nate once again went on the offensive.

"I have concerns about our systems being taken out of house. What security do you have in place to make sure we aren't hacked?"

"I agree that you have many firewall and security measures in place today. However, we have more expertise in this area. In addition to top level security, we have disaster recovery plans and procedures for every one of our clients." Selby looked to an attractive woman, who tapped at her iPad. Raine Presley, the company's chief security officer, had kept unusually quiet during the entire meeting and she wondered at her motives for doing so. "Miss Presley has also reviewed the plans."

"Raine," Ryder called, annoyed at his colleague.

"Hey, what?" Raine smiled up at Selby and then focused her attention on Ryder. "We're good. She's right. I'm not sure why this is such a big deal. We worked on this before...well, you know...the accident."

"And you approved this?" Ryder asked.

"You know as well as I do that Garrett has final say, but yeah, Evan and I were on board."

"Believe me, sir, I understand your reservations." Selby kept her voice soft and even, as if she were speaking to a scared animal. Both Nate's and Ryder's faces had reddened and she knew that having been confronted and potentially embarrassed, they needed to save face. "Lars and I know how important your data is to you. Your information systems are the delicate network, the fabric, if you will, that support your entire corporation. At DLar-Tech, we care for your systems as if they were our own. Agreeing to this solution will save you money. We're able to do this by leveraging skills across multiple customers. Your data is confidential and safe with us. IT is our specialty. We take over your day-to-day operations so that you can direct time and resources toward your core businesses."

Selby paused, and caught Garrett's sexy smile. She forced herself to meet the gaze of every last person sitting around the table, praying to God she'd get her hormones under control. Ryder opened his mouth to speak and she proceeded to finish her conclusions.

"When you contract with DLar-Tech, we offer top of the line service level agreements to ensure your needs are being met. It's a win-win. Basic financial and contract information is in the dossiers provided to you. E-copies of more detailed terms and conditions have been sent to you. If you have any more questions or concerns, you can contact either Lars or me and we'll get back to you right away."

"Thank you," Garrett said, stifling any further argument on the subject.

"You're welcome, sir."

"Please give us a few minutes. Selby?"

"Yes, sir?" Selby closed her laptop and collected stray papers. Lars had warned her ahead of time that she wouldn't be privy to a vote due to the conflict of interest.

"I'll be in to see you in a few minutes. Thanks for your

presentation," Garrett stated.

"Thank you." Her voice wavered slightly and she pushed a stray hair from her face. His approval wrapped around her like a warm blanket and the butterflies in her stomach did a happy dance. The flicker in his eyes told her that he'd remembered everything from last night and that whatever they'd started was far from over.

"And Selby…"

"Yes?" She gathered her things in her arms, carrying them protectively against her chest as if to block him from seeing the emotion brewing inside her.

"Hope you remembered what I told you to bring yesterday."

"Um, what?" *A bathing suit.* What the hell could he possibly be thinking?

"This won't take too long."

"Yeah, okay," she managed.

"Nice job." Lars patted her shoulder as the boardroom door shut.

"Lars, I don't know if I should stay on…"

"You're staying. Garrett needs you whether he knows it or not. And I need you to get things transitioned after the contract is approved."

"You think they'll sign?" she asked as they walked to her office.

"Yeah, I do. Nate's just being difficult as usual. And Ryder…well, they're all taking things hard, with Evan out of the picture."

"About that." Selby rounded her desk and placed her

things on top. She kicked off her high heels and fell back into her leather chair. "Evan. How well did you know him?"

"He's been...he was with Garrett for a long time. Even though he was the CTO, he was a jack of all trades. Ex-military. Helped Garrett when he first started going after the government contracts. He also worked with Chase on the science stuff. Had his hands in all sorts of things."

"Did you sky dive with him?"

"Of course." Lars paused and closed the door.

Selby opened her desk drawer, pulled out a piece of candy and waved it in front of him. "Lollypop?"

"It's ten in the morning, Selb."

"Yeah, I've been up since five and I'm runnin' on a few hours of sleep. Give me sugar or give me death." She laughed, unwrapped it and popped it into her mouth.

"You know that shit's not good for you," Lars pressed. "Red dye. Yellow dye. Corn syrup."

"Don't care, Lars. I just got baptized by fire, so bring it on."

"You did well today in there. Evan and I had this all hammered out before his accident, but we hadn't taken it to the board. Garrett's a yes."

"Hmm...well, he could have said so during the presentation. Would it have killed him to let Nate and Ryder know that this was a done deal? It's like he wanted me to go through every last detail of the feasibility study. I read Evan's notes. He'd paved the way for this project. But you would never have known that this morning." She sighed, considering how much she should share with Lars about what had happened last night. "Speaking of Evan, how close were you? I mean, we've known each other a long time and I never met him before. But when you talk about him...I don't know, it just seems like you all were really close."

"Yeah, we all were close friends. I met him after you and I got out of college. I guess I never introduced you to him for the same reasons I never introduced you to Garrett. It's not like you all have anything in common. And Evan was always the craziest out of all of us. It's not like you'd date the guy."

"How would you know?" she countered. *Not only did I date him, I kissed him and he tried to get me to steal for him.*

"Don't take this the wrong way, but it's no secret that you're kind of tightly wound. You're all about control. And some of us... we like being out of control."

"I just like being alive is all. Death isn't up there on my to do list."

"I'm just saying that Evan would not be your type." Lars paused, scrubbing his chin with his hand. He cocked an eyebrow and gave her a sideways grin. "You want me to be honest about this morning?"

"No. Lie to me. It's awesome." She knew his critique was coming but couldn't stifle her sarcasm. Lars always enjoyed pushing her buttons.

"Garrett's main concern about you is that you really don't get his company and why people want what they provide. You already know that some of the stuff they develop is used for the military, things having to do with the skydiving, advanced technologies. But some of their products are for everyday people who just enjoy the extreme adventures we partake in. The bottom line is that no matter what the numbers say on the deal or how much money his company brings in, this is still not a publicly held company. Garrett built this from the ground up. All those guys sitting around him know it and most of them helped him."

"How's that different than some of our other clients?"

"They are a part of the company. Nate. Yeah, he's a hardass but he loves climbing any mountain that he thinks is impossible to climb. Ryder, he base jumps. Almost every single person in that room with the exception of Janice, his HR VP, is heavily invested in Emerson Industries. They don't just work here. They get the business, know why their customers do what they do. I love ya, Selb, but you're an outsider."

"Fair enough, but then why ask me to do this job?" She couldn't understand for the life of her why Lars would put her in this position. Knowing that Evan had propositioned her to steal made the situation all the worse, but now it dawned on her that she was the persona non grata.

"Because you're the best. And Garrett could barely breathe, let alone run his company after Evan died. Honestly, things could get worse before they get better," he admitted.

"I'll do what I can, but I'm not taking shit from assholes who don't know our business. After reviewing the data, there's no question we can save them money. And you know we'll do it better." Selby wished she could ask Lars more details about Evan, but like Garrett, she sensed he was holding back on her.

Lars stood and stretched his arms above his head. Selby inwardly smiled, aware that he'd never be so casual in front of anyone else. A knock on the door jolted her back into reality, reminding her they weren't in their own offices.

"Miss Selby." Garrett's secretary, Norm, entered her office and set a silver shopping bag onto her desk.

"Um, what's this?" she asked, her eyes darting to Lars.

"Mr. Emerson said you'd forget, and asked me to bring you your things for this afternoon's assignment."

"Oookay." Selby smiled, aware that she'd deliberately left her suit at home. She reached inside the sack and retrieved a peach-colored bikini top. A laugh bubbled out of her and she shook her head. "I guess he wasn't kidding."

"Garrett never kids. Looks like he's about to clue you in as to what they do here."

"How's a bathing suit going to school me on a multi-billion dollar company?" Astonished, Selby dug further into the satchel and pulled out the rest of the suit, a sarong and flip flops.

"Garrett doesn't do anything half way." Lars smiled and stood. He smoothed down his trousers before making his way toward her door. "I'd suggest we celebrate tonight, but I have a feeling you might be too tired for dinner."

"I don't work for him, Lars." She gritted her teeth, wondering what Garrett had planned. Numbers and technology she could do with her eyes closed. Surprises were up on her list of things to avoid, along with spiders and mold-covered bread.

"You need to look at this as a learning experience. You'll do fine."

"I'm not fine."

"Tangerine is a good color on you." He laughed.

"It's peach, dumbass. And I don't see any good reason why I should be wearing a bathing suit while I'm at work," she huffed.

"Ah, but you've never worked for Garrett. Welcome to my world." Lars winked as he left her office.

Frustrated, Selby grabbed the bag off her desk and hurled it across the room. Everything about the situation was uncomfortable. She may have idolized his maverick business sense but she had no intention of getting caught up in his dangerous lifestyle. He could jump off the space station for all she cared, but whatever he was planning simply was not happening.

Selby pursed her lips around the candy, the rough edges scraping her tongue. She glared at the contents of the bag, which had spilled onto the floor, and tried to reason why she shouldn't just gather her things and walk out of the office. She suspected that whatever Garrett had planned would test not only her deepest fears but her ability to resist him. Every second she spent in his presence deepened her attraction for the charismatic billionaire.

She bit down into the confection, the sweetness dancing in her mouth. *Do not be afraid*, she told herself. *You can resist*, she repeated. All the while, she knew it was a lie. She blew out a breath and walked around her desk. As she fingered the silky fabric, it was as if she'd been ensnared in the web of his temptation. She untied the strings of the bikini top and held it to her chest, and laughed. If there was one thing she knew, it was that no challenge would go unmet. She'd punish Lars later, but this afternoon, she'd show Garrett that she wasn't scared of his games. Hell, people didn't go skydiving in bathing suits; whatever he had planned, how bad could it be?

Chapter Nine

Garrett shifted his Jeep into gear, the warmth of the sun shining on his face. He loved the convertible, aware that it wasn't the luxurious car she'd be expecting he'd drive. He glanced over to Selby, who gave him a nervous smile. Watching her command the boardroom had given him an erection so hard he thought he'd have to ice himself down. Jesus almighty, the woman was smart. Despite her obvious IT knowledge, Ryder and Nate had protested her lack of experience with their products. Having a fancy degree wasn't enough at Emerson. Hell, some of his managers had never even been to college. What they did have above all else was subject matter expertise.

At the meeting she'd looked to him to intervene, but he'd purposely kept silent. No matter what the fucking contract said, he couldn't keep her on if she wasn't able to prove her worth to his operation managers. He'd known full well that the IT staff would be retained no matter the results of the deal. He, Evan and Lars had hammered out the details long before today's meeting. But if she was overseeing the transition process, she'd have to hold her own ground with his team.

His executives would expect Selby to have at least a basic understanding of all the key aspects of his business, what drove customers to seek the thrill that only certain high risk sports could bring them. Unfortunately, Selby had no experience, nor did she have the desire to embrace the rush he sought practically every day of his life.

Garrett had talked to Lars, had Selby investigated. She didn't smoke, rarely drank. Living within the confines of the law, she'd never even had a parking ticket. According to Lars, she'd had a few boyfriends but nothing serious. The woman didn't engage in any sports, let alone any kind of high risk ones. Despite her conservative profile, she'd demonstrated both courage and tenacity.

As he made his way through the industrial complex and turned onto the gravel road, his thoughts were drawn back to how he'd planned to teach Selby more about Emerson Industries. He glanced over to her, noting that her expression was well hidden behind her sunglasses. Garrett gave a small laugh, enjoying how their banter appeared to vacillate between sexual innuendo and business. He'd told Lars he wouldn't sleep with her, yet he'd already tested the limits of his promise. The previous night in his office, he'd lost control, indulging in their provocative exchange, telling her he'd bed her. Worse, she hadn't said no, leaving the experience entirely on the table.

The audience at the meeting hadn't stifled their heated gaze. Although she'd averted eye contact, it was as if they were the only two people in the room. He knew it. She knew it.

This morning, when he'd woken up, he swore to himself that he'd resist temptation. But as Garrett's eyes darted from the white caps in the distance to the flimsy cotton fabric that had ridden up Selby's leg, exposing her tanned thigh, he knew it would be difficult to keep his resolve.

"Are we going to talk about the meeting today?" she asked.

Selby's voice drew Garrett's attention, jarring his train of thought. He cursed as the tires hit a pothole, and his eyes focused back onto the gravel road.

"Sure, what would you like to discuss?" he asked.

"Are you signing us on? Is it a go?" Selby kept her eyes on Garrett.

"Of course." He smiled.

"You planned on approving it?" Selby crossed her arms and took a small breath. "I was right. It was a test."

"Well, I wouldn't put it exactly like that. I wanted buy-in from the team." Garrett pulled into a small parking lot. A narrow path led to the beach, which beckoned a couple of hundred feet away. He switched off the ignition and turned to Selby. "I can see from your résumé that you're good. Lars thinks you walk on water. But I need everyone to feel they had a say. Evan…he wasn't just a C-level pencil pusher."

"I'm really sorry for your loss," Selby offered. Her palm touched his shoulder, causing him instant arousal.

"Thank you. Evan was close to a lot of people here, not just me. As far as today, no matter what qualifications you have on paper, I'm afraid it doesn't hold much water with the others. The people, my team, they all get what goes on at Emerson."

"I told you I studied…"

"And I told you last night that you need to understand our brand. I expect my execs to live Emerson. How else can they manage it if they don't get our product?"

"Not all executives who run hospitals are doctors or nurses. But they still run healthcare companies," she countered.

"Yeah, and that's workin' out real well." He rolled his eyes, leaned over and unclicked her seatbelt. "Last night…"

"I'm sorry I went in Evan's office."

"I'm not talking about that." Garrett jumped out of the Jeep and rounded to open her door. He reached for her hand and the heat sizzled his palm. Despite his promises to himself, he'd touched her already and didn't want to let go. "What I said about learning your limits, to feel the rush of adrenaline; some of us are like junkies, trying to get our next fix. Others are simply weekend warriors, reminding themselves that mortality comes for all of us. They're fighting back against the inevitable. And you need to learn."

"I can't date you," Selby blurted out, and pulled her hand away. She looked away to the dunes, avoiding eye contact.

"Why do you sing in that club?" He ignored her statement and changed the subject, forcing her to recall what she'd done to him.

"It relaxes me. I enjoy it. Besides, I don't get out a lot with my schedule. I like the people there."

"Why don't you get out? Lars pays you well, right?" He opened the trunk and retrieved a large backpack.

"I really shouldn't be telling you this...it doesn't matter."

"Everything about you matters, Selby. Why the gig at the club? No offense, but it seems so different than how you are in the office."

"It's just that I get anxious sometimes." She traced a small path in the sand with the toe of her sandals. "You might as well know. It's not like I can have any secrets, with you as my client. I'm surprised you didn't see it in the clearance paperwork."

"I haven't read it yet," he lied.

"I...I'm afraid of heights, small spaces. But mostly," she hesitated and her eyes met his, "look, no one's ever asked. It's never an issue because I try very hard not to put myself in situations that will exacerbate the problem."

"What problem?"

"Panic attacks," she confessed. "You don't need to worry about this, though. I swear to you it's under control. No medication either. I know it works for lots of people but in my job...I just can't risk interactions. I meditate. Get acupuncture."

"And sing? Hmm." He raised an eyebrow at her and

smiled. "In a corset?"

"Hey, there's nothing wrong with it. But I don't dance. That night…" She paused. Garrett gave a small laugh as her cheeks grew red. "Ugh…Lars. He knows I sing but he didn't tell me he was coming. I certainly didn't know it was you when I…well, you know what I did. I was just feeling a little flirty…pushing myself to go a little further with my act. It's therapeutic."

"So you don't actually strip when you're there?"

"No way. I mean, not that there is anything wrong with it. It's burlesque. Everyone is the same with their clothes off. It's a great equalizer."

"And you have experience with this? Public nudity?" Garrett resisted the urge to laugh, given her background.

"Well, no, but I've seen other people naked. It doesn't bother me at all. It can be beautiful," she said, her tone of voice indignant.

"So you're a voyeur?" he half joked. He'd hoped she was more of an exhibitionist, given her performance.

"What would make you say something like that?"

"You just said you liked to watch?"

"Well, yeah, but…wait, are you teasing me?"

"Maybe," he lied. He'd been entirely serious. The temptation to play with her in front of others taunted him. His cock jerked, and he shook his head. *Jesus, Garrett, not here.*

"You wanna know how far I'll go?" she continued, giving him a small smile. "What gives me a rush? That's what you asked me last night, right?"

"Yes, I did." He laughed. Neither of them had forgotten what he'd promised.

"I may not like heights, Mr. Emerson, but there's plenty I do like. Lots of things, as a matter of fact." She winked. "But I'm not going to tell you. You'll just have to find out for yourself."

"Garrett," he corrected her.

"I know who I'm addressing. Or do I? Is it my client who tests my knowledge in the boardroom? Or is it the man whose lips were on my skin last night? You know, the one promising me…what was that you said? A rush in the bedroom and out?" Selby teased playfully. She stopped as they approached the opening to the beach, and smiled at the sight of the ocean.

So his little IT expert liked to flirt? Or was she angry that he'd let her go a round with his executives, knowing full well he'd accept the deal? If she thought she'd throw him off kilter with her remarks, she was wrong. Sure, she was going to drive him to break his promise only hours after he'd made it, but he'd never let her see him sweat.

Garrett stopped mid-path and turned to face her. He lifted his sunglasses, his eyes devouring the sight of her.

"I'm happy you didn't forget our conversation." He smiled and nodded toward the surf. "I knew you weren't fond of heights, so I've got an easy lesson for you today."

"What makes you think I want lessons in anything?"

"Ah, Selby, lying doesn't become you." Garrett stepped closer, his chest inches from hers. She lifted her eyes to meet his but he caught the slight tremble in her bottom lip that she attempted to conceal. "You feel it already, don't you? We may not know each other that well yet, but I know you like being the best." She rolled her eyes, and he grinned. "If you want to be the best here…really know what's going on in this company, what drives my customers," he leaned forward, his lips near her ear, "what drives me…not just something you read in a business class. If that's something you want, then you'll want this. If not, I'm sure you can do a half-assed job and we'll eventually find someone to replace Evan. So what's it going to be?"

"Well of course I want to…"

"Answer me. We'll do this with your consent only. Otherwise, it's a moot point."

"Do what with my consent?"

"Anything. Everything. The other night…" He hesitated to show his cards.

Garrett's heart beat slightly faster, knowing he was pressing a sexual encounter with her. He still wasn't satisfied with her answers regarding Evan. Yet every time he was within ten feet of her, he yearned to touch her. Worse, he wanted her to know him, why he did what he did. He struggled with his warring emotions. He wasn't the kind of guy who had long-lasting relationships. Not many people were willing to put up with his dedication to work, let alone his infatuation with riding the crest of death. Only the people within his inner sanctum, ones who understood his thirst for danger, understood.

"I don't know. I mean…I told you. I'm afraid. I'm not

like you, Garrett," she explained, her tone serious. "There's part of me that wants to know. The other night…last night…I've just always had this rule not to date people I work with. Lars…"

"You work for Lars, not me. We both know that Lars lassoed both of us into this situation. Besides, I didn't ask you for a date." He smiled.

"What is this then?" She laughed.

"This is a lesson. If and when we go on a date, you will most definitely know you are on a date."

"Ah." She shook her head.

"This is your first lesson in feeling the rush. The one outside the bedroom." He winked.

"You assume we'll be inside a bedroom? You just said this isn't a date."

"You've sat in my lap. I had my hands on your thighs last night. Neither of which are dates, but they are an indication."

"Of what?"

"Interest. So what's it going to be, Miss Reynolds? Are you granting consent to our first lesson? And be warned, this is one of many." Garrett slid his sunglasses back down, giving her a wide smile. "Do you trust me?"

Selby blew out a breath and finally nodded. "Yes, okay. I'm trusting you to keep me safe. I'm not kidding, Garrett."

"You can always trust me," he responded.

Elated by her response, he began walking before his cock had a chance to stiffen any further. Holy shit, the excitement of teaching her about his lifestyle would wreck him, but at the moment he could have cared less. As they approached the rolling waves, he couldn't restrain his satisfied smile. If Lars was going to challenge him on this, he'd go head to head, because he anticipated that teaching Miss Reynolds was going to be one of the greatest highs he'd had yet.

In his effort to keep his promise to Lars, the one he'd already broken, Garrett had arranged to have his friend, Seth, teach the lesson. Seth Harris, VP of Aqua Operations, was a pioneer in big wave surfing. Garrett had met the champion while surfing at Mavericks five years ago, and he'd quickly become an integral asset to Emerson Industries. A millionaire in his own right, he sat on the board, leading both civilian and military aquamarine projects. Fearless with instinct, he'd developed new designs and technologies in the field.

"Hey, bro. What's happenin'?" Seth asked. His long wavy blond hair had been tied up in a bun. He tugged at his unzipped wetsuit, which hung low on his hips.

"How're the waves today?" Garrett bumped fists with his friend and glanced back to Selby, who wore a pained expression.

"Not too bad. A few little rip tides today. Pretty calm overall. Hey, Selby." Seth approached her, and she shook his hand.

"Hello."

"You ready to ride today?" He laughed, his eyes darting from Garrett to Selby.

"I've never done this before," she began.

"You swim, no?"

"Um, yeah, but not a lot."

"You live in California, right?"

"Well, yes, but…"

"Go to the beach?"

"Yeah, but…"

"So why haven't you surfed before?" Seth walked to his ATV and pulled out a black wetsuit. "I think I've got you sized about right. Go ahead and put it on."

Selby accepted it and went to sit on the ground.

"No, no, no. Come on over here. You don't want to get it wet or get sand in that. It'll be hard to get on, and it'll feel like shit. Don't want sand in your bits." He laughed.

"Go easy," Garrett warned. "Can I borrow your chair?"

"All yours. I've got the easy job today. Go about your business, sir." He winked at Selby. "Yeah, you can't wear that cover up."

"I figured as much." She smiled.

Garrett sat in the beach chair and opened his laptop. As it flickered on, he caught sight of Selby peeling off the sarong she'd worn over her bathing suit. His cock slammed to attention as her tanned stomach came into view. Unlike some of the women he'd dated, she was softer, her full breasts filling out her bikini top.

His lips tensed in a flat line as Seth knelt before her and glanced over, giving him a slick smile. His friend taunted him, aware that Garrett wasn't going. Seth's hands moved to her thigh, in an attempt to pull up the stretchy fabric, and lingered two seconds too long.

"I think she can manage," Garrett yelled over to him.

"Just helping her out. You okay?" Seth asked.

"Yes, I really appreciate you being so gentle with me. I've never put one of these on before," she said, glancing back at Garrett as if she was enjoying every minute of Seth touching her.

"As long as you're getting your needs met, I'm good with it," Garrett gritted out. Did his little hacker like games? To have another man's hands on her? Garrett blew out a breath and casually adjusted the painful erection that had nowhere to go.

"I'm just preparing for my lesson is all," she teased. "If you'd been my teacher, you could have helped me."

Shit. Garrett couldn't wait to play with her to see how far she'd take things. She might be afraid of heights, but she sure as hell knew how to push some boundaries. She'd only met Seth once and yet she was toying with them both.

"Here you go, almost in. Turn around," Seth guided.

She followed the direction, and Garrett tensed as he caught sight of the long scar that ran from the top of her left buttock up to her shoulder blade. He was no stranger to the occasional laceration, and was certain that whatever had caused it must have been serious. His curiosity piqued, he was unable to recall anything in her file about an injury. Her disclosure about her anxiety had come as no surprise, but he wondered if she'd been in a car accident or something far worse. As the scar disappeared under the latex and she turned around, her eyes locked on his. He knew he'd been caught staring when her smile fell flat.

He forced a small grin and waved but she'd quickly focused her attention back on Seth, who'd begun giving her instructions. His gut teemed with guilt as his business call connected, and he considered that he shouldn't have been so hard on her. The next lesson would bring pure pleasure, he swore. As he heard his name called from the speaker, his eyes fell to his computer screen.

Chapter Ten

Selby's stomach clenched when she caught him staring at her scar. He tried to play it off with his cool smile, but she knew he'd witnessed the mark on her soul that reminded her every day of the person she'd fought not to be, a victim, torn apart by a predator. While she'd grown independent and free spirited, the vulnerability of her childhood remained. Despite Garrett's carefree attitude toward it, she knew all too well that action was never taken without consequence. Her innocence stolen on a warm summer day, she blamed herself for the attack.

A fresh rush of shame rose to the surface and she swallowed it, repeating the silent mantra that a child couldn't be responsible for the actions of a monster. She hadn't invited the pain, asked for the strangling emotions that stalked her throughout the years. In her moments of strength, she'd concealed her weakness, pretended it didn't exist.

Not even Lars knew what had caused her first attack. Confessing her anxiety to Garrett had been somewhat liberating. While most clients knew the details of her health history, no one had ever broached the subject with her. When she'd told Garrett in the car why she sang, she'd experienced a sense of relief. Grades and money were of little consequence as she stood bare at the microphone. Under the spotlight, she became someone else; a sensual being who entertained, without feeling remorse or responsibility. It was an escape from reality.

Her attraction to Garrett and his charismatic demeanor continued to blur her judgment. After he'd cut off her nylons the previous night, she'd gone home, wishing he'd fucked her. Touching herself had provided little relief from the constant ache that plagued her. When he'd given her the bathing suit, continuing his promise of adventure, she'd tried to deny the excitement. She'd accepted his challenge, getting dressed in her office.

On the way to the car, she'd taken so many deep breaths she teetered on the edge of hyperventilating. But as they began to converse, she relaxed. A speck of the person she wanted to be shone through her hardened exterior. Flirting came naturally as he pressed her with questions. Given the right circumstances, she feared she'd follow him anywhere. Worse, when he'd asked for her consent, her first instinct had been to say yes, to give him whatever he wanted. She'd resisted, caving only after losing to her own internal struggle.

When she'd learned Seth was her instructor, her heart had dropped. Garrett was the one who'd promised her adventure, a lesson. He was the teacher she'd hoped would be at her side. When Seth had taken her hand, she stepped into the role of tease. As if she were on stage, she'd enjoyed Garrett's eyes on her as she donned her wetsuit…until he'd seen the scar.

Seth's voice broke her contemplation and her nerves rose to the surface.

"Lookin' good. You ready?" he asked her.

Nodding, she forced a smile. Her eyes darted to Garrett. Underneath the dark glasses, he appeared engrossed in his call.

"Nice job in the meeting today, by the way." He grabbed a couple of surfboards and started toward the water.

"Thanks," she replied nervously. Like a puppy, she followed him. *What the hell am I doing?* Sure she'd been an avid swimmer in the health club pool, but go for a swim in the ocean? Certainly not. In the Pacific? Not on the warmest day during an El Niño. Add sharks and giant alien stalks of kelp to her list of fears, and just hell no.

"Sorry they were hard on you. With Evan's accident, things have been out of sorts. Everyone's on edge. There's no replacing him, but the show must go on." He settled long planks flat onto the sand. "Garrett and Evan, they were pretty close."

"Were you close with him, too?"

"We were amicable." He winked. "But he and Garrett, they'd been together a long time. Lars told me…"

"Lars told you what? Wait, how do you know Lars?" A look of confusion crossed her face.

"We're friends. Got in some jumps together...stuff like that. Sometimes we get together for parties. I guess Garrett has mentioned our, uh, outings." He stepped on a board and knelt.

"No. I mean, I don't know him very well. I actually just started yesterday."

"You must be pretty special for him to let you come into Emerson like that. Take over for Evan." He waved her over and pointed to the board.

Without being told what to do, she stood atop the surfboard.

"That's it. Come on down here. Promise I won't bite."

"I'm not special per se, but I do have certain talents. As for letting me take over for Evan, it's only temporary. I did this as a favor to Lars." Selby found she was growing more comfortable, as if she'd finally found someone she could talk to. She considered asking him more about Evan, but he continued his train of thought.

"Clearances. Yeah, I get that's important. But lots of people have them."

"I'm good with IT. Computers."

"Hacking?" He laughed.

"Maybe," she hedged and gave him a small smile. "But the real reason I'm here is because of Lars. I work for him, but he's also a good friend of mine."

"He is?"

"You sound surprised."

"It's just that he's never brought you round, is all."

"You mean to your outings?" Selby wondered what

kinds of things they did together besides go skydiving.

"Yeah, our events." He smiled and lay down. "Get on your stomach like this."

"Aren't we going in the water?" she asked, but did as he told her.

"Soon enough. You like the water?"

"Ocean water? Not really."

"I see." He shook his head and blew out a breath.

"What?"

"You sure you want to do this?"

"No. I mean yes." She pressed her forehead onto the warm Plexiglas out of frustration and then stared at him. "Listen, Seth. I'm going to be perfectly honest here. I want this, but I'm not like you guys. My guess is that's why Lars hasn't introduced us before. This isn't my thing."

"I understand. It's not for everyone. Most of us, we breathe this company. Some of them get kind of intense with it. But don't worry, I'm not like that. Don't get me wrong. I love this place, everything Garrett's built. But if Lars says you can do the job, that's good enough for me."

"I really can help. It's not just because I'm trying to get the contract for DLar-Tech."

"I believe you. Look, all of Garrett's team members have experience within the field, but you don't need to do this to prove your worth."

"It's not about proving my worth." *No, I had to do that in the boardroom today.* "Maybe it's more about proving something to myself. But you're right, the kinds of things you guys do aren't something I'd ever do."

"Not everyone's cut out for jumpin' out of a plane. But this…" He gestured to the ocean. "We're just having a lil' fun today. No big deal. I promise I won't let anything happen to you."

She raised a questioning eyebrow at him and gave a small groan.

"I swear it. Seriously. And by the way Garrett's acting, I can tell he'd kick my ass if I did."

"Sorry, I don't mean to be a baby. I just get nervous." Selby couldn't believe that in the course of one day she was confessing her fears to two different men. This after going nearly ten years without talking about it with a solitary person besides Lars. She supposed that no one had ever pushed her to do anything remotely outside of her comfort zone. Garrett would never settle for anything less.

"No worries. Just pretend you're in Hawaii or someplace like that. Nice and easy, right. No matter what Garrett told you, he's not letting you go just because you can't surf."

"I know that but he's right. You guys. His company. There's something about what drives your customers. And as much as I get what you're saying about what that is, I don't really understand it." Selby gave him a small smile. "I can do this."

"You sure?"

"Yeah." Selby glanced over to Garrett. She'd never needed or wanted a man's approval but her stomach fluttered in excitement as he gave her a smile. Guarded behind his shades, he'd studied her. The heat of his gaze shot desire throughout her body. Her pussy ached. She brought a palm to her flushed cheek. *Fucking hell,* she thought. *How can I be thinking of sex at the same time I'm scared to death?* Garrett's words played through her mind. *Sex. Fear. These are the things that make us feel alive.*

Lie flat, up onto my hands and knees and stand. Selby repeated the instructions as she paddled out to what probably amounted to three feet of water. Despite Seth's assessment that the surf wasn't rough, Selby disagreed. Her stomach lurched as she glided over another swell. She tasted the briny water as the cold mist sprayed her face. She heard Seth whistle and she stopped, bobbing about right before the breakers.

"You ready? This isn't something you can learn online. You just need to commit to a wave and practice."

"Um, okay," she managed, her voice shaky.

Selby barely noticed the ice cold water that numbed her fingers. As if she were a live wire, her body hummed with excitement. A rush of water came and she paddled. He may have told her she couldn't have learned online, but she could damn well follow an instruction. She pushed onto her hands and knees. As she surged forward, she attempted to stand. Selby screamed for dear life as her feet slipped and she fell sideways into the water. Although she'd failed miserably on her first attempt, the challenge of almost succeeding drove her to try again.

By her fifth attempt, she'd grown more comfortable. She laughed with Seth while they floated, waiting for a wave. Selby glanced to the beach and caught sight of Garrett standing at the edge of the surf. She bit her lip, stunned that he'd taken off his shirt. She wished she was closer so she could inspect every inch of the rock-hard ridges of his abdomen. As his arms were crossed, she was unable to make out the details of the tattoos on his chest. The man was a specimen of fitness at a level she'd only seen on the magazine racks at the grocery store.

The water propelled her forward, bringing her attention to her ride. Once again, she pushed up onto her hands and knees. The swell rose higher, lurching her upward. Rationally she knew she was only rising a few feet, but the height caused her heart to race in fear. She could hear Seth's voice yelling at her from behind and she struggled to concentrate. Her legs burned as she pressed upward. Balancing her torso, she tightened her core. A rush of adrenaline tore through her veins as she coasted for several seconds.

She began laughing, the thrill of victory filling her chest. Out of the corner of her eye, she caught sight of Garrett clapping his hands. Losing her focus, she teetered. The wave closed and she toppled into the sea. Pounded into the sand, Selby struggled to surface. Like a rag doll, her body was tossed under the white cap. She held her breath, fighting against the tide, but no air came. A tunnel of darkness closed in and she resisted sucking in the salt water.

Chapter Eleven

Garrett had watched with fascination as Selby went off with Seth. After their discussion in the car he'd regretted asking his friend to help teach her to surf. He thought he must be losing his damn mind. One minute he swore he wouldn't take it any further; the next he was ready to make love to her the first chance he got. The only thing he knew for certain was that Lars was going to fucking kill him once he found out how deep his attraction had grown for the IT specialist who'd turned his world over in the course of a few days.

He blamed his uncharacteristic behavior on his grief. The intense arousal Selby spiked within him was a welcome reprieve from the crushing despair that had racked his mind over the past couple of weeks. Show no weakness, had been his motto. Yet losing Evan had tossed his psyche into an oblivion of malaise. Nothing could crack the bitter sorrow that shrouded him…until he'd met Selby.

Garrett was no stranger to insta-lust, but he'd never

had time for a girlfriend, committing himself to one woman. There were too many complications. He worked eighteen hours a day and his rare days off were dedicated to his sports. Even if he ever managed to find someone who'd put up with his insane schedule, he'd be skeptical of their motives. It wasn't lost on him that most women he'd met cared little about him and more about his wealth.

Regardless, there was something about Selby that drew him. He wished he could shake it. Becoming involved with someone who didn't share his passion for adventure would lead to disaster. But the flicker of curiosity she'd shown when he'd propositioned her was all it took to hook him into the game.

Garrett dug his toes into the wet sand, impressed that she hadn't given up trying to ride her board. Surfing had never been his specialty, but given that five-year-olds learned how to do it, it'd been the least dangerous thing he could think of to give her a taste of the rush. He resisted smiling when she yelled the f word as she tumbled into the ocean, grabbing her board as if she was ready to beat it to the ground. Despite whatever albatross she believed was wrapped around her neck, she'd temporarily broken free. Her spirit for success far outweighed her fear of failure.

His pulse raced as he caught sight of her press upward, finally balancing herself. Cheering her, he counted off the seconds she rode…*one, two, three, four, five*. As she fell into the turbulent break, he knew instantly she'd be in trouble. He took off running into the surf, the sixty-five degree water stinging his skin.

When he saw the detached board tumble by, he knew she'd gone down hard. A second wave broke preventing the water from settling. A rolling white top collapsed and he caught a flash of color. *Selby.* He dove underneath and managed to cling to a slippery ankle. Within seconds, he'd reached her limp body and kicked to the surface. To his relief, she choked and began coughing.

Garrett cradled her in his arms and shoved to his feet, carrying her onto the beach. By the time he'd set her onto the warm sand, she'd begun to pant for air. He fell to the ground, and brushed his palm to her cheek.

"Selby." Garrett didn't do fear, but his heart pounded as if he were fighting for his own life.

Her eyes blinked open and he could tell from the look on her face that she'd been stunned. A small trickle of blood seeped from her forehead and he inspected the tiny scrape, ensuring it was nothing serious. Seth handed him a towel and he gently dabbed the abrasion.

"Garrett," Selby whispered.

"Sweetheart, you're okay. Just a little shaken is all." Garrett wondered if he was referring to her or himself.

"Sweetheart?" She smiled.

"Yeah, that's right." He laughed. She had his number and that caused a fresh surge of nerves.

"I'm cold."

"You're just in shock. You're going to be all right." Garrett unzipped her wetsuit and peeled her out of it. He covered her with a towel and rubbed her arms. When his fingers brushed over her stomach, he froze, jarred by her voice.

"It was great."

"What?" Garrett adjusted her on his lap and bent down, putting his ear to her lips. The heat from her sun-kissed cheeks radiated against his own and he reprimanded himself as his cock stirred.

"I said it was awesome."

"I should have gone with you," Garrett began. He felt like shit for pawning her off on Seth. She could have been killed. She'd been in his charge and he'd failed her.

"I could see you. You distract me."

"Selby," he breathed. Overcome with emotion he'd held at bay, he pressed his forehead to hers and their eyes locked. "You were spectacular."

His thumb grazed over her soft skin, eliciting a small gasp. With their lips mere inches apart, the desire to kiss her had never been stronger. There was no going back once he tasted her. If there was one thing he knew about himself, it was that once he wanted something, nothing would stop him from attaining his goal. But Selby wasn't a *thing* to be had. She was a person with a heart and soul. After everything he'd just done, she trusted him.

"Garrett." With fire in her eyes, Selby blinked slowly and smiled. Her fingers glided over his arms, gripping his pecs.

"I shouldn't…" Whatever semblance of restraint he'd had gave way as her touch seared his skin. His lips met hers and he felt like he was jumping for the very first time. But unlike every carefully planned event he'd carried out, he was acting out of emotion.

Adrift in the moment, he took her mouth, his tongue brushing hers. He deepened the kiss until she moaned. Her thigh slipped against his, and he knew he'd never be satisfied until he was buried deep inside her. His fingers glided underneath the flimsy fabric of her bikini top, flitting over her hard tip. With his actions shielded by the towel, he cupped her full breast, his hardened cock prodding her belly.

"Garrett," she repeated into his mouth.

He went to break their connection and she protested.

"No, don't..."

He smiled into their kiss. His woman knew what she wanted and was taking it. *Jesus Christ, she'll ruin me*, he thought. Fuck every mountain he'd ever climbed. Selby Reynolds was the only rush he was looking for, one far more dangerous than he'd anticipated. The sound of Seth calling him forced him to break away. He glanced at Selby who wore a stunned expression, and he hoped he'd concealed his emotions.

"Yeah," he answered, tearing his eyes away from her.

"Dean's at the office," Seth told him, his voice serious.

"So?"

"He's got a warrant."

"Shit." Garrett removed his hand from Selby's breast, and the blush on her face told him she'd been as aroused as he was. He tucked the towel around her torso, concealing her nudity from Seth. It was not that he was a prude. On the contrary, he enjoyed public play every now and then, but he'd control when it happened.

"Selby, I hate to do this but I've gotta go. Are you sure you're all right? Your head," he gestured to the small scrape that had stopped bleeding, "how does it feel?"

"I'm fine now. Really. I was just out of breath."

"Drowning," he corrected.

"Okay, maybe a little. But you saved me." Selby pushed upward, careful to keep herself covered. She gave him a small knowing smile. "I'm going with you."

"You don't have to do that…"

"All my clothes are at the office anyway." She shakily stood as if to prove she was unharmed.

"All right, let's go." Despite the disapproving look on Seth's face, Garrett put a comforting arm around her and smiled as she relaxed into his embrace. "Seth…my stuff?"

"I'm on it. Go see what Dean's doing."

As they exited the beach, Garrett glanced at his friend once again, who shook his head and gathered the boards. He couldn't be sure why his friend objected, but he suspected it was for the same reason as Lars. They all guessed she'd never fit in with their friends, but after today, he was more determined than ever to prove them wrong.

Chapter Twelve

Selby, still shaken from the events on the beach, took a deep breath and stared at herself in the mirror. Her mind replayed what had happened. The thrill of her surfing accomplishment had been spectacular. Even her small brush with drowning hadn't dampened the experience.

Her fingertips went to her mouth, the heat of his lips on hers still fresh in her mind. With Garrett, she'd gone from elated to terrified to aroused beyond belief all in the course of thirty minutes. When his rough fingers thrummed over her nipple, she'd lost cognizance of where she was in space and time. She'd wrapped her leg around him with every intention of taking things further. Until Seth spoke, she'd barely been aware they were even in public. She hadn't remembered, and even once it registered, she hadn't cared. She had been in awe of Garrett before she'd met him, and it terrified her knowing he had the ability to make her lose control.

After their brief interlude at the beach, her no-dating-clients rule being smashed into a thousand pieces, the only hope she had of gluing her model of propriety back together was to find her replacement. She wasn't entirely sure she could date someone who flirted with death on a regular basis, but ignoring her attraction to him wasn't possible either. The only way she could forget was if she moved to the North Pole, because the heat that radiated from her body every time she was in the same room with the man wouldn't be cooled otherwise.

Selby had never been terribly adventurous in bed, and she expected that he'd do exactly what he'd promised; he'd teach her to embrace new levels of her sexuality that she hadn't known existed. A week ago, she'd have scoffed at the idea, but after today, an addiction to Garrett Emerson had been planted in her heart. She'd call it lust and pray that that was all it would turn out to be in the end. The odds weren't in her favor but as she recalled his searing kiss, she planned to roll the dice.

Selby glanced around the women's locker room, which looked more like a spa, and selected a comb. Removing its cellophane wrapper, she teased it through her long hair. Even though she'd shampooed, she swore she still smelled like the beach. After today, the ocean would never be the same and neither would she. It occurred to her that what had happened could change her life. Selby considered how the mere thought of heights could throw her into a panic, but today, under Garrett's careful watch and Seth's instruction, she'd done something she'd never have done on her own.

Her thoughts turned to the reason they'd returned to

the office and her stomach tightened. The police had been waiting for them as soon as they'd entered the building. She'd deferred to Garrett when he'd told her she wasn't needed, but she expected that by the time she dressed, they'd want to speak to her. She wasn't a fool. Evan had been in charge of information systems. After he'd asked her to steal information, she wondered if whatever he'd done had to do with why the police were here.

Once again, she contemplated whether or not she should tell Garrett about her previous interaction with Evan. What he'd said had been an insinuation, not a printed request. She feared neither he nor the police would believe her. Even the fact that he'd used a different name might seem unbelievable to them. Considering her situation, she reasoned she'd only divulge what she knew about Evan if the police asked.

Garrett plowed his fingers through his hair as Dean Frye, a fellow sky diver and assistant district attorney, presented his findings. Not only had they found poison within Evan's body, someone had tampered with his equipment. As Dean stood in front of him, he knew the next question that would come. Answers weren't easy.

"Look, Garrett, I don't like this any more than you do, but we need access to everything Evan was working on," Dean pressed.

"You're welcome to search his office, his files." Garrett sat behind his desk and folded his hands, steepling his fingers so they rested on his lower lip.

"Everything. We need everything."

"You know that's not possible. There are projects we work on that require clearances. Besides, what proof do you have that his death is linked to Emerson Industries?" As much as Garrett loved Evan, there was no way he'd divulge covert projects they'd worked on or technologies they were still in the process of developing. For the greater good, some secrets must remain unknown, even to the police.

"Jesus, Garrett. He was our friend. Don't you want to know who did this?" Dean looked to Lars, who stared out the window, his arms crossed. "Lars, come on. Talk to him for me. This isn't right."

"He was a brother to all of us but you know this isn't my company and what Garrett says…you know damn well there are things he works on that he can't tell you."

"No." Garrett held up his hands to halt the conversation. "This is my decision, not Lars'. The only reason he's here is because, like me, he deserves to know what happened to Evan."

"You both can't sit here and tell me that Evan didn't have his fingers in some secret spy shit."

"Government contracts," Garrett explained. He picked up a pen and tapped it on the desk, a habit he frequently had when deep in thought. "All of which are top secret. And you know what that means, Dean. These things…there are broader implications than Evan's death. If, and I repeat, if his death is in any way connected to Emerson Industries and something he was working on, I cannot disclose that to you. And to be perfectly honest, I'm not one hundred percent convinced that's the case. In twelve years of handling military projects, we've never had an incident."

"How about this? You show me everything, and we'll call it lawyer-client privilege," Dean proposed. "No one else in the department will see it. I swear it."

"I just told you that…" Garrett paused as a knock sounded.

"Don't you have a secretary? This meeting's private," Dean told him.

"Come in," Garrett barked. As Selby walked into his office, he averted his gaze to meet Lars'. Despite the jolt of desire he felt every time he saw her, he buried the emotion deep inside. Sooner or later he'd have to tell Lars about his plans to pursue Selby, but this was definitely not the time or place.

"Who the hell is this?" Dean asked. "Garrett, you're not taking this seriously."

"Selby, this is Dean Frye. He's the DA. He's investigating Evan's death. Dean, this is Selby Reynolds. She's on loan from Lars. She's working Evan's projects and recruiting a permanent replacement."

"This is a private conversation," Dean insisted.

"She stays. Sit." Garrett pointed to a chair. Selby's eyes widened at the command and her lips drew tight. He'd meant to order her in front of the others, so they were all aware who was running this meeting. Dean had gone too far, insinuating that he didn't care about Evan. Nothing could be further from the truth.

"Fine, but none of this leaves the room, Miss Reynolds, got it?"

"Of course," Selby responded. Her expression had grown cold and her eyes darted to Lars, who returned her gaze.

"As I was saying," Garrett continued. His focus faltered as he caught Lars nodding at Selby. While he'd been intentionally curt, it cut him to see her look to Lars for reassurance. He knew he was fucking things up six ways to Sunday, but at this point, he had to keep going. "Selby has all the pertinent files that contain most of the information about the projects Evan was working on. Before you leave tonight, you will have copies as well."

"But..." Selby went to interrupt and Garrett silenced her.

"You're here to listen, not speak." The flash of anger in her eyes told him instantly that he'd gone too far. Fuck, he was being a dick, he knew, but everything was going to shit faster than he could stop it. Selby had cleverly found the reference to the PFx Prototype he'd carelessly left in the files, and he was afraid she'd mention it in front of Dean. He'd need to make sure it was scrubbed clean before the DA got the files.

"Garrett," Lars interrupted in Selby's defense, "you can't talk to her like that."

"No, Lars. It's fine. You want silence, Mr. Emerson? You got it," she replied, her tone cold.

"Dean, you'll get what you need," Garrett continued. He'd make it up to Selby later, explain why he'd spoken to her the way he had. Right now, he needed to get Dean off his back and the police out of his building. "But you should ask yourself why this would happen now. Evan's worked on all kinds of secret, sometimes downright dangerous, projects over the years. What does someone get from just killing him? Seriously. Think about it."

"I've thought about it all right. I've also been to his house."

"What?"

"That's right. His house was torn apart. Someone was looking for something. I don't know what but my guess is that if they didn't find it at his home, it's in his office."

"I loved Evan, you know that. He taught me everything," Garrett gritted out, raw emotion causing his voice to waver. He'd hoped to keep the grief at bay, but the more they talked about his friend as if he'd done something wrong, as if he wasn't a person, the more it flooded his chest. He blew out a breath and shook his head. "But you and I both know he had enemies. How about starting with the long list of women he dated? His ex-wife. Have you questioned her? What about ex-girlfriends?"

"Yes, we're going to check them out too. But Garrett, this could've been an industry hit of some kind," he suggested.

"Jesus, Dean. Really, are we going to jump to James Bond shit? I hate to say it, but people get killed all the time. Sure, someone had to go to an awful lot of trouble to make it look like an accident, but still, it's not like it went unnoticed. We all know Evan wouldn't have made a mistake like that."

"What about the poison?" Lars asked.

"Atropa belladonna."

"What's that?" Lars asked.

"Deadly nightshade. It's a plant indigenous to many parts of the world including Europe and Africa but it grows here too," Selby offered before Garrett had a chance to answer.

"Its berries can kill, but it's the leaves that are even more deadly," Garrett added. Despite Selby disobeying his command not to talk during the meeting, he couldn't help but be impressed with her knowledge. Still, he considered that she needed to learn how to follow instructions.

"They used to make poison darts with the berries, but you're on target with how he died. It was ingested," Dean offered.

"How the hell could he have eaten it? Besides, I'm telling you that he was fine before we left. He gave me the thumbs up before he jumped. It was all good." Garrett pushed out of his chair and went to the floor-to-ceiling window. From his office, the sunset beckoned over the ocean.

"We don't know that yet, now do we?"

"Belladonna. It's been a while since I've studied this,

but as I recall, it causes hallucinations…affects the mind," Garrett said. "If he'd somehow eaten it, which I don't even get that part because I'm tellin' you he was fine, but let's just assume he ate it, something again he never ever does before a jump, I guess that might explain how he didn't see a problem with his gear."

"If they hadn't messed with it, the chute would have automatically deployed. He'd vomited prior to landing. But you know…the condition of his body. It was difficult to see what had happened at the time."

"Yeah," was all Garrett could manage. The sight of his friend's mangled body would haunt him forever. Evan had lost a hand as well as part of a leg. Face down, his skull had cracked wide open, exposing his brain.

"So about the files…"

"I'll get you what I'm allowed to share with you. You know this, Dean. There are some things you cannot see. No matter how much I want to share them, I can't. If I did, that'd be paramount to treason, something I'm not going to do, not even for Evan."

"All right, but I may need to take further legal steps."

"You do that. Hey, if you can get a court to get me to expose my projects, then so be it. But you don't have cause right now. All you've got is a theory that his death is related to work. No proof at all. And like I said, I think you have other people in his life with motivation."

"A woman thinking he was a dick is a far cry from murdering him," Dean countered. He slipped a folder into his briefcase and stood.

"People kill all the time for pretty much no reason. We don't know who he's been dating on the side."

"He hasn't brought anyone to the club. Sure he's played with a few of the women there, but he hasn't…"

Garrett shot Dean a look in an attempt to silence him. His eyes darted to Lars, who shook his head. He hadn't told Selby about Altura. He'd planned to tell her, to invite her to the party on Saturday, but he hadn't had a chance to discuss it with her yet.

"What?" Dean asked.

"I'll tell you later." Garrett caught Selby staring at him and he broke eye contact.

"We should be done here in a few more hours," Dean told him. As he went to leave, he hesitated. "One more thing. I noticed some glass in his office. Looks like a few specks of blood as well. Any idea how that happened?"

"I was in his office last night." Garrett's eyes darted to Selby's for only a second and then he firmly met Dean's gaze. "I was looking at that photo of us…remember when we climbed Denali? Selby came looking for me and I accidentally dropped it. We were cleaning up the glass, and she cut her hand. It's her blood you'll find in there."

"Yeah, I saw the mess. Just wondered what went on."

"I was going to clean it up but I forgot to tell housekeeping about it. Staff has been ordered to stay out, so no one's been allowed in his office." Garrett approached Dean and offered his hand. "Listen, I'm sorry to be a hardass but my hands are tied. We'll catch up on Saturday."

"I know this has been hard on you, Garrett. You know I'm damn sorry about Evan." Dean shook and released Garrett's hand, then turned to Selby and Lars. "Miss Reynolds, I'll meet up with you to get the files?"

"She'll be out to assist with them in a few minutes," Garrett answered for her.

He shut the door behind Dean and sighed. "Lars, I need to talk to Selby."

"I can't believe he was murdered," Lars exclaimed, ignoring Garrett's implied request for him to leave. "Do you really think he was working on something someone would kill for?"

"I can't believe any of this is happening either. And yeah, Dean could be right. But at the same time, I can't disclose secrets to someone who doesn't have the clearances I sponsor. It's just not happening. Speaking of which…Lars, can I call you later? Right now I have to talk to Selby. In private."

"Yeah, sure," Lars agreed.

Garrett inwardly protested as he watched Lars hug Selby goodbye. As she returned his embrace, Garrett wondered if their relationship had gone further than friendship. Not usually a jealous man, the thought of her with anyone else bothered him. He wanted Selby for himself, he thought. Despite sharing other women with Lars, there was something about Selby that made him think that wouldn't ever happen.

As Lars waved goodbye and left his office, Garrett steeled himself for the conversation with Selby. He'd been stern with her, perhaps going as far as to embarrass her in order to establish dominance. It was how it had to be. In business, he'd seek her valuable opinion on many matters, but in the end, all decisions were his and his alone to make.

"Selby, we need to get a few things straight," he began.

"I was wrong," she interrupted.

"What?"

"I was wrong about you. Today at the beach. Just now," she said. "Why keep me here in the room? You want me in here for a meeting where I'm obviously not welcome. Then you tell me to shut my mouth as if I'm a child. Seriously, is this some kind of test again?"

"Sit down," he told her.

"No. I'm a grown woman. You may think just because you run this company that you get to treat people like shit, but I have news for you, Garrett, that doesn't work with me. The next time you want to embarrass me, just do me a favor and don't. I can't believe I thought…"

"Selby," he said softly. He reached for her hand. She went to tug it away but he held firm.

"No."

"I'm sorry, okay? Look there are some things with us that aren't negotiable." Her fingers softened and he sat on the edge of his desk. He waited for her to look at him but she defiantly looked away to an empty chair. "When Evan died, I knew that something terrible had happened. No, not just terrible. I knew that there was no way he'd make a rookie mistake or fuck up his gear. Today when Dean came in here asking for files...I didn't want you to say anything that would give him reason to press further with his request for information."

"But why wouldn't you want him to know?" She finally locked her eyes on his.

"Because some of the technologies we develop are top secret. Granted, some of them aren't, they're civilian products for the fun of the sport. But there are projects we have that will create things to help our country. Things that help protect our protectors. I know damn well there are people out there looking to steal government secrets, and I'm not going to make it easier for them. I trust Dean with my life, but the people he works with..."

"He's with the police."

"Exactly, and most of them we could trust, but you and I know there's a process for establishing clearances. People are vulnerable to blackmail. Corruption. I can't do that."

"Why did you lie about what happened in Evan's office?"

"I don't know...I just don't want you involved in this. And honestly, your reasons for being in there last night involve a laptop that I'm not willing to turn over to Dean as of yet. I don't know what's all on it, but I knew if they discovered he'd been murdered, they'd be looking for it.

I'm certainly not going to tell Dean you were snooping around Evan's office and drag you into this."

"I wasn't snooping," she insisted.

"Yeah, you kind of were. Don't bullshit a bullshitter, Selby." He raised a questioning eyebrow at her.

"I already told you what I was looking for."

"Yeah, and I told you it was confidential. And I would have told Dean the same thing."

"I understand, but you can't talk to me like that." Her bottom lip wavered, her eyes flickering in anger.

"I'm sorry, but again, I give the orders, sweetheart. You, on the other hand, take them. I think we reviewed that rule already."

"That's not fair."

"I'm sorry for the way I said it but I couldn't risk you saying anything else to Dean."

"Okay, but what happened today…"

"Come with me on Saturday. We're having an event. A few investors will be there. I think it's important you meet more of the Emerson family."

"But you and I…on the beach…we need to talk about what happened."

"We do, and that's why I want you to come to the party. I could sit here and tell you about the circle of people who drive this company, the people who were Evan's friends, but I want to show you."

"But today…" she stammered.

"Today," he began and then laughed. "Today, you scared the ever loving shit out of me."

She laughed and shook her head.

"But you were amazing. And because of what happened today, I need to show you who I really am, so you can meet the venture capitalists who helped me create Emerson Industries. I think it's time." Garrett knew introducing Selby into the group would be tricky. Lars wouldn't be pleased, and he expected, from Seth's reaction, that he'd be less than thrilled. Yet his instincts never steered him wrong. Selby had shown courage today, had even somewhat forgiven him after he'd publicly reprimanded her in front of Dean and Lars. Moreover he wanted her more by the hour. The only way he'd be able to enjoy it was if he thought they had a chance of having a relationship. Until she accepted his inner sanctum, it was meaningless to go any further.

"Time for what?"

"It's time you learned about Altura." As the words hung in the air, he hoped that Selby wouldn't disappoint him.

Chapter Thirteen

For the rest of the week, Selby kept her nose down, meeting with employees affected by the transition to DLar-Tech. After her earlier conversation with Garrett, she'd wanted to ask him details about Saturday's event. But when she'd gone to see him, he'd been conveniently busy in meetings. Selby had grown cautious, aware that she didn't know him that well. Although he'd nearly brought her to orgasm with just his smile, the way he'd spoken to her had planted a seed of doubt. Lust in itself, including a fascination that bordered on obsession, hadn't meant she'd chosen wisely as far as relationships went.

Garrett had insisted on sending a car to pick her up from her condo. The extravagance of being ushered into the black stretch limo shouldn't have surprised her, but still, she'd been caught off guard. After riding in Garrett's Jeep, she'd been lulled into thinking his down-to-earth transportation extended into other parts of his life. She'd forgotten that he wasn't just anyone. As she ran her fingers over the soft leather interior and stared out the window, she was reminded that he lived in a world that wasn't like her own. Wealth in and of itself wasn't unfamiliar. She worked for rich clients every day of the week. But she'd never kissed one, and without a doubt, she hadn't slept with one.

As the car turned into the sprawling estate, she was astounded by the breathtaking fountains that were lit up in shades of red and white. The colossal waterfalls appeared to wax and wane as if they were dancing to Tchaikovsky. She imagined the 1812 overture playing in the distance, creating a well-coordinated waterworks display. As a child, she'd learned how to play piano, mastering several compositions. While she'd always been partial to Mozart, she'd fallen in love with the ballets, immersing herself in both the Nutcracker Suite and Swan Lake.

The limo slowed as it approached the main home, its circular cobblestone driveway lit up with luminaries. A waiting bellman opened the door, and she swallowed the nerves that had built in anticipation of her arrival. Trepidation was soon replaced with awe as he assisted her out of the car. She glanced up to the spectacular mansion, which appeared like a modern fairytale castle. Its massive stone arches led to a wooden door which was flanked by turrets.

As her escort guided her up the steps, Selby teetered in her platform wedge sandals, and wished she'd worn flats. She adjusted her dress, concerned that perhaps she was showing too much cleavage. Although the royal blue minidress displayed a plunging neckline, the sexy teaser was offset by its long sleeves and wispy silk skirt.

Her breath silently caught as the door opened into candlelit dimness, and she had visions of entering a haunted house. She fought back the butterflies as she obediently followed her guide into the abyss. In the silence, her heels clicked on the black Spanish marble, reverberating throughout the mansion's spacious lobby. Although she hadn't seen a soul as they navigated toward the back of the home, she detected the distinct sound of a bass beat in the distance.

Selby's stomach nervously clenched, as she wondered what kind of party was occurring. She wished she'd pressed Garrett for details. Selby didn't do surprises. She did her job well because she prepared for all scenarios. Yet tonight, there'd been no file to review, no numbers to check, no data to process. The only thing she knew was that a special memorial for Evan had been held the previous evening. Garrett hadn't invited her and she hadn't offered to go.

A pang of guilt stabbed at her given that she hadn't been completely honest with Garrett about Evan. She hated lying but she still hadn't found any concrete evidence that Evan was involved in wrongdoing. Everyone had secrets, albeit some were more dangerous than others. Garrett had lied to his friend, the DA, about what had happened with the picture and the laptop. After years of friendship, Lars had failed to disclose his relationship with Garrett and the club to which they belonged. It was as if he'd hidden a whole part of his life, making her wonder if she knew him at all. *Deceit. Secrets. Danger.* It appeared they thrived on it. As the assumption lingered, she considered how easily she'd concealed her own truth. She was becoming what she despised.

"This way, ma'am," the butler announced, jarring her from her spiraling thoughts. As they arrived in front of a set of intricately carved doors, her heart pounded. Whatever lay beyond the exotic entrance, she needed to face it with courage and grace.

"Mr. Emerson requests you wear this, madam." Selby watched with interest as he reached inside his jacket, retrieved a sparkling item and held it up to the flickering light.

"What's that for?"

"It's a masquerade event," he explained, displaying a silver mask adorned with white crystals.

"Um, yeah, okay," she agreed. As if her evening hadn't been cryptic enough, guests were donning masks?

"If you could just turn around for a minute, I'll tie this for you," he offered. "If you wouldn't mind lifting your hair?"

"Of course." Selby did as he asked and held the cool metal in place as he fastened it underneath her hair.

"Well done." He turned to the door and gave her a warm grin.

"Thank you." Selby's nerves had soared out of control. She suspected that whatever happened tonight would change her life.

"Welcome to Altura."

The doors opened, and she stifled the gasp that rose in her throat. Selby stepped into the great room, astounded by the sight. Hundreds of glass balls, illuminated with tea lights, descended from the cathedral ceiling. A band played in the corner, several couples dancing on a small parquet floor. Blood-red leather chairs and sofas accented small round tables adorned with white tablecloths and exotic orchids. On the left, several people sat on mahogany stools along a brass-topped bar. A cool breeze drew her attention to a wall made entirely of glass, which opened onto a veranda.

As if in a daze, her eyes studied the elegant party. Slowly, she ventured into the room, weaving her way through the tables of guests. She squealed as a pair of strong arms wrapped around her waist, warm breath on her ear.

"What are you doing here?" Lars whispered.

Recognizing his voice, she spun around and gave him a small smile. This was his hidden world, she knew, and he hadn't invited her.

"Garrett asked me to attend," Selby told him.

"He shouldn't have done that."

Selby stood firm, despite his annoyed expression. Over the years, she'd seen him both frustrated and determined, but never angry.

"It's not like I asked to come. Garrett invited me." She crossed her arms, irritated that he hadn't welcomed her.

"Dance with me." It was a command, not a request.

Selby marched to the parquet floor, allowing him to take her in his arms. The music slowed to a ballad and she began to plead her case.

"Please don't be mad, Lars. You're the one who got me into this."

"I'm sorry, it's just..." He exhaled loudly. "Look, Selby, the people in this room...you're not like them."

"Gee, thanks. Nice."

"I didn't mean it like that. But come on, you know you're not big on any kind of adventure. These folks are here because they share a passion. You wouldn't understand us. What we do...it's not something you are ever going to do. We've been friends for a long time, but Garrett shouldn't have brought you here."

"Everything we do has a risk. I'm afraid to fly but I still do it anyway. And do you know why? Because at the end of the day, data speaks, bullshit walks. I know full well that I have a better chance of dying in a car accident than I do getting on a 747."

"Well, your chances are a helluva a lot greater when you base jump. Try more like one in sixty."

"True, but you haven't died yet, and there are things I do that are a little risky." She guessed that singing at the club wouldn't rank very high on Lars' list, but as far as she was concerned, it counted when it came to bravery.

"Get real. You can't even go down an escalator without saying five Hail Marys and holding on for dear life. This club," he gestured to the people dancing around them, "the people here tonight...they embrace it all. Pushing the envelope of what we're supposed to be doing." He paused and added, "Including sex."

"What?" Selby had fully expected the 'we like to do dangerous things' lecture, but hadn't expected him to talk about sex.

"Look around." Lars spun her in a circle to the beat. He whispered in her ear. "The couple in the corner. It's Chase and Penny. Do you see them?"

Selby glanced to a man and woman who sat in darkness. She could barely make out their silhouette.

"They're fucking."

"What? No they aren't," she protested. As she glanced again, she observed the slightest movement.

"Yes. Yes they are."

"But Garrett said they're investors…"

"They're the originals. His venture capitalists are his closest friends. We helped him build his dream, and in the process, we all prospered."

"That's good, right?" Selby asked, still trying to catch a better look at what exactly the couple was doing. She swore Lars was just messing with her to get her to leave.

"Some work at Emerson. Most do. Some, like me, have our own companies with close partnerships with Emerson. A few," Lars nodded to the band. "See the twins?"

Selby caught sight of the lead singer, who wore a tight black t-shirt. He tightly gripped the microphone, his heavily tattooed arms bulging every time he flexed. A similarly handsome man played drums.

"They're recent doctoral grads from MIT. They were

interning with Evan. Now they're helping Chase out with a few things."

"Why didn't you tell me this involved having interns?"

"Because *you* don't have any. You're there to help recruit Evan's replacement and expedite the outsourcing. Nothing more, nothing less."

"I know that," she replied. Her lips pursed as she considered that once again Garrett hadn't disclosed all the facts of the situation. Her whirling temper was thwarted as Lars stopped dancing and held her tight.

"What's going on between you and Garrett?"

"Lars," she breathed. Her head fell to his shoulder. Jesus, she wished she could lie to him, but she couldn't.

"He wouldn't have brought you here if you weren't…are you sleeping with him?"

"No," she protested. "And besides, even if I was, it's not like it's any of your business."

"I don't want you to get hurt, is all. It's why I never introduced you to him. I knew how you admired him. Women lie down and spread their legs the minute he says hello, and you aren't going to be one of them."

"Are you kidding me?" Selby exclaimed.

"Look, he's one of my best friends but he's not like you. You're innocent. You don't have this addiction we've got."

"Lars, I appreciate your advice but I'm not that girl you dated in college. I can handle myself." Or so she hoped. Despite her confusion over Lars' concerns, she wasn't leaving.

"Just be careful, okay? I know you, Selby. I've seen you during an attack."

Selby's stomach lurched as he mentioned her weakness. Garrett, no matter how smitten, hadn't seen her at her worst.

"The things we do aren't for you," Lars insisted, his voice firm.

"I surfed today," she said defiantly. So what if she'd only stayed up for all of five seconds? It still counted.

"Yeah, Seth told me. I knew they'd push for you to do something to get to know the customer a little better. But surfing? Come on. You know that kids do it, right?" He shook his head and laughed. "It's just a small sliver, baby. Unless you're planning on goin' with us on our next base jump, this place isn't for you."

"She's my guest." Selby heard Garrett's commanding voice behind her, and excitement flushed through her veins.

His hand glided over her shoulder, and tingles ran down her arm. She caught a glimpse of anger in Lars' eyes, but her focus was drawn to the debonair billionaire who'd invited her to the party. Her breath caught as her eyes devoured him. Dressed in black slacks and a white shirt, his strong muscular forearms pressed through his rolled up sleeves. A lock of his dark brown hair brushed over his forehead. He emanated sex without trying, his cool casual style apparent in his every movement and word.

"Garrett, Lars was just telling me about your, um, your club." Her arm broke out in gooseflesh as he trailed his finger down it. Although covered by fabric, she swore she could feel the burn of his touch straight through her dress.

"Was he now?" Garrett's eyes darted to Lars and back to Selby.

"Yes, he was telling me about your investors. Lars..." she went to address him but he'd walked away toward the bar. She shook her head, upset that he'd left angry. They never fought and it broke her heart to think he'd be irate about her seeing Garrett.

"Don't worry about him. Everyone's a little tense after last night. He's going to be fine." Garrett brought the back of her hand to his lips and kissed it.

"I...Garrett," she stammered.

Selby glanced around the room and caught sight of both Seth and Nate staring at her. As much as she yearned to throw herself into Garrett's arms, she hadn't expected public displays of affection at a company event.

"Selby?" He gave a small chuckle, tugging her toward the door.

"Where are we going?" she asked as he led her out onto a large balcony. It overlooked a magnificent waterfall that spilled into a swimming pool. Large glowing orbs the size of beach balls floated along its surface.

"It's too noisy inside."

"What is this place?" she asked in wonderment.

"This is Altura."

"Altura? And that means?" She gave a confused smile.

"Altura. As in, height, altitude. We fly where others don't."

"You live here?"

"No, this is for Altura activities. The investors…"

"Venture capitalists."

"At one time, but we're a family of sorts now. If they aren't connected to Emerson Industries directly, they help with beta testing, quality assurance, things of that nature."

"So everyone here knew Evan?" She reached for her mask but he stopped her, placing his hands over hers.

"Leave it on." He took her hands in his. "We've mourned. Tonight we celebrate."

"And the masks?"

"Evan was born and raised in New Orleans." Garrett went to move toward the railing and Selby stood firm. He raised an eyebrow at her. "What are you doing?"

"I don't like heights. You know that. I told you…" Selby attempted to pull her hand from his grasp, but he held it firmly.

"It's safe, Selby. Much safer than surfing," he joked.

"I know that, but I'm not going. I'm good right here."

"Do you trust me?" he asked.

"Yes, but I don't think I should," she joked, a small smile blooming on her face.

"Here's your choice. You can keep your eyes open and take it all in while we go over to the railing. Or you can close your eyes."

"What?" Selby's pulse raced as her eyes darted over to the ledge.

"Two choices. What's it going to be? Eyes open. Or eyes closed." He closed the distance between them and placed his hands on her waist.

"You like giving choices, don't you?" She recalled him asking the same question when she'd cut her hand. "What makes you think I'll choose either?"

"Because of my rules, Miss Reynolds. This is a company event, correct?"

"You've got to be kidding me."

"Oh no. I'm quite serious, in fact."

"You enjoy testing me, don't you?"

"I won't pretend not to, but we have unfinished business. If you'd like to deny my request, I'd be happy to give you a punishment of sorts instead."

"I don't think so," she scoffed.

"I do." Garrett reached around and cupped her ass. She squealed, but never moved to leave. "Have you ever been spanked, Selby? Because I'm thinking you might need one. You seem to have this habit of not listening."

"I...I...that's not something I'm into..." she stuttered. He must have been joking, but his hard smile told her he was entirely serious.

"Maybe I'll even let Lars watch. Is that something you'd like?"

No one had ever spoken so dirty to Selby, and her pussy dampened at his words.

"What's it going to be? Open or closed?"

Selby stared at Garrett, considering her next move. She was incredibly turned on by him, but fear held her back.

"Answer me," he told her. His eyes smiled but his intense stare warned her to obey.

"Open," she whispered.

Selby could hardly believe that after all these years of avoiding heights, she was agreeing to what he asked. It terrified her that he used his words to push her, to arouse her. She wanted to deny him, to deny herself the fantasies she'd never allowed herself to have with another man. But even as she grew wet from his suggestion, she couldn't bring herself to admit to him that she wanted it.

"Very well. Don't worry. I'll never let anything happen to you," he promised. He reached for her hand, and slowly walked with her toward the railing.

It wasn't lost on Selby that Garrett shielded her view. She came up behind him, clutching his shirt with her free hand and trembled in fear as he placed her palm onto the iron bar.

"Take a deep breath. You're doing fine, sweetheart." He turned to face her, and she forced her fingers to open, releasing the fabric. "That's it. Put your other hand here."

As he settled her grip around the cold metal, Selby closed her eyes. She felt the warmth of his body behind her, the hardness of the rail brushing against her stomach. Blinking her eyes open, she continued to shake as the pool came into view.

"I can't do this. Garrett, please. You don't want to see me like this."

A memory of being rushed to hospital flashed in her mind. It wasn't the first time, it wouldn't be the last. It had been a gorgeous day. She'd gone on a hike, traveled several hundred feet upward before she'd realized heights were a trigger. The sight of Los Angeles had been spectacular until she'd gone to walk back down. *I'll fall. I'm up so high. I can't move.* Paralyzed, she'd cowered to the ground. The pain in her chest wouldn't cease. She knew it was another panic attack, but was at a loss as to how to control it. Garrett's soothing voice brought her back into the moment.

"I see you. Maybe better than you see yourself. You're beautiful." His hands never left her body as they grazed over her arms onto her shoulders, then trailed down her back until they rested on the sides of her thighs.

"I'm scared. I can't do this." Selby shook her head.

"But you wanted to do this for me, didn't you?"

"Yes," she admitted.

"Why, Selby?"

"Are you trying to distract me?"

"Maybe, but the thing is, I want to get to know you. I want more than just working with you."

"But you hardly talked to me in the office this week. Ever since the beach…" He hadn't looked at her with the slightest interest.

"By asking you here tonight, I've given you more access to my life than ninety-nine percent of the people in my life. This is who I am…if you want to be with," he hesitated, "if you want to be with me, then there are certain things you'll have to accept. Lars…"

"He's so mad at me." Selby tried to turn her head to face him, but his hands held her thighs still.

"Lars is pissed at me, not you."

"He says you're going to hurt me. Are you?" she asked. "Are you going to hurt me, Garrett?"

"Never." His lips brushed her hair. "But I will push your limits of what you think you're capable of doing. You're brilliant. Even though you hold onto these fears so tightly, I know you can embrace what we do."

"I don't know if I can. Lars says I don't belong here. That I'll never be right for you. But when I'm around you…" she whispered, "you make me feel…alive."

"I want to fuck you right here. Will you let me do that?"

"What? Garrett…" Selby laughed. *Jesus almighty.* She couldn't believe that she was three stories up, overlooking the pool and that her first instinct was to say 'yes' to public sex. Before she had a chance to answer further, his hands slipped underneath her dress. She gasped as his palms glided up her belly and cupped her bare breasts.

"No bra?"

"No, I…"

"Have you fantasized about my hands on you?"

"I can't tell you that…"

"You have, haven't you? Tell me." His hand trailed down her abdomen, slipping into her panties.

"Please…I can't…" Selby moaned as Garrett's fingers pressed through her wet lips. He plunged a thick digit into her core, and she cried out. She'd yearned to have him touch her, had imagined it a million different ways, but never had she thought he'd take her at the party.

"I was right…look at how wet you are, my brave girl.

You know what I think, Selby?" His lips moved to her neck.

"Oh God," she cried as he pumped another finger inside her.

"I think you crave this…like a seedling waiting for the sun, you're going to bloom."

Selby clutched the rail. His warm breath teased her ear and she shook her head, wishing she could deny his words. But as his thumb flicked at her clit, any ability to lie failed her.

"I want you so much," she breathed.

"That's better," he encouraged.

"We shouldn't," she panted.

"We should."

"Someone could see us."

"It's secluded."

"I…ah…" Selby's orgasm built and her eyes darted to the deserted deck. Although they were concealed in the shadows, music blared in the distance.

"Or would you like someone to watch? Do you want them to see you come?"

"No, I just want…" Selby attempted to stop her pussy from clamping down on his fingers at the mention of exhibitionism, but her effort was thwarted as he rocked his erection against her ass.

"Fuck, you surprise me…it excites you. Don't worry, sweetheart." He kissed her ear. "We've got plenty of time for that. But right now, I just want to make you feel good…any fear you felt is gone right now, isn't it?"

Selby's head lolled over as he pinched at her clitoris. He added a third finger, and she cried his name out loud. She was helpless to stop it; her climax consumed her. Her hands gripped at the bar as the violent spasms racked her body. Without warning, he withdrew his fingers and she whined. The crinkling sound of a condom was all she heard before he spread her legs with his knee.

"Open for me," he whispered into her ear.

"Garrett," was all she could manage as he entered her from behind.

Selby's arousal spiked as he filled her to the hilt. The sweet pain of her channel stretching brought her into focus. She wanted him more than the air she breathed. Selby had never done anything like this before, but the more he tested her, the more she embraced the rush he gave.

"Oh shit…no, no, no…don't fucking move," he said. "Selby…you feel so good. Jesus."

"Don't stop," she told him as he stilled.

"I'm creating a monster." He laughed and slowly did as she asked. He withdrew slightly and plunged back inside her. With one hand, he gripped her hip and wrapped a strong arm around her waist.

"Ah….stop." Selby heaved for breath as he slid deep inside her. She pressed her bottom back against his pelvis, wanting to take every inch he gave. "Talking."

He pinched her nipple and she squeaked. "Punishing you is going to be so much fun."

"Yes…" Selby began to quiver as she tightened around

his cock. The tip of his length stroked her nerves and she began to shake. "Harder…fuck me…now."

Garrett grunted, pounding into her from behind, and as she turned her head, he kissed her, forcefully taking her lips with his. She returned his demanding kiss, desperate to connect further. Selby had lost cognizance of where she was as he fucked her, and she knew that she'd become addicted to all that was Garrett Emerson. There'd be no going back after what she'd done.

He increased the pace, and Selby cried into his mouth, her orgasm slamming into her. Her body trembled in ecstasy and went limp as she was overcome with pleasure. Garrett slammed into her from behind, his flesh against hers and he called her name out loud, coming hard.

As Garrett slid out of her, Selby rested her forehead on her arm, trying to catch her breath. She stared down over the railing and realized that for the first time in her life, she wasn't afraid of heights as much as she'd thought. But she was more terrified than she'd ever been in her life. Not only had she just engaged in near-public sex, she'd given Garrett a part of her soul.

"Selby," he said, bringing her into his arms.

Her heart melted as he embraced her; his lips pressed to her temple, slowly making their way to her own. Gently, he kissed her, and emotion bubbled in her chest. He'd fucked her roughly, and now, in the quiet moments after, his sweet lips made love to her all over again. A small tear escaped as Lars' words played in her mind. Without meaning to, she'd given him the power to crush her into a million pieces. Despite her confusion, she knew she was helpless to stop herself from making love with him again. Lost in his kiss, she let herself fall without a parachute.

He slowly broke away, his lips inches from hers. He stroked her hair, his forehead pressed to hers.

"Are you okay?" he asked.

"Yeah," she replied. Selby wanted to ask him a thousand questions but she hesitated.

"There's something about you," he began. "I don't know what's going to happen between us, but I want you to know I meant what I said. No matter what Lars thinks."

"Okay." She nodded, still shaken from their encounter.

"Will you come home with me tonight? I want to have time alone with you…to get to know you better. Now that I know you can surf, I'd like to see what else you can do," he joked.

She laughed. "You mean you weren't impressed by my mad surfing skills?"

"More than you can possibly imagine." Garrett scanned the empty balcony and focused on Selby. "I know you can't understand just yet, but bringing you here…to this place. It's important to me."

Selby regarded Garrett as he opened to her. Like his company, he'd built Altura. But unlike the many strangers who passed through its doors, this was private. His inner sanctum that he only shared with those he considered family.

"Thank you for sharing it with me. I know you didn't

have to do it."

"I'm gonna warn you that a few people might be pissed because I did. This place is just kind of for our group. But don't take any shit, okay? I wanted you here and that's what matters."

"Got it." She gave a small smile, accepting that she was an outsider. His comments explained the cold look Seth had given her when she'd arrived.

"So do you want to come home with me?"

"Yes." Selby nodded. She found it intriguing how Garrett was dominant but also gentle, unafraid to expose his vulnerability to her.

"Let's go find Lars and say goodbye. He's a pain in my ass but I don't like leaving things the way we did."

"Me either." Selby also wanted to smooth things over. They'd been friends for such a long time, and she hated that he'd been so angry with her.

"Garrett," she smiled. "You were right."

"Hmm?"

"I definitely forgot about how scared I was." She laughed.

"See? Stick with me, kid. You'll be jumping out of planes soon."

Selby and Garrett stood holding hands, gazing into each other's eyes. She swore it felt as if he could read her every secret thought, and it occurred to her that that was exactly what she yearned for, to have the kind of relationship where she could share everything, no matter how embarrassing or arousing. A woman's voice called to

Garrett from the entrance and the spell was broken. Selby went to drop his hand but he held onto her.

"Selby, this is Blaire. Blaire, this is Selby."

"Hello," Selby said, taking note of the woman's appearance. Tall and thin, her raven hair had been streaked with red highlights. She wore a skin-tight metallic silver-colored tube dress. She towered on four-inch spiked heels but deftly managed them, as if she'd been a seasoned stilt walker.

"I need to talk to you." Blaire ignored Selby and continued, "We're running into issues with the Strata line. I'd like to talk to you in private."

"Are you kidding me? It's Saturday night. I appreciate your dedication but it's been a long day. Can it wait until Monday?"

"I just need five minutes of your time. Please," she pleaded.

Selby observed how the woman leaned in toward Garrett, batting her eyelashes at him. A pang of jealousy stabbed her, and she attempted to thwart the ugly reaction. Garrett's eyes darted to Selby, who gave him a sympathetic smile.

"I don't understand why we need to talk now."

"I've been trying to get with you all week. Between her," Blaire's angry gaze landed on Selby then focused back on Garrett, "and the mess with the police, Norm wouldn't let me in to see you. Five minutes. I promise."

"Go ahead, Garrett. I'll find Lars," Selby offered.

"Are you sure?"

"Yeah, really, it's fine. I want to talk to him alone anyway." It wasn't exactly true but she knew that he'd been busy at work, setting aside anything that wasn't in a critical path.

"Okay, I'll come find you inside when I'm done. You sure you'll be okay?" he asked.

"I can hold my own."

As they made their way back into the ballroom, all eyes fell on her. She ignored their stares, and accepted a small kiss from Garrett before he left with Blaire. Heeding his warning that she wasn't welcome, she stepped toward the bar and focused on her task. Alone, Selby steeled her nerves, determined to find Lars.

Chapter Fourteen

"Bottled water, please." Finding an empty barstool, Selby sat down. Her feet were killing her. She'd walked around the room twice, but hadn't been able to find Lars

The bartender poured it into a wine glass, reminding her of the money that surrounded her. As she brought the rim to her lips, she was startled by the weight of hands on her shoulders, causing her to accidentally dribble droplets onto her dress. She peered behind her and saw one of the twins smiling down at her.

"Selby, right?" he asked, sitting next to her.

"Yes, Selby Reynolds. I'm filling in for Evan." Selby wasn't sure why she felt the need to explain her role at the company, but she guessed it was because everyone in the room most certainly belonged there...except her.

"I'm Cormac O'Malley." He nodded, studying her.

"I understand you used to work for Evan. I'm sorry for your loss."

"Yes, and thanks." Cormac accepted a fresh draft from the tap and casually took a swig. "So, are you Garrett's girlfriend or something?"

Mid-sip, Selby coughed. Again water sprayed down onto the front of her dress.

"Well." She paused, unsure of how to answer. "I'll go with 'or something'."

"So you're available, then?" He smiled.

"Um, I wouldn't say that." She laughed.

"She's not his girlfriend," he declared to his brother who approached. "I win the bet."

"I don't believe it for a minute."

"Hey, Selby, this is my younger brother, Beckett."

"By a minute. Don't believe a word he says." He winked. "So, is it true?"

"Is what true?"

"You and Garrett," he drawled. "Are you dating? Maybe they're just having sex?"

"What's wrong with you?" Cormac asked, giving his brother a punch to the arm. "Ignore him. He has no manners."

"What? It's not like half the people in this room haven't done it." He rubbed his arm. "That's gonna leave a bruise. I have delicate skin."

Selby laughed.

"She's not like us. This is her first time here, you dumbass." Cormac looked to Selby and nodded. "He pretty much checked his brain cells at the door."

"Fuck off," Beckett retorted.

"See, no manners. Like a rock."

"Now what makes Miss Reynolds so special that he'd

bring her here without ever going on one outing with us?"

"Don't be mean to her. She's pretty." Cormac leaned in and sniffed her. "And she smells nice."

"Sorry." Beckett shrugged.

"But back to my question. Are you his girlfriend?"

"Friends with benefits?"

Cormac smacked his brother again.

"What? We all just saw." Beckett rubbed his arm in response. "Damn, that hurts."

"Ignore him. Please," Cormac pleaded.

"No, it's okay. Garrett and I…um…it's complicated." She gave a closed smile.

"Ah…that means she's available," Beckett noted.

"Definitely." Cormac nodded.

"I didn't say that…"

"You're dating then?" Beckett asked.

Selby sighed. Pressed for an answer, she wasn't certain what she meant to Garrett. They'd kissed. They'd fucked. And she wanted to continue doing more of the same. She prayed her infatuation would wane, but something told her that going home with Garrett would do little to quell her growing attraction to him.

"Have you seen Lars?" She changed the subject.

"Did you date Lars?" Cormac asked.

"I…uh." Selby vacillated between telling the truth and making up a lie. Her conscience forced her to admit her past. "Yes. A little. In college. But that was a long time ago. And it wasn't serious."

"Ah ha!" Beckett said, pointing at Cormac. "The plot

thickens."

"Sorry, there's really no plot. So, have you seen him?"

"Look at you," Cormac said. "Right out there with it. I like this girl."

"I like her too. Do you want to dance?" Beckett asked.

"I found her first."

"Guys, as much as I'd love to stay, I really need to talk with Lars."

"I'm crushed." Beckett held his fist to his chest, feigning distress.

"He's up in the main house."

Selby gave him a confused smile. "Sorry, where?"

"Right where you came into this room…just turn left. He may have gone off to make a call or something. Not sure."

"Thank you so much. It was a pleasure meeting you." She smiled and offered her hand.

"Welcome to Altura," Beckett said with a grin. Taking her hand, he kissed the back of it.

As he released it, Cormac surprised her by giving her a quick hug.

"We know you don't do the things we do," he whispered in her ear. "But if Garrett trusts you enough to bring you here, then so do we."

"Thank you. I appreciate it. Maybe I'll see you at the office."

As Selby waved goodbye, a warm feeling settled in her chest, knowing that not everyone hated her presence at Altura. As a recruiter within IT, working to help outsource

IT departments, she never belonged and was used to being an outsider. It had never bothered her…until now.

Selby shut the heavy door behind her, relieved to be away from the din. Unsure of where she was going, she made her way down a long hallway. Although it was dimly lit, she was still able to admire the framed black and white prints that lined its walls. The clang of pans drew her attention and she caught sight of a waiter's white apron strings just as he turned into a room. Voices to her left grew louder and she swore she heard Garrett.

She trailed her fingers over the smooth wooden chair rail, and took note of the intricate carvings which etched the crown molding. The opulence was beyond her comprehension. Even though she'd known that Garrett hadn't always been rich, a self-made man, she wondered if he'd had a hand in the design of the building. The ornate details led her to believe the mansion had been built long ago, yet modern designs were weaved into its Victorian architecture.

As she approached, a sliver of light shone through the doorjamb, and it occurred to her that she might be interrupting Garrett's meeting. A woman's voice drew her curiosity, and she took a deep breath, startled by her tone. Selby wished Lars had stayed at the party as she tiptoed towards the room. If she hadn't felt like an interloper before, she'd now officially become an eavesdropper. She wondered if the meeting Garrett was having with Blaire had developed into a staff meeting, and decided she'd briefly interrupt.

But as her feet propelled her toward the entrance, something felt off, the whispered voices trailing into moans. She knocked, causing the door to swing open. Selby's heart shattered as she caught sight of Blaire, standing bare in front of Garrett. The stretchy fabric of her tube dress had been pulled down to her waist, exposing her breasts.

"Garrett," she cried, her hands reaching for his belt.

"Blaire, what are you..." Garrett's words trailed off as the door's edge slammed into the wall.

"I'm sorry." Selby stumbled backwards. *Making love meant nothing to him. I mean nothing to him. You're going to be okay. Just walk away.* The loop played in her head as she attempted to remain calm.

"Selby, wait." He went to go to her but Blaire held him tight.

"No...I've gotta go." Tears rose to her eyes.

"This isn't what it looks like. Dammit, Blaire, get off." Garrett grabbed her wrists and removed them from his pants. He turned to Selby, who silenced him with her hand.

"Don't...just no." She backed out of the room, almost tripping as she bumped into Lars. He caught her in his arms and righted her on her feet.

"Selby, where are you going?" He glanced at Blaire,

who glared at Garrett. She adjusted her dress, slowly covering herself. "Garrett, what the fuck is going on here?"

"Let me go." Selby broke free of his hold and ran.

Reaching for the ribbon under her hair, she tugged off the mask, and discarded it on the floor. She stifled a cry, unable to believe she'd allowed herself to care about Garrett. Ridiculously rich, he could have any woman he wanted. It wasn't as if she'd thought having sex had been any kind of a commitment, but he couldn't wait ten minutes to fuck someone else? And he'd planned on taking her home?

Selby heard Garrett call her name, and she glanced back to see Lars grabbing onto him. The sound of their arguing voices escalated throughout the house. She flung open the front door and scanned the parking lot. A dozen stretch limos were parked around the circle but she wasn't sure which one had brought her. She approached the bellman, concealing her shaking hands.

"I need to go." She swiped her fingers under her eyes, attempting to stem the tears that continued to flow.

"Are you okay, ma'am?"

"A car. Which one's my car? I need to leave right now. I'm going to be sick." As humiliation set in, her stomach rolled, the contents of her dinner edging up her esophagus.

"Are you sure you don't want to go inside?"

"Car! Now!" she demanded.

He blew a whistle and a driver immediately pulled forward. Selby didn't bother waiting for him to open the door. She ran to where it had stopped and jumped in the back seat. She called out her address and was relieved when the limo started moving. As they pulled away, she caught a glimpse of Garrett and Lars in the driveway. They'd quarreled, and she knew it was because of her.

Selby flicked up the privacy screen and bent over, putting her head between her legs. Helpless to control her emotion, she sobbed. *God, I'm so stupid.* She felt like an idiot for allowing him to lure her into his 'I'll teach you the rush' bullshit. He'd been playing her all along, and Lars had known exactly what he'd been doing. It was why he'd been so angry that she'd gone to the party. He'd told her to stay away from Garrett, and she hadn't listened.

She wished she could blame him for putting her in this situation, but pursuing Garrett had been of her own doing. He'd simply asked her to help his friend, one who'd suffered a loss. She was supposedly the expert, who could assist his company. Instead, she'd lost her mind, engaging in unprofessional behavior. Not only had she just fucked her pseudo-boss, she'd withheld information about a dead man.

By the time the car pulled out of the estate, she'd made her decision. As soon as she got home, she was quitting. She couldn't go into the office, pretending she hadn't screwed him at a party. She prayed Lars wouldn't fire her, that she'd retain her consulting position. She'd get down on her knees and beg his forgiveness, take any account that was available…any engagement except for Emerson Industries.

She shoved back into her seat and curled her legs under

herself. As her crying subsided, she reached for a tissue from the console. She glared at her surroundings. The extravagant limousine reminded her of Garrett. This was his life, not hers. It was likely he'd paid for the transportation for all of the guests, including the entire expense of the soirée. It was nothing for someone like him, just a drop in the bucket. His everyday working man Jeep had been a ruse to lull her into thinking he was just like everyone else. But nothing could be further from the truth.

Wealth. Power. At the snap of his fingers, he could have anything or anyone he wanted, anytime, anywhere. There were no limitations in his world. It now made perfect sense why he continued to test death. It was the last remaining frontier. He skated along the unattainable edge of infinity as if he owned the universe. He was beholden to no one. No matter how attracted she was to him, she knew she didn't belong within the confines of his reality.

Lars had known all along who Garrett was, the kind of daredevil, playboy lifestyle that intoxicated him like a drug. And he knew Selby. Complete opposites, they'd never have a chance in hell of being compatible. Unlike Garrett, she had bills and responsibilities that had nothing to do with employment. She wasn't afforded the luxury of waking up in the morning and deciding not to go to a client. Avoiding risk, her idea of excitement was watching a horror film and hoping she'd be able to go to sleep. Hell, she hadn't been on a roller coaster since she was a kid.

She sighed and shook her head. Selby's tears had dried,

but her stomach still churned with anger that he'd gone to another woman within minutes of taking what he'd wanted from her. Recalling their encounter, she cringed, embarrassed that she'd been used. She hated how much she'd enjoyed having sex with him. She hadn't just liked it; she'd loved it. No man had ever in her entire life made her feel the way Garrett did. But it had all been an illusion.

It was no wonder the twins had asked her status. They'd probably known exactly what would happen to her. Garrett had probably fucked hundreds of women on the terrace, playing at his domination game. Her only regret in leaving was that she hadn't called him out cold on what he'd done to her. She excelled at controlled conflict in the boardroom, but this situation wasn't in the office, and it had been far from controlled. She felt like a plane spiraling into the ground, even though her final explosion had been less than dramatic, as she'd run.

The car slowed in front of her condo, and she slipped off her shoes. She could hardly wait to take a shower. She wished she could extricate thoughts of Garrett from her heart as easily as rinsing the scent of him from her skin. As the limo stopped, she opened the door, ignoring the driver who rushed to get there first. She waved him off, but gave him a small thank you before running to her building. She punched in the code, and entered.

On the way up in the elevator, fresh tears surfaced. Confused, she wondered when she'd become such a terrible judge of character. While dominant and commanding, Garrett had been caring toward her, insisting that he wanted to get to know her. He'd invited her to a place he claimed was his inner sanctum, one not seen by many people in his life. Even the twins had made a reference that she was special, implying that Garrett didn't bring just anyone to Altura.

Her lips pursed in anger. She couldn't believe that she was even trying to understand what had just happened in any other way than how she'd seen it with her own eyes. A ding alerted her that she'd finally arrived on her floor. The doors opened and she strode to her condo, impatient to get inside. Tapping at the security pad, she entered the code. The handle clicked open and she blew out a breath.

"What the hell?" Adrenaline shot through Selby's body as she took in the sight of the overturned sofa. Black dirt splattered across the floor, plants had rolled onto their sides. Her desk had been ransacked, her personal laptop smashed onto the stone tiles.

With her first instinct to call the police, Selby remembered she'd accidentally left her phone charging in the kitchen. She gasped as she took in the sight of the mess. The cabinets had all been opened, vitamin and prescription bottles scattered across the floor. Her heart sank when she looked at her charger, the phone missing from its docking station. She carefully navigated around the shards of broken ceramic plates and spied the edge of her cell peeking out from under the refrigerator. Carefully, she bent to grab it, her fingernails tapping at the edges. *An inch further*, she thought. When it was within her reach, she retrieved it.

"Please work, please work," she repeated, praying it would recognize her fingerprint. As the biometric lock released and the phone flared to life she exhaled in relief. "Thank God."

Although the web of cracked glass made it difficult to see, she managed to type in 911. Selby's hands shook as it rang. The operator clicked onto the line, and she heard the sound of footsteps. The phone fell from her hands as the blow came to her head. As blackness claimed her, she called Garrett's name.

Chapter Fifteen

"You just couldn't keep your dick in your pants, could you?" Lars yelled at Garrett. He plowed his fingers through his hair and paced. "I asked one thing of you. To leave Selby alone. And you just couldn't fucking do it."

"It's not like that, Lars. Come on, you know me," Garrett countered.

"Yeah, I do know you. I know you could have any woman you want, but you had to have Selby. Why her?" Lars held up a silencing hand. "No, just forget it. You always want what you can't fucking have. Or was it all just for fun? Well, guess what? Selby's not a fuck toy you can just stick your dick in and throw away."

"It's not what it looks like. I told you I didn't touch Blaire. I'm not going to say it again. You know how she is." Garrett paused, still in shock over what had just happened.

When Selby had caught them, he'd been trying to convince Blaire to return to the party. After a brief discussion about product issues, she'd pressed him for sex.

At one time, they'd had an on again off again affair, but they hadn't had sex for over a year. They'd never been more than friends with benefits, but everyone in their entire club had known they'd played on occasion.

Garrett was pissed at himself for ignoring his instincts against meeting with her. Immediately, he'd been suspicious of Blaire's motives. He'd known there were certain members of Altura who'd take umbrage with Selby's presence. She was an outsider who'd never so much as looked at a parachute, let alone used one. Having sex at the party had been a spur of the moment decision. He'd deliberately selected a more secluded section of the terrace to make love to her, teasing her with the possibility they'd be watched. While he knew it was possible they'd been seen, he'd thought they'd gone unnoticed. Still, he'd tested the waters of what excited her, giving in to the fantasy. He wasn't entirely opposed to the idea of exhibitionism, but tonight he'd wanted her all to himself.

Ever since they'd met, his thoughts had become consumed with dark fantasies, all involving one Selby Reynolds. He'd prayed he'd be satisfied taking her just once, getting it out of his system, but their brief interlude had taken his interest to a higher level. She'd enjoyed being dominated but had turned on a whim, reminding him exactly who held the power.

He'd meant what he'd said to her; he wanted to get to know her better. A conversation here and there hadn't been nearly enough time. After their explosive encounter at the party, he'd craved more. Ravenous, his desire could only be quenched by making love to her again.

What had started out as a somber week had turned into a celebration of life, and Selby had given him the motivation to shove away the grief that had paralyzed him ever since Evan had died. He'd seen the light in her eyes when she'd surfed, and again when she realized she'd overcome her fear of the balcony. He couldn't be sure what had happened to Selby to make her develop so many deep-seated fears. They smothered her so badly that she'd become a prisoner in her own world. He was no psychologist, but he knew more than anyone what it took to overcome fear, to have faith in situations that didn't deserve a shred of hope.

Garrett whistled loudly for the bellman, having decided to go to Selby. There was no other choice than to explain to her what had happened. The look of disdain she'd given him, running from him as if he were the devil himself, cut him to the core. While it might have been true that he could have any woman he wanted, he didn't just fuck every one he met. On the contrary, he'd been selective and cautious, going out of his way never to inflict pain on a woman. He cursed, wondering how little she thought of him that she'd even believe he'd be capable of doing that to her.

Lars' booming voice drew his attention and he shook his head.

"Where the hell do you think you're going?"

"I'm going to talk to Selby," Garrett told him.

"No. Just leave her alone. I'm beggin' you. Don't you

think you did enough damage tonight?"

"I can't leave things like this. I know you don't believe me so just get out of my way." Garrett pushed past him and Lars grabbed onto his arm.

"Please. Just stop." He released his friend but followed him to the limo.

"I can't. You don't get it, Lars. I care about her."

"Are you kidding me? You just fucked her for the first time out on the balcony. Yeah, that's right. I saw you. That's real romantic."

"Fuck off." Garrett opened the car door and leaned on the top of it. "It's not like I planned it. Shit, okay, yeah, have I been thinking about how much I wanted to do it? I'm not going to lie to you. Ever since I met her, I haven't been able to get her out of my head, and then you," he pointed to Lars, "you are the one who insisted she come work for me. I could have let it go. But no. She's gotta take over for Evan, which you knew damn well would mean we'd spend time together."

"She was the right one for the job."

"Maybe you're right but there's something between us. And I want to find out what it is."

"G, I know you. You've never dated a woman for longer than a month. There's always a reason why. They're too needy. They don't get your business. They're after your money. You name it, you have an issue with them. You already know Selby's not like us. And you damn well know that's why I've never brought her around here."

"I'm not sure how to put this. You know I care about

you but this is happening whether you like it or not. Despite what you think, I won't hurt her."

"You already fucking did," Lars exclaimed.

"Again. Listen up. This. Is. Happening. You can accept it or not. We'll be friends either way, but this thing between Selby and me; I have to see it through. Maybe it's nothing. Then we can both go our merry ways and you can celebrate. But you're not stopping me." Garrett didn't bother saying goodbye as he jumped into the back seat. What he didn't expect was that Lars would follow him.

"What are you doing?"

"I'm coming with you."

"I don't need a babysitter. What I do need is to talk to her alone."

Lars slammed the door shut and reached for a bottle of aged whiskey.

"Fine, suit yourself. But you're not staying while I talk to her."

"I'll wait outside, then." Lars fingered two tumblers, twisted the cap off with his teeth and poured the golden liquid into them. Handing one off to Garrett, he took a long swig and coughed. He wiped his mouth with the back of his hand and stared out the window. "If you hurt her again, I'm going to fucking kick the shit out of you."

"I get that." Garrett sipped the liquor, pleased that Lars was finally starting to calm down.

"I mean it. You know I can, too."

"Yeah, sure you can. Fantasyland must be nice. Maybe I'll visit someday." He gave him a small smile.

"You'd better apologize."

"What the hell do you think I've got planned?"

"I'm serious. Like down on your damn knees. You are an idiot, by the way, for thinking Blaire wanted to talk about business," he told him. The corner of his mouth lifted into a lopsided grin.

"Yeah."

"The woman is badass but all she ever thinks about is sex. And you are so busy with your dick hanging out you can't think straight."

"Perhaps."

"And ya know they're not going to be too happy about you bringing Selby to the party without warning. So it's not like you're going to get any sympathy points from the rest of us."

"Yep."

Garrett rubbed his forehead with his fingers. He could hardly argue with Lars. He'd fucked things up with Selby and knew his friends weren't going to be happy either. It had been his rule that they could bring no one to Altura without the person having gone on at least one jump with them. The only exceptions to the rule were people like Seth, who first had proved his commitment by training some of the group on big wave riding. They each had their specialties, sports they preferred, but they all had a common goal of pushing the thresholds of athleticism.

Selby had no interest in the things Altura offered, yet he'd brought her anyway. No matter the logic that told him it'd never work, there was something about her he just couldn't let go.

He glanced to Lars, who stared at him as if he could read his mind. Garrett gave him a small smile and took another swig. He imagined it would be a tough sell. Selby might not forgive him, but if there was one thing about Garrett, he never gave up. His determination had caused him to excel in many situations, ones where the odds hadn't been in his favor. In business, Garrett always succeeded. When it came to Selby Reynolds, failure was not an option.

Chapter Sixteen

Garrett had gone ballistic when they entered Selby's apartment and he'd found her. She'd been sitting in glass, her back propped against the refrigerator. Despondent, she stared into the opened cabinets, and when his gaze met hers, she'd begun crying. Although she'd been awake when they'd arrived, she had no recollection of what had happened. With a knot on the back of her head, she'd woken against the tiled floor. Selby hadn't resisted when he'd scooped her up into his arms, cradling her to his chest.

Although paramedics had been called to the scene, Garrett contacted his personal physician, who soon arrived at her condo as well. She'd complied with their tests, wincing in pain as they cleaned the tiny cut on the back of her skull. When the doctor examined her, he determined it was unlikely that she'd incurred a mild brain injury. *Watch for signs*, they'd told him. It wasn't as if he didn't already know the symptoms of a concussion. Although they took precautions during their sporting events, head injury was always a possible outcome. Selby claimed her vision wasn't blurred nor was she nauseous, but Garrett was aware that issues could occur well after the initial incident.

The police officers had briefly questioned her. All she'd been able to remember was reaching for her phone. Before leaving the apartment, Garrett had texted Dean, requesting that he oversee the investigation. He'd told him of his suspicions that the break in at her apartment was related to Evan's murder. Save for her closet, the entire condo had been torn apart. A slew of questions whirled in his brain as he tried to figure out what had happened. How would they have known she was at the party? How had they entered her apartment when there'd been no sign of breaking and entering? What had they been looking for? Although her laptop had been smashed, the flat screen TV was undamaged. He suspected the person had been searching for something specific. When she'd come home early, she'd interrupted them.

Garrett had grown concerned that she hadn't resisted when he'd suggested that she go home with him. After what had happened, she would have never agreed without an argument, but he suspected she was in shock, unable to process the attack. On the car ride home, she'd fallen asleep in his arms. He'd brought her into his room, determined not to leave her side. When Lars had insisted he stay, Garrett hadn't argued. In truth, it terrified him that something could happen to her, and he wanted him around in case of emergency. He'd laid her in the bed without removing her clothes. She'd already been violated and if she woke up, he didn't want her thinking he'd taken advantage.

Garret had dozed off as well, exhausted from the day's events. She slept on his chest, curled into his embrace. He stirred as a stream of light speared into the room. Reaching for the remote, he activated the automatic shutters. They sealed over the wall of windows, plunging them into darkness. With a flick of a switch, a splatter of starlight appeared across the ceiling.

In the soft glow, Garrett stroked Selby's hair. He couldn't remember the last time he'd slept with a woman in his arms. She moaned, and he steeled himself for the conversation he'd expected when he'd gone to her earlier. She'd been too traumatized to fight, but he knew she'd come around. As her eyes fluttered open, he froze, waiting for her to react.

"Where am I?" She tilted her chin upward and glanced at Garrett, then once again closed her eyes. "Garrett."

"Hey, sweetheart, how are you feeling?"

"How long have I been sleeping?"

"About seven hours. Lars and I brought you back here after…"

"Where's Lars?" Selby lifted her head, scanning the room.

"He's in the other room. How's your head? You feel sick? Headache?"

"No, I just feel tired. My head is hurt?" she asked, reaching for the small lump.

"It's just a small abrasion. No need for stitches. Do you

remember the doctor telling you that?"

"No. Maybe, I guess. It's like a blur. I was in the kitchen. My apartment," she whispered. Her fingers clutched at his shirt as if he was her rock.

"I'll have it cleaned up," Garrett told her. After the police had finished investigating, he'd pay to have it completely restored, painted, new furniture, the works. He'd spare no expense to right her world.

"No, I can do it." Her voice wavered.

"It's already taken care of."

"It was locked."

"Sorry?"

"It was locked," she repeated.

"What was locked?"

"My condo. I have a code. No one knows the code but the custodian."

"They're going to question him."

"Adam wouldn't break into my apartment," she insisted.

"The police are looking into it." In truth, he'd already asked himself the same question.

"My phone was under the refrigerator. I called 911." She looked up at him, recalling what had happened. "And after that...I don't remember. You were there. Lars."

"It's going to be okay, Selby. Why don't you get some more rest? You got knocked pretty hard. Last night..."

"Last night...at the party..." Selby's eyes widened, and she pushed out of his arms. She swung her legs over the edge of the bed but didn't move to walk away. "No, I shouldn't be here."

Garrett scrambled to sit next to her, his knee brushing hers. He moved to put his arm around her but thought better of it. They'd have to work this out, there was no other choice. He had to convince her that he hadn't cheated.

"I know you think you know what you saw last night, but nothing was going on," he began. She scooted over a few inches and glared at him in disgust as her memories became clear. "Please don't look at me like that. I'm telling you you're wrong."

"I know you're used to getting what you want, Garrett, but I'm not an idiot. I saw you. I saw her. How can there be any explanation other than what was going on in that room?" She shook her head, and stared toward the bedroom door, eyeing the exit. "It doesn't matter. Listen, whatever I thought was going on between us…I was wrong. You don't need to worry about it, because I quit. I'm done. I'm going to beg Lars to forgive me, which hopefully he will. I'll plead a case of naivety and stupidity, and then we never have to see each other again."

"Jesus, Selby, I'm telling you that I was not making a play for Blaire," he insisted.

"Really? So I just imagined seeing you and her? Her boobs? Hmm…thank you very much for clearing that up. Not only am I stupid, I'm crazy. Nice."

"Would you just listen for five minutes?" Garrett scrubbed his chin. He'd known it would be difficult to get her to understand, but the conversation wasn't going at all how he'd planned.

"Knock yourself out. I'm still quitting."

"I think it's pretty obvious that Blaire was hitting on me..."

"What was your first clue? Oh yeah, she wasn't wearing a top."

"Selby, I care about you, but you need to listen to me. First of all, when you came in last night, I was not touching her. Think back. Were my hands on her at all? Was I touching her?"

Selby shrugged.

"No, don't give me that. Answer me. Was I touching her?"

"No." Selby crossed her arms defiantly, and trained her eyes on the floor.

"Exactly. Second, and this is the most important point, do you really think so little of me that you actually think I'd be with you one minute and turn around and go fuck Blaire the next? Seriously, I'd just told you that I wanted to get to know you."

"I saw her."

"I would never do that to you. What you saw was her coming on to me. I swear I had nothing to do with it."

"Garrett," she began.

"Selby, I know we haven't known each other very long, but I meant what I said. I want to get to know you. Now, do I know where this is going? Not a fuckin' clue. But I told you I wouldn't hurt you and I meant it."

Selby put her head in her hands and sighed. Garrett

recognized that she was softening her position and moved to kneel before her. Gently, he spread her knees open, settling himself between her legs. He took her cheeks in his hands, wiping the tears brimming from her eyes.

"I'm sorry about what happened last night," he apologized.

"Why did that woman think she could do that with you? Is she your girlfriend?" Selby asked, her voice uncertain. She clutched his wrists and closed her eyes.

"I'm not going to lie to you. We both have pasts. Have I had sex with Blaire? Yes, but it was a long time ago. Over a year, as a matter of fact. But we never dated. She is not, has never been my girlfriend."

"I haven't dated a lot of people," Selby confessed. "I don't do what you do. I can't just be okay with you…"

"I know you think you know me, the rumors. When you start to let me in, I'll let you in. But for now, whatever you think about me, I'm not some asshole who fucks a different woman every day of the week. And I'd certainly never do what you think I was doing. That's not me," he whispered. Garrett's head moved toward hers until their foreheads met. "I've meant every word I've said to you since we've met. Do I want to push you…test your limits sometimes? You bet your sweet little ass I do. But I'm not playing games. I would never do that to you. Please, I'm sorry about what happened."

"I'm sorry, too." Her eyes locked on his and they held a long gaze.

"She's nothing to me. A friend, that's it. You, on the

other hand...I can't get you out of my head."

Garrett stared into Selby's green eyes as if they answered all of life's questions. Sensing she'd forgiven him, he gave her a small smile. The strong soul inside her had recognized the truth in his words. She blinked, and his heart tightened.

As silence set in, Garrett thought of all the reasons he should let her go. He'd promised not to hurt her and setting her free would ensure that would happen. But as his eyes fell to her lips, he wondered if he was the one who'd be destroyed.

As Garrett kissed her, Selby's defenses shattered. She'd never been so aroused, so devastated, so out of control. His strong lips took hers, penetrating through any doubt she'd had. She was exhausted and confused, but his kiss erased the hideous events of the evening and brought forth the rush of desire she'd repressed. Selby gave in to her deepest craving, allowing him into her heart.

His tongue gently probed her mouth, and she moaned at his soft intrusion. Underneath his gentle kiss, an explosive sexual tension simmered. As she moved to reach for him, he wrapped his fingers around her wrists and retreated. Breathless, she opened her eyes to see him staring at her. A long moment of silence lay between them and her heart pounded against her chest as she wondered what he had planned.

"Don't stop," she heard herself saying.

What was it about this man? Like a drug, she needed him now. She'd never been jealous, desperate for someone. But when he'd come for her at her apartment, she hadn't thought twice about going into his arms. Despite what she'd witnessed, he represented strength and security. Realizing he hadn't been with another woman, she was slightly more terrified of her growing emotions.

"I'd love to continue, but I'm thinking maybe we should take a shower. Your dress..." He reached for the torn hem. "And I've been in these clothes all night."

"Okay." Her voice was soft as she agreed. Selby's body tingled in anticipation, aware she hadn't seen him naked yet.

"Can you walk?" he asked. He shoved up to stand and brought her hand with him. "I can carry you."

"No, I'm okay." Selby slowly stood. A tremor of dizziness ran through her and she grabbed his arm. As soon as it came, it left and she went to release him.

"Hey, I've got you. Come here." Garrett lifted her, cradling her against his chest.

"You don't have to carry me." Embarrassed, she buried her face in his shirt. God, she'd never felt so weak in her life.

"I'm going to, though. Even though the doctor said you looked okay, we need to watch you for signs of a concussion. I plan to keep a close eye on you." He gave her a wicked smile and carried her into his bathroom.

"A close eye, huh? Is that what you call it?" She rubbed her fingers over his wrinkled shirt and breathed in his masculine scent.

"Yes, close eyes. Close hands. Close lips." He kissed the top of her hair. "It's all good."

"So that's how they're treating head injuries these days. Warm showers? Tell me more, Dr. Emerson." She laughed.

"I was pretty good with a pair of medical scissors, wasn't I?" Garrett flicked on the lights and carefully set her on her feet.

"Yes, I suppose you were…" Selby lost track of what she was saying as she took in the sight of her surroundings. A gas lit fireplace roared to life against the far wall. Its flickering light illuminated the black soapstone walls of the bathroom. She heard Garrett give a command and soft red lights glowed in the ceiling, while water rained down from all sides of the shower. Through the spray of water, the orange fire danced in the background.

Garrett turned to her, his expression serious. Without saying a word, he unbuttoned his shirt. It fell to the floor, revealing his ripped abdomen. As if her hands had a mind of their own, they reached for him. She gazed into his eyes, trailing her fingers over his shoulder.

He unbuckled his belt, sliding it out of his pants, and within seconds he stood fully nude before her. Selby wanted more time to just stare at him, to memorize every inch of his spectacular form. She glanced at his hard length, and quickly raised her gaze to his, giving him a shy smile. Her nipples stood to attention as if saluting the general who was about to take command. Her heart beat faster, as she was unable to anticipate his next move.

Garrett reached for the hem of her dress, and in one smooth movement, he easily guided the blue fabric away from her body. Allowing him to remove her thong, she stood bare before him. Without words, he took her hand and led her into the hot spray. Serenity blanketed her mind as he brought her back to his chest and began to massage her shoulders. She moaned and before she knew what was happening he was washing her hair. Water droplets danced over her skin as she arched her back, her chest pressing upward. He tilted her head into the soothing rain, rinsing away the lather. Strong soapy hands slid down her arm, and Selby yearned to turn to him. She went to move, but he settled a hand on her waist, holding her in place. The tip of his cock prodded the crevice of her bottom, focusing her attention.

"Tell me what happened?" Garrett asked, trailing a slippery finger down the long scar on her back.

Selby froze, having forgotten it was there. She hadn't planned on having this conversation with him tonight.

"What's wrong? You can tell me." His wet lips pressed to her neck.

"It was an accident." Her voice trembled. Once again she tried to turn, but he held her in place as he continued to draw a line on her raised skin.

"I can see it was an accident. I don't imagine surgery would leave this type of scar."

"Playing doctor again?" Selby attempted to change the conversation.

"Nope. You kind of get experience with scars in my business. I like to think of them as souvenirs. They remind us of how tough we are."

"Not everyone wants to be tough." Memories of her childhood attack would never leave her. She could only be so lucky to forget.

"Did someone hurt you?" The tone of Garrett's voice grew serious.

"Sort of. It was my fault," she hedged.

"You don't like to let anyone in, do you?"

"What do you mean?"

"You're strong. Smart. But you're also a little closed up. Your fears. It's almost as if something made you afraid. Or someone."

"I'm just cautious."

"You don't need to be afraid of me."

"What makes you think I'm…?" Selby's words trailed off as Garrett's hands brushed over her breasts, caressing them.

"When you're ready, you can tell me what happened. But you will tell me eventually. Do you know why, Selby?" he asked, pinching her nipples until she gave a small moan. Her head lolled back onto his shoulder as he touched her.

"Why?" Her voice croaked. Selby's body was set on fire as his hands glided down her belly. She wanted to tell him, to admit what had happened to her. But the shame was too great to bear.

"Because you will trust me to be the man who not only makes you come so hard you see fucking stars, I'll be the one who you can rely on in your darkest moments. I want to be that man for you. But until that happens, we'll continue to get to know each other."

Selby gasped as he rocked his erection up against her ass, sliding his fingers down into the crease near her inner thighs. His hand grazed over her skin slowly, this time flittering directly atop her pussy. As Garrett washed her bared mound, thoroughly cleaning her folds and gently swiping over her nub, Selby thought she'd come undone.

"Garrett," Selby groaned as he withdrew. He opened her lips to the spray, sweeping away the bubbles. The water splashed onto her exposed clit, and it swelled in arousal.

"I want to do everything to and with you," he whispered in her ear.

"Yes," she replied, tilting her hips upward.

"No one will ever have you the way I will, Selby. Not only will you trust me someday, you'll beg me to listen to every secret you're keeping. By the time we're done, you'll get that I don't do things half way. Not in business, not with you. Now sit."

"What?" Selby, only halfway listening, had gone numb with desire. She whimpered as he released her folds, bringing an abrupt end to the quivering sensation he'd caused.

"Sit," he repeated, turning her so she faced him.

"What are you doing?" Selby asked as he guided her onto the smooth stone seating.

Garrett went onto his knees. Water droplets fell down his face as his eyes locked on hers.

"Open your legs. Let me see your pussy."

Her dominant lover had returned, and her body obeyed his sweet command.

"I've wanted to do this ever since you teased me that night at the club. You're a very dirty girl, sweetheart. And I can't wait to show you how to release your inner beast."

Selby smiled as his dark eyes met hers. Her skin tingled as he ever so slowly slid his fingers onto her inner thighs, inching toward her mound. His thumbs wiggled through her labia, brushing over her entrance, causing her to pump her hips upward as if she were making love to an invisible lover.

"That's right. You want me to suck you, baby. Because I really want to. I'm so hungry for this beautiful pussy of yours. But first..." Never taking his eyes off hers, he brought his lips to her clit. He blew gently until she moaned. "You're going to tell me what you want me to do."

"Garrett, no...please just do it...don't stop," she protested. Jesus Christ, he'd make her mad. His erotic tests would never end, she thought.

"Touch your breasts," he ordered, his thumbs caressing her inner lips.

"I can't...oh my God...please," she begged. Selby averted her gaze but continued to pump her hips as he massaged her. Every time he moved his thumbs upward, he ever so slightly grazed her clit.

"Do it. Touch your breasts." His smile brought a soft veil to his demand.

Wanting to please him, she brought her hands onto her chest, her fingers flicking her nipples, and was immediately rewarded as he slid a thick finger into her tight core.

"Ahh...yes."

"You are so beautiful. I can't wait to fuck you, sweetheart, but first I want to hear you tell me nicely what you want." As he spoke, his lips brushed her mound.

Selby could manage the occasional 'fuck me', but to tell him what she really wanted, how she wanted it...to articulate oral sex went far beyond her comfort zone. But she knew that was exactly the point. He'd push her further and further. A soft slap to her inner thigh drew her attention and she set her eyes back on his.

"Say it, Selby. I'm right here," he instructed, his fingers continuing to plunge inside her core.

Selby moaned as he spread her folds wide open, the warmth of his breath on her skin. She pinched her nipples, tilting her pelvis toward his mouth. Aching with arousal, she gave in to his request.

"Lick me, Garrett," she told him, keeping eye contact.

"See how easy that was?" Darting his tongue through her lips, he lapped at her.

"More..."

"More what?" Garrett asked, pressing his mouth to her lips.

"Lick my pussy….ah yes, like that." Selby nearly fell off the slippery seat as he did as she asked, laving at her ripe bud.

"That's it, sweetheart. Fuck, you taste good." Garrett plunged two fingers into her.

"Faster, right there," Selby screamed as Garrett did as she asked, flicking his tongue faster and faster as he fucked her. Her orgasm built, and her channel tightened around his hand. "Suck me…suck my clit. Ah yes. I'm coming. I'm coming."

Selby shook as her climax claimed her. She reached for his head, raking her fingers into his hair. As if holding on for dear life, she pressed his face into her pussy. She quivered, every muscle in her body convulsing as he made love to her with his mouth.

"Garrett, Garrett, Garrett," she repeated as it subsided.

He raised his head, his eyes locking on hers. She gasped for breath, kindled by the ravenous flare of his gaze. He gave her no quarter as he placed his hands onto the ledge and pressed upward, his lips taking hers. Tasting her own juices, she kissed him back in a feverous frenzy. He wrapped her legs around his waist and lifted her up into the air.

As he stood, he stumbled backward into the spray until his back touched the wall. Selby reached around his neck, hoisting herself higher until she felt his cock prod her entrance.

"Condom," she heard him say as he tore his lips from hers. He bent and reached for a shelf outside the shower.

"Hurry," she responded, sliding her clit against his slippery stomach. Holy hell, this sexy as sin man had driven her insane, she thought. Never in a million years would she have been so far gone as to have had unprotected sex. She breathed in relief as she heard the wrapper tear open. Why the hell he kept a condom near the shower was a question for later.

"I can't get enough of you," she heard him say right as he slammed her down onto his rock-hard cock. Selby groaned in pleasure as he stretched her channel. Breathless, she reveled in his strength. Her heels dug into his ass as she held on for dear life.

"Garrett, please…please…" she begged. With every forceful thrust, his crown grazed along her band of nerves, bringing her closer to orgasm. He gripped her hips, holding her firmly in place as he pounded up into her.

"Selby…fuck yeah," he grunted. "You…I want all of you."

Selby gasped as his fingers traveled down the crevice of her bottom, tracing a circle along her puckered flesh.

"Garrett," she breathed. Unaccustomed to his touch, she tensed.

"Relax, sweetheart," he told her, gently pressing his forefinger. "Let me in."

"I don't know…ah," Selby cried. She bit down onto his shoulder as he slid it in slowly. She barely felt the sting as he pushed into her.

"I'm going to fuck you here, too, baby. See how good it…" Garrett lost his words as he rocked up into her.

"Oh my God." She relaxed into the dark sensation, allowing him to fill her. Slowly, he withdrew and forcefully pressed both his cock and finger into her. Selby undulated her hips into his thrusts, her swollen clitoris brushing his pelvis. Her core tightened around him as her orgasm tore through her.

"Yes, sweetheart. Aw hell," he grunted, coming hard.

Selby lost herself in all that was Garrett Emerson. As she floated down from ecstasy, her jaw released his shoulder. His fingers lifted her chin and he kissed her gently. Like she'd been possessed by the devil himself, she'd let go, releasing her inhibitions.

Slowly their lips broke apart, but he kept his forehead pressed to hers. When she opened her eyes, her heart leapt. His intense stare told her he'd capture her soul, take everything she was and she'd be grateful he'd done so. She prayed she'd survive her greatest adventure; Garrett Emerson.

The silence stretched and was only broken when he reached to turn off the spray. He lifted her off of him and removed the condom with one hand. After tossing it into the trash, he reached for towels and gently patted her dry. Selby couldn't take her hands off of him as he blotted away the moisture, paying careful attention to every last inch of her skin. When he'd finished, he gave her a small smile, surprising her as he lifted her into his arms. She lay her head on his shoulder for a few seconds and protested with a moan when he set her down onto the bed.

"Be right back," he told her.

When he returned from the bathroom, he brought her into his arms so that she rested her head on his chest. Curling into his embrace, she brought her thigh across his legs.

"Garrett," she whispered. The emotion in her chest rose to the surface and she struggled to keep it inside. "I've never been with anyone like you."

"Me either. This thing with us...it feels like I can't get enough." He brushed his hand over her wet hair.

"It was amazing." She pressed her lips to his chest, terrified that she'd fall for him. He was unattainable. Like the wispy edges of a wonderful dream, he'd disappear from her life.

"We should get some rest."

Selby closed her eyes, unsure of what words she wanted to hear from his lips. It was as if he'd destroyed her for all other men. She didn't believe in love at first sight. But after being made love to as if she were a goddess, no man would ever measure up to him. Sexually he'd pushed her far past her comfort zone, and she'd delighted in every sinful moment. Selby could fall for him hard, she knew. As she drifted off to sleep, she relaxed against his naked body, wishing she could stay there forever.

Chapter Seventeen

Garrett woke, his body tightly spooned against Selby's. He contemplated the past twenty-four hours, wondering how things had escalated out of control. Pushing the envelope of where she'd go sexually had started off as a game of sorts. He sought to teach her the high that came with risking everything. But with each lesson, he was the one who'd been schooled. When she'd done as he'd asked, telling him to lick her pussy, he'd just about exploded right then. He laughed to himself, recalling how she'd bit him. Like a wild animal, she'd gone feral, losing herself in the moment. She could kill him, but he reasoned he'd love every second.

He inwardly cursed, aware that he'd almost fucked her without a condom. They hadn't talked about seeing each other seriously, let alone having unprotected sex. Yet in the shower, all he'd wanted to do was bury himself deep inside her, his bare skin touching hers. If he were truthful, he'd admit that an unfamiliar desire to date her exclusively could threaten to overtake his current lifestyle. The thought of it was ridiculous, he knew. Until now, his entire life had been wrapped in Emerson Industries and Altura, but as she stirred in his arms, he briefly considered what it would be like to let go.

This morning, all he wanted to do was make love to her again. His lips grazed over Selby's neck, his tongue brushing onto her skin. She tasted like honey butter, salty and sweet. Her nipple peaked underneath his fingertips and his arousal spiked. Garrett's hand glided down to her mound, and without saying a word, she parted her legs, giving him access to her already drenched pussy. He plunged a finger into her core, testing her readiness, and she rocked into his hand.

"Hmm, Garrett," she moaned.

"Give me a minute," he said, reaching for protection.

Using his teeth, he tore it open and slipped it onto his hard length. Garrett rolled Selby onto her back and her eyes blinked open at him. She gave him a sleepy smile and his heart caught. For the love of all that was holy, he'd never seen a more beautiful sight. Her tousled hair spread all over the pillow, her hands off to the side.

"Good morning, sweetheart," he said, guiding his cock to her entrance.

"Good morning." Selby closed her eyes and moaned as he slowly pressed into her. "Ah, yes."

"You are so damn sexy, woman." As he rocked into her, fully sheathing himself, he dropped his head to her breast, suckling a taut tip. "Hmm...delicious."

Garrett gave equal attention to her other nipple,

eliciting soft cries. She raked her fingers into his hair, cradling his head to her chest.

"You feel so good inside me," she told him.

"Not nearly as good as you feel around me." He lifted his gaze to meet hers, and his chest filled with emotion. *Jesus Christ almighty, I could make love to this woman all day and it would never be enough.*

Garrett kissed her, sucking her bottom lip, and softly nipping it. As she moaned and raised her hips to meet his, he thrust upward, brushing his pelvis against her clit. His fingers wrapped around her wrists, and he pinned her arms to either side of her head. As she exposed her neck to him, his lips moved to her collarbone.

"Garrett, I'm…yes, yes, yes," she mumbled as he took her.

Writhing underneath his muscular torso, she screamed his name. Her pussy pulsated around his cock as she came hard. Plunging into her, he lost control as she fisted his shaft. The waves of his release claimed him, and he pressed his lips to hers, passionately kissing her. Slowly breaking contact, he opened his eyes and caught her wanton gaze. Selby blinked and gave a small laugh.

"Something funny, Miss Reynolds?"

"I never get these kinds of wake up calls when I travel on business," she teased.

"I certainly hope not."

"I could do this with you every morning," she said. As if she realized what she'd implied, she averted her gaze.

"So could I, sweetheart." Her eyes darted to his and the

reticence lingered before he continued.

"How are you feeling this morning?"

"How do I feel?" She smiled. "I feel great."

"Do you want to sleep a little more?"

"Hmm…maybe."

Garrett knew she needed more rest, and he probably did too, but more than that, he needed space. It was far too soon to commit to her, but in his heart, it was exactly what he desired. For the first time in his life, he could picture himself making love with this one woman every morning. The thought terrified and thrilled him all at once. He needed time to think about what was happening between them. Instead of broaching the topic, he pressed his lips to hers a final time and lifted himself off her. Quickly disposing of the condom, he swung his legs over the bed and retrieved a clean pair of pajama pants.

"I'm going to make us something to eat."

"Okay." She yawned and snuggled into the covers.

Without saying more about it and digging a deeper hole, he dressed and shoved onto his feet. Garrett tucked the sheets over her naked body and smiled as she curled onto her side, drifting back into her slumber. As he closed the door behind him, Garrett considered how she could have been killed. He texted Dean, and hoped for an immediate response. They needed to figure out how the hell they were going to keep her safe.

Chapter Eighteen

Garrett began cooking brunch, which he'd describe as pretty much anything he could find in the kitchen. Ever since he'd left the bedroom, he'd been thinking about how incredible it had been making love with Selby. Although Garrett had been with other women, no one had ever made him feel the way she did. From her strong will to her playful sexuality to the way she challenged him, he was drawn to her. As she let him inside and he gained her trust, the bonds of intimacy strengthened between them.

Over the years, most women he'd dated had been after his wealth. Not only had Selby appeared less than impressed with his money, she'd even threatened to quit, and he'd known she'd meant it. It infuriated him that she'd been attacked, and he had a sick feeling that it was tied to Evan. Given Emerson's strict security, he couldn't understand what they could have been looking for or why someone would think either Evan or Selby had taken it from the office. No one was allowed to so much as bring a cell phone into or out of the building, let alone any other kind of electronic device. She hadn't been given access to Evan's laptop, and any confidential information would have to have been accessed via internal servers. All saving capabilities on laptops and PCs had been disabled, so downloading to an external drive was impossible.

Bacon grease popped from the pan, breaking his train of thought, and Garrett jumped back to avoid being burnt.

"What are you doing?" Lars asked, rounding the corner from the hallway.

"What does it look like? I'm making breakfast. Well, brunch really." He grabbed a towel and wiped his hands.

"Where's Laura?" Lars sat down on one of the bar stools, his voice laced with surprise.

"I gave her the day off. I've got this." Garrett went to the coffee machine and held up an empty mug. "Want some?"

"Okay." Lars wore a look of confusion as he watched his friend pour him a cup and slide it to him across the counter. "What is going on with you?"

"Nothing. Just making food." He went to the refrigerator and opened it. After several minutes of searching, he retrieved a dozen eggs. When Garrett turned, he caught Lars' baffled expression.

"What? I'm cooking."

"Yeah, I see. But here's the thing, G. You never cook. Like ever. What the hell is going on?" Lars took a sip of his coffee and set it down. He scanned the room, noticing that Selby was missing. "Where is she?"

"What are you talking about?" Garrett began cracking open eggs, pouring their contents into a bowl and discarding the shells into the sink. Several pieces fell into the mixture and he began picking out the broken shards.

"Who the hell do you think I'm talking about? Selby. Where is she?"

"She's asleep." He began to whisk the yolks, focused on his task.

"No. Tell me you didn't."

"What?" Garrett set the bowl back on the counter.

"You had sex with her again, didn't you?"

Garrett shrugged, and gave him a shy smile.

"Exactly what the fuck is wrong with you? Didn't we just have this discussion last night? You said you wouldn't hurt her."

"I won't." Garrett's tone turned serious. "You don't understand."

"What's to understand? I brought her to you because she's the best at what she does."

"Yeah, you took me to a club where she sat on my lap."

"I did that to help you to get out of your funk, so you could see she wasn't just some desk-jockey. She had no idea who you were or why I brought you there."

"I may be grieving but I'm not the one who's dead. That night…" Garrett plowed his fingers through his tousled hair and shook his head. He began rummaging through several cabinets. "I didn't go looking for her. This is not my fault. You introduced me to her."

"So she could go to work for you. Not so you could

fuck her. Jesus, Garrett. We just talked about this. You can have anyone you want. Selby is special." He paused and sighed. "I thought she was pissed at you, anyway."

"She was. But we talked and things are cool."

"See, that right there. That's what I mean. She catches you with your pants down and all you do is throw her the charm and what? She forgives you?"

"First," Garrett slammed a pan down onto the stove and turned around to face his friend, "I did not have my pants down. We already talked about this. Blaire came on to me. And second, I'd never do that to Selby...not ever. She's what you said. She's..."

"What?"

"She's special, okay? I just...I can't let her go right now." Garrett focused on igniting the gas flame.

"And what's going to happen when she doesn't like you base jumping or jumping out of planes or taking off on a moment's notice to face climb? What's she going to do then? She's not like us. I keep telling you that but you don't seem to want to accept it."

"I don't know. It's not like Altura is the only important thing I do. Maybe I'll cut back on some events. I'm pretty busy now anyway."

"Are you kidding me?" Lars shook his head and laughed out loud. "I never thought this would happen...not to you."

"What now?" With his back turned, he shrugged, throwing his hands up in the air.

"You like her."

"Fuck yeah, I like her. I keep telling you that. I think it's pretty evident."

"I can't believe this."

"What, Lars? That I actually am capable of liking someone? I don't even know where this thing is going with us. Would you give it a rest?"

"Be real with me. I'm not even joking. You really like her, don't you? No fucking around. Garrett Emerson doesn't cut back on jumping for anyone anytime. She's in your head," he pressed.

"Holy shit, Lars. What do you want me to say?" Exasperated, he blew out a breath and grabbed the bowl. He dumped the contents into the frying pan and it sizzled. "Yeah, okay. I like her a lot. I just told you that. I know this isn't optimal. I get you don't want me to hurt her, that you're her friend. I'm sorry."

"Just please don't treat her like the others. Now listen, I'm not judging. I get why you treat dates like paper plates."

"That's a little harsh. It's not like I have sex with all of them. That's not who I am."

"But you don't ever see a girl for more than a week. Don't lie."

"It is what it is. You know the position I'm in. Can I get beautiful women? Yeah, sure. But they aren't like Selby. She's different." Garrett turned to his friend, and set his palms on the granite countertop. "I keep telling you that I don't know what's going to happen. It's not all about me or what I want. As you just pointed out, at the end of her contract, or even before if we replace Evan, she might not want me. She could decide that this is all too much for her at any point. She could cut things off."

"I'm not trying to be a hardass. It's just that Selby and I, we've been friends a long time. It's not like she hasn't dated over the years but it's never been serious. I think because she's kind of reserved. She keeps things inside and is super controlled but that's why she's good at what she does. She's hyperfocused."

Garrett paused, listening to his friend talk about Selby in a reverent manner. He'd known something had gone down between them but he suspected that Lars' feelings ran deeper than he'd admitted.

"Hold up a sec. I've gotta ask you. You're grilling me over here about how I'll treat Selby, and I get that you've known her for a long time, but do you have a thing for her? Because if you do, Lars, I don't know...I love you, you know that. And I know we've shared women before, but Selby...I don't know if I could do that."

"Look, I am not gonna sit here and tell you I feel nothing. But at the same time, whatever we have, it's not love, love. If that's what you're asking. So if you're in love..."

"Holy shit, bro. No throwin' around the 'L' word, okay? I think we've gotta reserve that for another day and time because I just can't go there. But if you're telling me you're in love with her..." Garrett blew out a breath. The eggs started smoking and he turned his attention back to cooking. *Jesus fucking Christ.* As if he didn't have enough problems.

"I didn't say that I was in love with her, but I do love her. Why the hell do you think I'm so pissed off at you? She's not just some employee. She's my friend." Lars stood and went to the microwave to warm his lukewarm coffee. He set his cup inside and pecked at the buttons. "I'm just sayin' that I care about her. Do I find her attractive? Who wouldn't? But that ship has sailed for Selby and me. I think we're better off as friends."

"Are you a dick in the box?"

"No. I mean, if she'd do friends with benefits, I may have considered it. But she's not like that. Which is exactly my point. You know everyone in Altura's pretty open about sex. Selby isn't."

"Maybe you don't know her as well as you think you do," Garrett countered. He'd seen how Selby had come alive under his touch on the balcony. She'd thought someone might catch them and had loved every second.

"What's that supposed to mean?" Lars retrieved his mug and took a sip.

"I'm saying that maybe she isn't as introverted as you think. Last night at the club…she may not be as open as the rest of the crew, but she's not a prude either." Garrett reached for a plate and worked while he spoke. "I just think she's scared. But scared isn't the same as not having courage. Oh no. My girl got out there and surfed the other day. And it wasn't just that. She wiped out and hit it hard. And when she got out? She wanted to go again. You know what that tells me? It tells me she's brave."

"I didn't say she wasn't. I'm just saying that she's my friend and I don't want you fucking with her head. But my guess is that it's already too late for that." Lars sniffed the air. "Do I smell brownies?"

"Yeah." Garrett laughed.

"What the hell?"

"I thought she might want something sweet."

"Who the hell eats brownies for breakfast? You suck at cooking."

"It's brunch. And yeah, I'm making my girl something to eat anyway. And your lazy ass too. So how 'bout you help me?"

"Nice. Okay, what can I do?"

"Wash the strawberries. Grapes too."

"On it." Lars went to the refrigerator. "Laura's going to kill you for messing up her kitchen."

"Yeah, I know." Garrett gave a small laugh. "She'll forgive me."

"So have you heard from Dean yet?" Lars turned on the spigot and began to work.

"He texted me. They're still at her apartment. I don't want her going over there until the place is completely cleaned up."

"Have you talked to her about it yet?"

"I told her I'm taking care of it."

"Okay."

"I'm not going to put her through anything else. I think whatever happened over at her place is related to Evan's death. I don't know the who, the how or the why, but I just know this has to do with Evan. And it pisses me the fuck off."

"Did Selby take anything home from the office? I can't imagine she'd ever do that, but why else would they look at her place?"

"No way. She's only been given a few paper files. Everything else is on company servers and it can't be downloaded. As far as I can tell she followed protocol. That's the confusing part. If someone knew Evan, really knew him, they'd know his work habits. Our security protocols are every bit as stringent, if not more so, than other government contractors."

"They had to be watching her."

"Yeah."

"She's going to want to go home."

"Not happening." The timer went off and Garrett turned off the oven. "She's staying with me."

"Did she agree to that?"

"She will."

"G, you can't just order her to stay here."

"I won't have to. I'm very persuasive." Garrett gave his friend a sly smile. "She's in danger. She'll see reason."

"She could stay with me. You know my security's just as tight as yours."

"No. Not up for discussion. She stays here."

"I'm kind of enjoying this. And here I was worried that Selby was going to get hurt?" Lars laughed.

"What the hell's that supposed to mean?" Garrett donned an oven mitt and retrieved his pastries.

"Nothing. You just seem awfully possessive is all."

"She stays here."

"Okay, just ignore me. You're a little invested is all. But whatever."

"You're a dick." Garrett told him, understanding exactly what Lars was accusing him of. Sure, he was being protective, but it was in his nature to care for those in his charge. She could have been killed. There was no way he was going to admit to Lars that his feelings for Selby were any more than a casual attraction.

"Yeah, fuck you too, G."

"Jesus, what's with you? First you worry I'm going to hurt her and now you think, what?"

"Someone's got it bad is all I'm saying. It's going to be fun to watch you go down."

"Shh…" Garrett held up a hand as he heard footsteps approaching. He'd set clothes out for her on the bed, and hoped like hell she was wearing something. "Can you please keep some of this to yourself?"

"Yeah, yeah. Do not fuck with her, though. I meant that part." Lars grabbed a large knife from the block and began slicing off the stems.

"Duly noted." He scraped the browned eggs onto a plate, held it up to his friend and smiled. "Not bad, huh?"

"Lookin' good, Emeril."

"I am good. Eggs and brownies. Breakfast of champions." Glancing at the mess he'd made, he laughed. "Yeah, Laura's going to kick my ass."

As Selby came into view, he froze. He knew Lars was

watching, that he should perhaps conceal his feelings. But as she approached, it was as if they were the only two people in the room. His cock stirred, seeing her in his t-shirt. Her hard tips peaked against the draping fabric. She tucked a strand of her long blonde hair behind her ear, glanced to her bare feet and then up to him again. He smiled as her eyes met his.

"Come here, sweetheart," he said, reaching for her hand.

Without speaking, she fell into his embrace and his entire body responded. *I'm so fucked*, he thought. His lips grazed over her hair. She smelled of their lovemaking, reminding him of every mind-blowing second they'd spent together the previous night. She brushed her cheek against his bared chest, the warmth of her hands caressing his back.

He should have cared even a little bit about the conversation he'd just had with Lars, but the only thing that mattered was Selby. Guiding her chin upward, he leaned to kiss her. Gently his lips took hers, delicately tasting her mouth. He ran the back of his hand over her bottom, fingering the hem of the shirt. He deepened the kiss, tugging up the fabric, surprised when he discovered she wasn't wearing the shorts he'd left out for her. Palming her soft globes in his hands, his erection prodded her belly.

A cough from Lars drew his attention, and he slowly receded. His thumb caressed her cheek, his eyes on hers.

Garrett knew he was so far beyond gone with this woman. It wasn't as if he hadn't kissed a woman in front of Lars before, but the moment had been far too intimate, emotions surfacing between them.

"Good morning," Lars commented. He gave them a small grin as if he'd enjoyed the show, and continued eating his eggs.

"How do you feel?" Garrett asked Selby. He smoothed his fingers gingerly over the back of her head where she'd been hit.

"Good." She smiled.

"My shirt looks good on you." He released it, his fingertips lingering on the back of her thigh. "Did you see the robe? Shorts?"

"Yeah, I saw. Thanks." She rubbed her torso against his as if she were a purring kitten.

"I like it." He laughed.

"People. You all do get that I'm right here, don't you?" Lars called over to them.

"Sorry, Lars," she said. As she spun to face him, she kept her body close to Garrett's.

"I'd say get a room, but seein' as I'm the guest…" He shook his head and laughed. "Are you really okay?"

Selby nodded. "I'm fine."

Garrett attempted to follow the conversation as Selby brushed her bottom into his erection. If he didn't know any better, he'd think she was enjoying his state. Playing with fire in front of Lars wasn't a place she should go, he thought. If she wanted public sex, he'd give it to her. Patience was his friend, and later he'd test how far she'd go. But as much as he was tempted to bend her over the counter and fuck her right there, he considered that she'd better eat. With her attack, he was more concerned about her health and less about his dick.

"Are you hungry?" Garrett asked, placing a kiss to her neck.

"Yes." She winked. "Very."

"For food, woman?"

"Yes and yes." She laughed.

"Maybe you were right about her," Lars commented with a grin.

"Right about what?" she asked with a curious lilt to her voice.

"He says you're more adventurous than I thought."

Garrett gave him a pointed look and mouthed the word, 'no'.

"Now, I on the other hand insisted that you are Selby Reynolds, you know, the girl I've known since college. The one who hates elevators. Refuses to go skiing. No risks ever."

"Hmm…and what does Garrett say?" Selby broke free of Garrett's arms and snatched a berry out of the bowl. She turned to him, leaning her back against the counter, and seductively slid it between her lips.

"I say," Garrett smiled and caged her with his arms. His legs straddled hers but he didn't move to kiss her, "that you're repressing your inner wild child. She wants to play, and does when encouraged to do so. She just needs the right man to keep her safe and teach her how."

"Is that right?" she flirted. Biting the strawberry, she

held the other half to his lips.

"I'm always right." He gave her a sexy smile. As he took the treat into his mouth, he snatched her wrist and held it in place, sucking the juices off her fingers. She flittered them against his tongue, causing a fresh surge of desire. He withdrew them, licking the tips. "See?" His eyes darted to Lars and back to Selby. "My point is proven."

"I didn't say she was celibate. I said she wasn't adventurous. Hey, it's not a bad thing. It's just the way she is."

"I disagree. Am I right?" Garrett asked.

"Maybe," Selby answered coyly. "Or maybe I'm both. Or maybe I'm enjoying finding out."

Garrett's cell phone buzzed, drawing his focus to a text. Releasing Selby, he retrieved it and slid his finger across the screen.

"It's Dean."

"The district attorney?" Selby asked.

"Yeah, they're still at your place."

"I should go," she said.

"No, you should eat something. You're staying here with me." Garrett set his cell down and reached to plate her food. He set it onto the counter next to Lars.

Selby raked her fingers through her hair and paced away from the kitchen island. He imagined she was stressing about the attack and went to her.

"I'll go to a hotel. I need to go to my place to pick up some things. I need my clothes, shoes....shit, I need to get my car." Selby ticked off her to do list.

"Relax." As soon as Garrett said the word, he knew it was a mistake. Telling her, a woman, to relax was the antithesis to any goal he wished to achieve and would surely result in a negative outcome. But as he went to correct himself, she interrupted.

"Don't tell me to relax. Someone broke into my place. I've got to get my things." Selby's voice grew louder.

"We'll get your things." Garrett crossed the room to meet her. "It's going to be all right."

"What is going on here, anyway? You think that last night is somehow related to Evan, don't you?" Selby didn't move to accept his comfort.

"Do I think what happened is tied to Evan's death? I don't know for sure but it's likely. But I still don't know why the hell someone would kill Evan. Do we work on some top secret things? Yes, we do. Are some of them worth killing over? Perhaps. It's not like it's unheard of. That's why we have clearances and people with them can't just travel wherever they want outside the country. You know that. But if they killed Evan and went after you, it seems like they still don't have what they want. And here's the thing…" Garrett hesitated in front of Lars and pointed to him. "You did not hear this."

"Hear what?" Lars held up his hands and got up to make more coffee.

"I told you I have Evan's laptop," Garrett said, his eyes trained on Selby.

"Yes. And you also said you wouldn't give it to me."

"Selby, seriously." He paused and took a breath. "I get

that you came in here with clearances, but one of my best friends had just died. You really think I'd trust you on day one with the secrets that might be in his files? No offense, but that wasn't happening."

"You're always asking me to trust you," she challenged.

"That's different and you know it. I was waiting to get to know you better. Get a feel for if I could trust you. I needed to get a read on you before I let you have at it."

"Excuse me? Is that what you've been doing with me? Getting a feel for me? Has this all been some secret test?" Selby spat.

"What's happening between us has nothing to do with it. Listen, would you have trusted me that day Lars marched you into my office? Don't even bother answering because I know that you wouldn't have. Hell, you didn't even want to work for me."

"That's not true."

"Don't lie to me, Selby." His tone grew serious.

"Fine, maybe. But I idolized you. Not literally of course, but you were a case study. The chance to work for you would have been amazing if Lars over there hadn't brought you into the club."

"I never judged you," he insisted.

"Doesn't matter if you did. We didn't get off on an equal footing."

"You broke into Evan's office," Garrett accused her. Selby averted her gaze, which caused Garrett concern. They both knew it was the truth, but her excuse for doing so still rubbed him the wrong way. He'd like to think that after everything that had happened over the past week, he'd learned more about her, that he could trust her with the information. He wasn't sure what caused a flash of doubt, but he just as quickly buried the notion that she could be anything but honest with him.

"I didn't break in. I knocked and entered."

"Let's not mince words. You went looking around when you couldn't find what you wanted in the information I got you."

"Maybe. I could have hacked into your servers, which I didn't."

"She could do that," Lars called out from the other side of the room.

"Close your ears, Lars."

"Just sayin'. She can hack just about anything. She could have taken the files without you ever even knowing."

"Would you please shut up?" Garrett walked to Selby and took her hand. He both hated and loved the sizzle that traveled up his arm, all from just touching her skin. "Selby, listen. Whatever happened to Evan…I'm not going to let anything else happen to you. I want you to stay here so I can protect you. I'll bring more guards on the property. More at work, too. Maybe we'll just work from here to be on the safe side. I need time to think about it. Last night, all I could think of was you."

Garrett sensed Selby was about to interrupt, so he continued.

"I have Evan's laptop. The one that he kept in his

office. He didn't have another one, because you know you can't take it out of the building. If he needed something at home, he could always virtual network into the office, but no one can save anything externally. Technically you can't even do it from the office, but it seems like someone is looking for something. It has to be data. I don't know how or why Evan would have ever saved anything or even if he did it, but I need you to look at it for me. No one else has seen it. I've gone through the files but I don't see anything out of the ordinary. But then again, I'm no IT expert either."

"Of course I'll help you, but Garrett, do you really want me here? I could go stay at a hotel or I don't know, I could stay with Lars?"

"No." Both Garrett and Lars responded at the same time. Garrett couldn't believe she'd even suggest that she would live with anyone else. Uncomfortable with his reaction, he recognized the foreign emotion, one he couldn't fathom he'd ever feel over any woman: jealousy. "No. You're staying with me. No arguments."

"You can't just boss me around. If I want to leave, I'll walk out that door right now. This is an agreement or I'm out of here."

Garrett took a deep breath and walked back to the kitchen. His anger surged at her demand. What didn't she get about the fact that someone could have killed her? Why would she ever want to stay with Lars after what had happened between them? He settled his palms on the counter and locked his eyes on hers.

"You're right about me not being able to boss you around in your private life, but I care about you." Garrett's eyes locked on hers. "I just watched my friend die. I will not let that happen to you. So when it comes to where you'll be safe?" Garrett strode over to Selby, invading her personal space. As he took her hands, his expression grew serious. "You'll stay with me."

The possessive tone of his voice surprised him, but he wasn't leaving it up for discussion. The thought of her sleeping and eating with Lars didn't sit well. She could have her own room if she wanted, but she'd stay at his mansion.

"I...I'll help you. But I can't stay here forever," she agreed, sadness lacing her words.

"You'll help me?"

"I'll help." Selby wrapped her arms around Garrett, burying her face into his chest.

Garrett returned her embrace, and cradled her head against his chest. He caught the judgmental look on Lars' face as he did so, and considered that Lars had been wrong to worry. Perhaps it wasn't he who'd hurt Selby. She hadn't further protested staying with him, yet she implied that she wasn't interested in a long term relationship. While the idea of him dating anyone longer than a few weeks in itself was newsworthy, her statement stabbed in his chest.

Chapter Nineteen

When Selby woke, she'd happily recalled erotic memories of her night with Garrett. Her heart tightened as she pulled on his t-shirt, breathing in his scent. She'd decided to forgo panties, hoping to tease Garrett. He'd been confident in his lessons, she mused. He'd pushed her and she enjoyed the thought of tantalizing him the way he'd done to her.

But the conversation in the kitchen had turned sour after Garrett had insisted she stay with him. It wasn't as if she didn't want to spend more time with him. On the contrary, she'd been delighted waking up in his arms. But the attack weighed heavily on her mind. The reality that she'd almost died was setting in, that her home had been destroyed. After brunch, Lars had agreed to go to her condo to get her clothes, and other important belongings. Although she'd offered to go with him, she felt a wave of relief, not having to go back to the apartment. A killer remained on the loose, and violation was still fresh in her mind.

Her thoughts drifted to Evan, and guilt coiled in her stomach. She hated the dead man, regretting the day they'd ever met. Once Garrett found out she'd withheld the truth about Evan, he'd probably toss her out on her ear. Regardless, she suspected that Evan had a hand in his own death. Garrett was only just starting to trust her, and she needed time to figure out the right way to explain things to him. It was vital she had access to Evan's laptop if she had any hope of discovering tangible evidence to present to Garrett. She knew it was entirely possible Evan had cloaked data beneath the layers of everyday applications.

Selby sat in Garrett's palatial office, scrubbing the laptop for surreptitious anomalies. She'd done the cursory checks, and now was delving deeper, running programs to find hidden files. Selby didn't expect it to be easy. If Evan was half as good as Garrett said he was, she'd have to work harder and smarter to find whatever he'd created.

After several hours of going through every last folder, she suspected that he could have been hiding secrets on Emerson's own network. Connecting to it, she initiated a series of cybersecurity tools. Selby always worked bottom to top, keeping it simple, moving toward more complex solutions. As she launched the program, she hoped the sniffer would follow down a path, granting her access to files she hadn't yet seen.

The door creaked open, and she gazed up at Garrett.

"Any luck?" He gave her a sympathetic smile, having realized that this project wasn't as easy as he'd hoped.

"Nothing so far. The laptop itself seems pretty clean. I don't see anything out of the ordinary. But that's in line with protocol. If he was going to store something, he may have put something on here that can access other files at Emerson. I'm running some programs to see how hard it is to get into your files using his laptop."

"You're breaking into the company servers?"

"Yeah, I mean, we've got to give it a go. I hope you don't mind but I started up your laptop too."

"But I have a password," he said.

She gave him a wide smile. "Yes, you do."

"You hacked into my laptop?" He sat on the corner of the desk and propped his well-worn cowboy boots on the edge of a bookshelf. Craning his neck, he stole a peek of the screen.

"Yes, I did." She laughed. "I know you know this, Mr. CEO, but you should be using strong passwords."

"You mean 'Emerson123' didn't cut it? For the record, I added an extra couple of characters."

"I saw. Very clever, but you don't know who you're dealing with."

"A dangerous cybercriminal I'm sure. Very dark."

"I could be if I wanted, but I've never been interested in being a black hat, thank you very much. I wear my white hat proudly."

"Why do you need my laptop?"

"I'm trying to tunnel into Emerson from Evan's laptop and yours, because I want to see if there are any deviations. Can I get in from one? Both? This work isn't always clear cut. I may need to try several things before I figure out what's going on here."

"Do you have time to take a break?"

"As a matter of fact, I do. I've got a diagnostic running."

"I had Norm bring you something to wear. It's in the bedroom."

"Okay," she said slowly, curious that he'd called his male secretary to buy her clothes and within hours they had been delivered. She couldn't even imagine what it must be like to be Garrett Emerson, the world at his fingertips within seconds. "I don't have shoes, though. Where are we going?"

"Selby, Selby, Selby." He took her hand in his and stood, bringing her with him. Wrapping his arms around her waist, he smiled. "First, you do need to learn how to trust me. Would I ask you to go out with no shoes?"

"I suppose not." She laughed.

"And second, as to the where. Well, that's a surprise." Garrett leaned in and captured her lips.

He kissed her, his talented tongue brushing into her mouth. She moaned as he gently sucked on her bottom lip, teasing her. By the time he broke away, she was dripping wet with arousal. Selby's heart raced. The man had a way of turning her from a competent professional into a bowl of jelly within seconds. She went to reach for his belt but he wrapped his strong fingers around her wrists.

"You have no idea how badly I want to fuck you right

here on my desk, sweetheart, but I've got something even better planned for you." Garrett grazed his lips over her temple and released her. "Now go get dressed. We're going to have some fun."

Selby squealed as a slap landed on her bottom. She wished she hated it, but it only made her want more. With an ache between her legs, she stuck out her tongue and feigned sadness. She was promptly rewarded with another satisfying smack to her other cheek.

Clarity struck and she realized how deep in she was. Never in a million years would she have considered letting a man spank her, and yet it seemed as if all Garrett had to do was mention a fantasy, and she'd join him. As she made her way to the bedroom, she considered the past week. She was the same person inside, but he'd ignited a flame. And like a drug, she had to have him and looked forward to every minute until the truth was exposed.

Selby stopped short of entering the enormous barn and took in her surroundings. On the way from his mansion to the stables, she'd been impressed with the spectacular beachfront property. From the majestic pool area, which overlooked the Pacific Ocean and the adjoining fields, she couldn't stop wondering what it must be like to live in such opulence. As they approached, she breathed in the air, a mixture of both the sea and horses, and she rooted her feet to the dusty ground.

"What are you doing?" he asked.

"Nothing. I just..." Selby stumbled on her words as her childhood memories flashed in her mind. Growing up in the country, her parents had built a modest barn to house her pony. She'd been in the woods playing with friends when the stranger approached. Garrett's hand to her arm interrupted the horror that she recalled as if it were yesterday. She jumped, and blinked, remembering that she was no longer a child.

"Hey, are you okay?" Garrett gave her a concerned look and put his arm around her.

"I'm fine," she lied. Selby leaned against his chest, and let him lead her into the barn.

"Do you ride?"

"A long time ago. You?"

"A little." He smiled and approached the chestnut Belgian Warmblood. "This is Mocha. Hey girl, how's my baby? Who's a good girl? You're a good girl. Come give me some love."

Selby smiled, surprised at the way he spoke to the horse as if she were a baby. A new side to Garrett was revealed to her as he gently petted and whispered into her mane. He waved Selby over and she slowly approached.

"Mocha, I want you to meet my friend. This is Selby." He winked at her and focused his attention back onto the great animal. "She's going to be staying with us for a while. So make sure you tell the others to be nice."

"How many horses do you have?" The enormous mare

towered above Selby. She yearned to touch her but was cautious.

"I've got six here. But I sponsor many more."

"What do you mean?"

"They're all rescues of sorts. Mocha, here, was a jumper. But like many horses, she was injured. She's recovered now, but she can't compete. When that happens, sometimes they go up for sale. Sometimes they're bred. But sometimes if they're too injured or if the owner can't afford the vet care, they might be put down."

"How did you start adopting them? Do you compete?"

"Me? Oh no. But you know how it is. You go to these charity events or whatever, and you meet a few people who are involved with horses. I was at a competition with a friend when someone told us about a horse that needed a home. I have the room here, so I thought I'd help him out. Next thing you know, I have six here. I have a nonprofit set up for other rescues, too. But this girl, here? She's my baby."

"Where are they all?"

"Most of them are out in the field. Seth was coming by today to round up Angus. He's probably out on a trail."

"So I take it you don't personally muck out these stalls?"

"Yeah, no. I've got staff. Don't get me wrong. If I have a day off, I don't mind getting my hands dirty, but you know how it is over at Emerson. It's not like I have a lot of time." Garrett regarded Selby with a critical eye and set his hand on the stall. "I know you probably think that I was some kind of a trust fund baby, but that's not me. I didn't come from money. All this," he looked around the modern, cedar barn, "it's new to me. Fifteen years ago, I was getting through college on school loans. Mom and Dad didn't have a pot to piss in, but I worked hard, got lucky."

"I read about you in school."

"So you said. But the struggle…I'm sure they always gloss over that part. All those people at Altura, they supported me in a dream to make something out of an idea. And now we develop products and services while doing what we love."

"Where's your family now?"

"Mom and Dad moved to Costa Rica. Retired. My baby brother, Erik, is out sowing his oats. He used to work here but we had a small falling out."

"Sorry to hear that."

"How about you?"

"My mom died. I'm not in contact with my dad. He kind of left us. Mom wasn't exactly mother of the year but at least I had her when she was alive. So it's pretty much just me now." Thoughts of her mother broke her heart but she tried not to dwell on what she couldn't change. She hadn't heard from her father in years and had no plans on initiating contact. The last she'd heard, he was working as a dealer in Atlantic City.

"You wanna feed her?" Garrett changed the subject. "I'll be right back."

Selby eyed Mocha and inched closer. Slowly she

reached her hand toward her, and gently stroked her forehead. The horse whinnied in response.

"You are a good girl, aren't you?" she whispered.

"She likes you," Garrett said from behind her.

Selby laughed. "She's sweet. Sometimes I get a little scared. They're so big."

"True. You need to treat them with respect and they'll respect you back. Here." Garrett handed her some carrots. "She's spoiled but she's earned it. You remember how to feed them? Hold your hand flat. That's it."

Selby presented her palm, and Mocha quickly gobbled down the treat. She smiled to Garrett, who watched their interaction.

"Did you mention that Seth is here?"

"Yeah, I let a few of my friends ride them. He loves Angus."

"Thank you for showing me your horses."

"We'll go riding soon. After yesterday…"

"I feel okay," she assured him.

"All the same, I'd feel more comfortable waiting. Better safe than sorry."

"Did I just hear the word safe from you? I thought you were all about the danger." Selby gave him a flirty smile.

"I'm about maximizing risk, while minimizing injury."

"You're a paradox."

"I'm a simple man, actually. Take us. I'm enjoying our lessons, but I won't take you further than you really want to go."

"About last night…" Her gaze fell to the floor.

"Last night was amazing," he answered.

"Yeah, it was." Selby shifted nervously on her feet, lifting her lids to meet his gaze.

"You know, Altura, my horses…all important parts of my life, but you, Miss Reynolds, you've been on my mind a lot lately."

"We should probably get back up to the house. I need to check that diagnostic."

"I'm not talking about the laptop. I'm talking about us. You. Me. Last night on the terrace. When I mentioned being watched you didn't stop me."

"I could hardly have stopped you," she protested. Selby's cheeks flushed at the mention of what they'd done.

"Not true. I would have stopped if you'd told me to. But you didn't." His eyes turned dark, his sexy smile giving her the chills. "Why did you agree to do it?"

"I don't know. We were off to the side, sort of hidden. It's not like I was naked, anyway."

"But still, we had sex at a party," he pressed. Garrett took her hand and led her over to the tack room.

"I've never done anything like that before. But there was something exciting about it. It's taboo, the idea that someone could watch." She considered what Lars had told her about the couple who'd been making love at the soirée. "Lars said that Chase and Penny were fooling around, too. I couldn't see anything but when he told me…let's just say I wasn't turned off by the idea. I'm not sure why. Maybe it's just curiosity. I may not do all those things you guys do, but I'm not a prude."

"Which was exactly my point to Lars." Garrett took her by her hands, backing her up toward the wall.

"Lars knows me." Selby's bottom brushed up against the bale of hay and she glanced back at it.

"Perhaps, he knows you as a friend." He shrugged, placing her hands onto the hay. "But I know you as a lover. And I'm going to make love to you right here."

"Are you now?" Selby shivered, wondering what he had planned. The devilish look in his eye told her that he'd long forgotten about the work that she'd been doing in his office.

"We're going to find out together just how far we can take each other." Garrett bunched the fabric of her long skirt up in his hands.

"I see why you bought me this now." Selby glanced at her clothes and noted that Garrett didn't respond to her comment; he only smiled and raised a knowing eyebrow at her. "I'm not sure this is the best place for you and me to…you know…"

"Fuck?"

"Yeah, that." She laughed at his bluntness. "Didn't you say Seth is here? And you have security too?" Her pulse increased as she said the words out loud, realizing his intentions.

"Yes, I did. Let me see you." Garrett locked his eyes on hers as he dragged the fabric up her legs. Exposing her, he rolled it upward, tucking it into her waistband. His fingers trailed down her thighs and froze when he realized she wasn't wearing underwear. His lips brushed her ear and he whispered to her, "No panties again? Selby, Selby,

Selby...I was right about you."

"Yes," she breathed. Desire shot through her body as he kissed her neck. She flattened her palms onto his chest.

"I'd say that I want you like this all the time, but I don't think I'd get any work done knowing you were walking around the hallways of Emerson with no panties." Garrett stepped back to admire her. She went to cover herself and he intervened. "No. Put your hands down. I want to see your pussy."

"Garrett. Seriously, someone could see me." Although she protested, she did what he said.

"Spread your legs open for me." Garrett unzipped his pants.

"What if he sees us?" Wetness dripped down her inner thigh as she glanced over his shoulder. As loath as she was to admit it, the thought of being caught excited her. Her breath stopped as Garrett pulled his cock out of his pants and stroked himself.

"Touch your pussy," he told her.

Selby went silent at his demand. She should say no. Every rational cell in her brain told her to stop as her hand delved into her folds. Drenched in her juices, she flicked her fingers over her clit and she moaned.

"You're so fucking sexy, do you know that?" Garrett took two large strides over to meet her. He fisted his fingers into her hair and guided her mouth to meet his.

Selby gasped as he kissed her. His demanding, possessive kiss told her he owned her, and caused her to shiver at his touch. She swept her tongue against his, amazed at how this man could drive her mad with one command. Giving him access, she opened to him.

He grabbed her wrist and wrapped her hand around his cock. Replacing her fingers with his, he plunged a thick digit into her core.

As he pressed it into her, she groaned into his mouth. Another finger stretched her open, and she cried his name. Her climax set off like fireworks and she struggled not to come.

"Garrett, oh my God." Her body shook, but she refused to release his shaft from her grip.

"Fucking yeah," he cried. Tearing his lips from hers, he bit at her neck.

The orgasm rocked through her body, leaving her shaking. She snuggled into his chest, licking at the skin on his shoulder. As he withdrew his fingers, he smiled at her, pressing them into her mouth. She tasted herself, and she nipped and twirled her tongue around them as if she was sucking his cock.

"You're a very naughty girl."

"You do this to me," Selby responded. She was reminded that she was in the stables, a cool breeze grazing over her mound.

Garrett reached for the pile of blankets and tossed them over the hay.

"Isn't this what you've always wanted?" He gave her a wicked smile. "To be free?"

Selby's breath caught as he spun her around and bent her over the bales. He spread her legs wide open, exposing her to the room. Her face settled onto the soft fabric and she panted in anticipation. His cock brushed the back of her thigh, and she moved to accept it. A firm slap landed on her cheek and she cried out.

"What are you doing?"

"Patience. I want to look at you." His palm flattened on her back, pinning her in place as he glided his fingers over her ass.

"Garrett, I can't wait."

"Tell me, would you like me to fuck you here?"

Selby's pussy ached with desire as his slippery finger circled her puckered flesh. She groaned. Jesus, she'd never had sex there, but every time he touched her, her core pulsated in arousal.

"Hmm…no words, huh? I've got a toy for you," he told her.

"A what?"

"Something to get you ready for me, because you know what, Selby? I think you do want this, but are afraid to ask for it."

"Garrett, please don't make me say the words. Last night…" Selby recalled how he'd made her tell him to lick her pussy, and a fresh wave of arousal rolled through her. She squirmed against the blanket.

"Last night, you seemed to enjoy it when I did this."

Selby gasped as he slid the tip of his finger inside her back hole.

"So I think we should try a few toys, yes?"

"Toys?"

"If I'm going to fuck you here, and I am. Well, it's better to show you."

Selby moaned as he withdrew. She went to stand but was reminded to stay in position as his palm stilled her. She heard the crinkling of paper and swiveled her head to see him retrieving a pink object from a black and gold bag.

"This," he told her.

"Cold," she cried as the cool gel dripped over her bottom.

"It's very small. Just a starter, really. Just relax and push back."

"What are you..?" Selby asked, her words trailing off as the slick object penetrated into her bottom. "Garrett…I don't know if…oh hell."

"Breathe. Yes, like that. You're doing great."

Selby sucked a breath, doing as he told her. Her core ached as her bottom became full, the object stretching her.

"There you go." Garrett adjusted the plug. "You are so beautiful."

"I need you to…please make love to me," Selby begged. As the words left her lips, she knew, if she was honest, that was what she wanted. She buried her face in the blanket, realizing that she could fall for Garrett.

"There's something about you…you make me want to play. No more work."

"Play with me…play now," she whispered. Selby nearly came undone as he plunged a finger inside her pussy. She glanced up to see him tearing a condom open with his teeth and she wondered what it would be like to have him inside her with no barrier.

As he swiped his crown through her wetness, she was brought back to the moment. She widened her stance, readying to accept him. He slowly sheathed himself, and she knew he was being careful not to hurt her. Reaching for him, her fingertips dug into his hips.

"Easy, sweetheart," he groaned. "Are you okay?"

"Yes, just please…" she released a giggle, "please move."

"I'm going slow, but it's so damn hard. How's your bottom?"

"I feel full but it feels so much tighter. Oh yeah," she cried as he began to increase his speed.

Selby clutched at him as he pumped inside of her. The head of his cock brushed along her sensitive nerves, causing her to tighten around him. She wasn't sure what made her look, but she caught Seth's eyes as he passed by the entrance. In a blink he was gone, but she knew he'd seen them. She should have felt embarrassed, she knew, but instead, her channel clenched down around Garrett. As he slammed into her, she reveled in his strength.

"I love playing with you," he grunted.

"Harder," she demanded. She was so close.

"Where have you been all my life, woman?" Garrett increased the pace. "I can't hold back, oh shit…"

"Yes, like that. Fuck me," she screamed. Her fingernails raked his flesh as she took him inside. She came hard, his cock stroking her core. She gasped, realizing that she'd come without him ever touching her clit. Like a fucking god, he'd taken her to Nirvana and she didn't want to return to reality.

He leaned over her, covering her body with his and taking her mouth. Softly, he sucked her lips, prodding his tongue through them. As she tasted her lover, she knew she'd never been with a man who could make her feel the way Garrett did. Nothing would ever be the same. When she told him the truth, he'd never forgive her. She fought the tears that came, falling down into their kiss.

"Hey, baby. What's wrong?" Garrett whispered. He quickly removed himself and the toy. "No tears. Come on now."

Selby made no move to get up and within seconds he was gently cleaning her bottom with a warm towel. She wiped at her eyes, trying to stuff her emotions away. Garrett tugged her skirt down, and lifted her into his arms. The blankets fell to the ground and he slid down until he was sitting on them. Pressing his lips to her head, he stroked her hair.

"Selby, talk to me. You're scaring me."

"I'm sorry…"

"No, I'm sorry. We won't do that again if you don't like it," he said.

"No…it's not that. I loved it, all of it." She paused. "I just…no one has ever made me feel like you do. You do things to me, Garrett. This thing between us…it's just intense."

"It is, but that's not a bad thing."

"You don't know me." Selby shook her head. Worry

crept into her thoughts; once he found out, everything would change.

"I'm getting to know you. That's how this works. I share things about me. You share things about you. We see how it goes. This thing we have going?" Garrett pressed his lips to her hair. "I haven't been in a relationship in a long time. I'm not even sure how to do one."

"I wasn't asking for anything," she said.

"I'm not saying you are. But this is what I'm talking about. We're getting to know each other. My lack of relationships is one of those things you should know. I'm a busy man. I do what some people think are crazy, dangerous things. This is who I am. I'm not sure you want to even hook up with someone like me, but at the same time, I know already I'd have a hard time letting you go. I know we haven't known each other very long, but I care about you. When we're together, it's unbelievably hot. But I can't make any promises about things or how things will end up between us."

"I can't make any promises either," Selby stated.

She cuddled into Garrett's embrace, wishing she could seal her heart. Selby was developing feelings for Garrett and it terrified her. Just one more minute in his arms, she told herself. One more minute to fantasize about a life with a man who was unattainable. One more minute to feel safe and warm, reveling in the ecstasy of the moment. Giving up Garrett Emerson was going to eviscerate her, but until the inevitable came, she'd soak up the memories, learning how to feel, for the first time in her life.

Chapter Twenty

Garrett sat across the room, observing Selby as she pecked away on the laptop. Focused on her task, she hadn't spoken in thirty minutes. He glanced down to his iPad and pretended not to notice how she'd gone silent, completely obsessed with her work. Selby Reynolds intrigued him more than any other woman he'd ever met. Although she seemed reluctant to admit her desire to explore her sexuality on new levels, her body came alive under his touch.

Making love to her in the barn had been an incredibly erotic experience and he had a hard time thinking of anything else. After testing her willingness to engage in anal play in the shower, he'd hoped she'd go further. While she'd been working earlier, Norm had picked up his order for him. As he'd suspected, she'd been responsive to the toy he'd selected, splintering apart under his touch. Even her awareness of Seth's presence, the idea of being watched, had turned her on and he looked forward to exploring every aspect of Selby's adventurous side. What he couldn't have anticipated was her tears. Seeing her weep was like a blade to the gut. Like a switch, she'd gone from shivering in ecstasy to crying. He couldn't deny the intensity of their encounter, yet he suspected she was keeping something from him.

It would have been perfect if he'd been able to tell her that he'd date her exclusively, that they'd have a future. But the words didn't surface. He should have told her the truth. That he was scared to death. That she was a game changer, one that he was struggling to control. Lars had called him out on his feelings earlier and he'd been on target.

Garrett accomplished every goal he'd ever set. Financial targets had become an easy attainment. He'd become ridiculously wealthy, to the point where he gave away millions of dollars a year to charities. Extreme sports were the only things that remotely challenged him, but in the face of meeting Selby, it all paled in comparison. The only thing that would sate his craving was total possession of the woman who'd crawled into his heart.

"Garrett, we need to talk," she said, interrupting his racing thoughts.

"What's up?"

"So I ran the same exact tool on both computers." Her eyes never left her screen as she spoke. "The reason I did that was because even though I'm not detecting anything unusual on Evan's device, that doesn't mean it's not there. The important thing is that when I try to break into Emerson, I get pretty much nothing."

"That's good, right?" Garrett crossed to her and sat on the edge of his desk. She turned the screen so he could view it.

"Yeah. It's good but you can see here," she pointed to the glass, "I was able to tunnel just the slightest bit into Evan's department. I'm not sure what that means but it's not good."

"I thought you just said you couldn't get in."

"I'm not in. And on your PC, I didn't get anywhere at all. It looks a-okay. But here. This isn't right." She pulled her hair upward and twisted it into a bun. "I'm using basic hacker programs. But my guess is that if I work on this a little more, I could get in, as in all the way into his department's data."

"Go on." *What the hell did Evan do?* He hated that even the smallest doubt had emerged. Still, he'd defend him until all the facts were unearthed.

"The question is, can I get files to download when I get there? If I can do that, you have a major problem. Basically I could just steal whatever's in there."

"Are you implying that Evan stole data?" The shock in Garrett's voice registered at the same time he asked.

"Garrett." She hesitated. "I think maybe you need to give me a little more time to see if I can even get in. Let me work on this. I'll get something custom going to try to block the tunnel. If it works, then we can cross that bridge when we get to it."

"Evan wouldn't steal from me," Garrett insisted, his voice stern.

"I didn't know him...personally."

"I did know him. He helped me build this company and I'm telling you there is no way. I don't care if you can get in or not. He would have had a reason."

"I'm not sure what you want me to say. I'm just doing what you asked me to do." Selby rested her palms on each side of the laptop and stared at the screen. "Sometimes we don't know people as well as we think. Sometimes people keep secrets. With no evidence, I can't say what he did or what he didn't do. All I know is that someone killed him. They could have killed me." Selby sighed and locked her eyes on his. "Someone is looking for something. And it must be pretty damn important."

"I agree, but there are lots of people out there who want to steal company secrets. Competitors."

"Terrorists."

"Sure. And that's why Evan had us locked up tight. He isn't the kind of person who would steal, let alone be a traitor. He wouldn't do that." Garrett shoved onto his feet. "You didn't know him. Besides, he's the victim here. I don't know why you'd spend any time thinking he did something wrong."

"I didn't say he did." Selby blew out a breath and focused back on the computer, typing. Her lips tensed, and her eyes flared with anger. "I'm just saying sometimes we don't know people. Sometimes the people closest to you are your enemy."

"Not Evan." Garrett regarded Selby as she refused to make eye contact. It was the first time he'd seen her truly angry, and it didn't surprise him that she was controlled even when she got mad.

"Whatever. This is going to take a few hours," she noted.

"I'll be back," he told her, leaving his office.

He didn't care what Selby thought. There was no way Evan would have stolen data. Thanks to the asshole who'd killed him, the real criminal, his friend would never get the chance to defend himself.

As Garrett came into the great room, he caught sight of Lars sitting on the sofa, staring at his cell phone. A tote bag with Selby's belongings sat next to him.

"Did you have any problems getting in the condo?" he asked, falling back into an oversized chair. He crossed his feet on the ottoman.

"No. Dean was still there, though. I guess they closed up early last night and came back again. He said he hadn't found any fingerprints. He let me take some clothes and shoes. I grabbed some jewelry that I found scattered on the floor. Selby doesn't wear a lot of bling, but I figured that she wouldn't appreciate people stepping all over it." Lars held up a small plastic baggie filled with shiny items. "Drove her car back here, too. It's out in the driveway."

"Did Dean find anything?"

"Yes and no."

"What does that mean?" Garrett asked.

"Well, he knows how they got in. They found a small remote camera lodged into the crevice of the molding in the hallway. He thinks they watched her enter the codes.

Probably used the same method to get in the building then set the camera up in the hallway and waited a few days to come back," Lars replied.

"Doesn't she have security cameras? They should be able to grab an image of the guy."

"They have them outside, but it'd been disabled. It was done in a way that the super never noticed. I'm sure there's hours of footage where no one's coming or going. He never saw anything."

"Whoever's doing this is intelligent. They're not just your average criminal," Garrett surmised. He pinched the bridge of his nose and then rubbed his forehead.

"Agreed. This is a deliberate, well-planned attack."

"But they didn't kill Selby."

"If they had a camera, they knew she'd left her place. But how did they know how long she'd be gone?"

"Maybe he was going to kill her but when she called 911, he backed out. He didn't know if her 911 call could have alerted the super."

"But he could have killed her," Lars countered.

"Yeah, I know," Garrett agreed. She'd been rendered unconscious but if the intruder had hit her with greater force or on the temple, she could have died. "I'm thinking we should stay here tomorrow."

"Is Selby feeling okay?"

"She seems focused." *Pissed off.* Garrett inwardly shrugged. He hadn't meant to come down so hard on her, but when it came to Evan, he was off limits.

"That's Selby for you. It's why people want her."

"She's mine now, though."

"Possessive much? Jesus, you have it bad for her, you know that, right?"

"I'm just saying she works for me. Maybe I'll steal her from you permanently." Garrett attempted to thwart Lars' line of questioning, but as the words left his lips, he considered that perhaps that was what he really wanted. She'd already effortlessly taken over Evan's IT initiative.

"She's not mine to steal. Selby does what she wants. What she sees in you, though, I'm not sure. Yeah, you've got the whole 'I'm a good-looking billionaire' thing going on, but that shit doesn't work on her."

"She's not like other girls."

"Exactly. Maybe that's why you're all hung up on her. You enjoy the challenge. Not only can you mold her into your fantasy sex goddess, you have no worries that she's into you for your money."

"Fuck you," Garrett shot back, indignant that he'd insinuated he'd be playing with her like a neophyte porn toy. "For your information, Selby's already a fucking goddess as far as I'm concerned. Maybe she just hasn't found the right person that she's been comfortable with. Maybe I'm the first person who really gets her and what she wants. Did that ever occur to you? She trusts me."

"Oh my God. You are so far gone." Lars laughed.

"You're a dick."

"Yeah, well, I love you too, man. I can't help it. I'm going to enjoy every fucking second you fall for her. Ah, the great Garrett Emerson is going down hard." He smiled and tapped at his cell phone, ignoring the look of contempt that Garrett gave him.

"I'm not falling for anyone. I like her. Big difference."

Lars rolled his eyes and gave a small chuckle.

"I like her a lot. What's wrong with that?"

"Nothing. I'm happy for you, I am. Despite your name calling, I meant what I said. I love you both. As long as you don't fuck it up." He sighed.

"Nothing is happening that requires fucking up. Selby's working for me. Thanks to you. Whatever's going on between us is just...I don't know...it's just happening. We're two people who are attracted to each other. Nothing more, nothing less. Don't go looking any further into it, okay?" Garrett's phone buzzed and he pulled it out of his pocket. "Besides, I've already told Selby all this. We're cool. She knows the score."

"Does she really? What exactly did you tell her?"

"Selby knows..."

"Hello, Selby's right here," she stated, coming around the corner. Selby put a hand on her hip and brushed her hair from her eyes.

Both men sat straight up, startled and embarrassed they'd been discussing her within earshot.

"Hi." Lars laughed, his eyes darting to Garrett, who shook his head no.

"So did you find anything?" Garrett asked, changing the topic. He couldn't believe he'd let Lars bait him into talking about how he felt about Selby. The glare Selby gave him told him she'd heard the tail end of their conversation.

"I'm in." Selby avoided Garrett. Walking around the sofa, she took a seat next to Lars.

"You're in...as in you're into Emerson?" *Fuck no.* Garrett couldn't believe she'd tunneled into his company. His entire corporation could be at risk if word leaked that they had a breach of security.

"Yeah. So far I can't download any files, but I'm sure if you give me a little longer, I'll figure it out."

Lars' face went flat as Selby spoke. "What did you run?"

"The standard tools didn't work, but that partial crack gave me an in. You know I've got a few of my own things I can try. But honestly, I wouldn't have been able to get in on any other device. Evan's got something enabled that creates the hole. So I guess the good news is that I wouldn't consider it a widespread leak. Not unless Evan gave whatever he used to another user. I guess it's possible he could have done that, but I doubt it."

"Could have been worth killing for," Lars stated.

"True, but Lars, give me a break. You and I both know Evan would not do that. For all we know, he was doing exactly what Selby just did. Maybe he was white hatting. We don't know."

"Could be," Selby agreed.

"Someone went after Selby and was looking for something. Maybe the laptop? Maybe someone knew or suspected what Evan was doing?" Garrett scrubbed his chin, walking through in his mind why Evan would have hacked Emerson.

"He would have had to tell someone," Lars surmised.

"I think we need to take things one step at a time. I know I just said I think I'll be able to download the files, but until I actually do it, it's just a possibility. If you give me a little more time, we'll have more evidence."

"I fucking hate this," Garrett commented, glancing at the text. The color drained from his face as he read it. "Something's happened to Cormac. We've got to get going."

Chapter Twenty-One

The scent of disinfectant permeated the air as they entered the emergency room. Selby grew dizzy as the memories rushed back. Screaming, she'd begged them to let her up from the table as she bled out onto the gray concrete floor. The masked adults around her spoke in what sounded like a foreign language as they discussed how best to suture the laceration on her back. No amount of pleading or crying made a difference as they cuffed her small wrists. As the first prick of anesthetic stabbed into the wound, she saw stars. From her shoulder to her buttocks, they administered the shots. Five minutes into the torture, she'd seized in anxiety. She gasped for air as her tiny heart pounded. Her chest felt as if an elephant was sitting on her, and she accepted the darkness that finally came when the sedation was administered.

It had been years since her last attack, but she'd been no stranger to the emergency room. Throughout college, she'd been taken several times. It wasn't until she fully understood the nature of her condition and how to better control the stress, that she'd been relieved of going through the hellish experience of sitting in the waiting room, and later being poked and prodded by medical staff.

The sound of Garrett's booming voice brought her thoughts back to the present, and her stomach dropped as the doctor approached. When they'd refused to let them back to see Cormac, Garrett had called for the administrator to intervene. Apparently, he'd recently donated several million dollars toward their new cancer center. A brief conversation was all it took, and they were through the locked doors. As they made their way through the ER, Selby took note of several officers, who'd gathered outside one of the rooms. A doctor stopped them before they had a chance to go any further.

"Mr. Emerson?" she asked.

"Yes, that's me. What happened?" Garrett demanded. "Is he going to be all right?"

"Sir, please. Just a minute." The doctor's eyes dropped to the ground and then back to Garrett's. "I'm Dr. Ross and I was on call when the ambulance arrived. I'm not sure of your relationship to the victim, but his brother knows you're here and gave me permission to talk with you…I'm very sorry to tell you but he's gone."

"What do you mean, 'he's gone'?" Garrett's expression immediately grew solemn as he registered the news. "No…no, this can't be happening."

"Garrett." Selby placed her hand on his shoulder in an attempt to comfort him.

"He was attacked at his home, stabbed. Abdominal

wounds...they can be difficult."

"Was he alive when they brought him in?"

"Apparently he'd made it outside his house. By the time he arrived, he'd lost too much blood."

"What about surgery?"

"I'm afraid he was DOA. We tried to resuscitate, but there was nothing we could do for him."

"Jesus Christ," Garrett breathed. Tears brimmed from his lashes and he swiped at them with the back of his hand. "I've got to see Beckett."

"Go," Selby told him.

Garrett opened the door to the room. Lars took her hand in his and they followed. Beckett sat at the bedside with his head laid on his brother's arm. A nurse brushed past Selby, and shut off the machines. She gave Beckett a sympathetic nod as she covered the bloodstained sheets with fresh linens before exiting the room, leaving them alone.

Selby bit her lip, watching Garrett take Beckett into his arms. The young man wept into his shoulder, and Selby looked to Lars, who'd also begun to cry. Nothing could make it better, she knew. There were no words in death's final moments that relieved the emptiness that filled your heart when a loved one passed away. The horrific manner of his death only compounded their devastation. Selby wrapped her arms around Lars, offering him her silent condolences.

As Garrett's friends from Altura filtered into the room, Blaire's cold stare reminded her that in this private moment, she was indeed an outsider. As she released Lars, she quietly mourned the loss of a man she'd only met once. Their interaction had been brief but pleasant as she recalled the twins' friendly banter. Although she backed into the shadows, she could overhear Garrett questioning Beckett.

"Did you find him?"

"Yeah, we were supposed to go to dinner. When I arrived all the lights were off. He was just there on the deck...the blood, there was so much blood. Why would someone do this?" he cried.

"I don't know." Garrett's eyes met hers, and Selby knew he was lying. Both Cormac and Beckett had worked for Evan.

"Did you see anyone in the house?"

"No, I didn't go in. I just stayed with him until the ambulance came. They couldn't save him. He told me he loved me and I..." Beckett sobbed and fell into the chair, putting his face into his hands. "I can't believe he's gone. This is so fucked up."

The door cracked open and Dean entered.

"Cormac...he was murdered," Garrett said.

"Yeah, I heard from my guys. Beckett, I'm so sorry." Selby noted the caring tone of Dean's voice. While he'd argued with Garrett that day in the office, he was their friend.

"We need to talk." Garrett nodded to Dean. "Be right back."

As they left the room, Selby followed. She found a

bench to rest on while Garrett and Dean discussed what had happened to Cormac. Lars came up beside her and sat down, letting his head fall back against the wall.

"I'm sorry, Lars. He seemed like such a nice guy."

"He just got his doctorate. He loved Evan. I'm telling you, Selby," he whispered, "This is all related to Evan's death. Please tell me you'll stay at Garrett's."

"I told you I would," she assured him.

"If anything happened to you, I'd never forgive myself. You didn't ask for this assignment. I got you into this mess. If I had known for one second that this would be happening, there's no way I'd have got you involved."

"There's no way you could have known. You even said you thought that Evan's death was an accident. But Lars," Selby wrung her hands, gathering the courage to tell him about Evan. "I have something I need to tell you and Garrett."

"What?"

"I don't want to say it here, but there is something else. Something about Evan I need to tell you. And Garrett isn't going to want to hear it. We fought today about his involvement in whatever's happening. He thinks Evan was completely innocent, but I'm telling you, I don't think he was. The fact that I could get into Emerson. They're a government contractor. You know I'm good but still, that's some serious shit. Whatever Evan did to that laptop…he's got something on it. Something that shouldn't be there."

Dean and Garrett approached, and Selby went quiet.

She swore she would tell Garrett everything as soon as they got home. A second man was dead and she suspected that until the attackers got what they wanted, it would continue. Garrett gave her a suspicious look as if he'd heard her talking to Lars and she avoided eye contact. She knew that he didn't want Dean knowing about the laptop, but sooner or later they'd have to tell him. The web of lies had grown exponentially, and something had to give. She steeled her heart, aware that once she told Garrett the truth, he might never talk to her again.

Selby stood nude in front of the mirror, wiping the moisture from her body. Garrett had insisted that she and Lars return to his mansion while he helped Beckett make arrangements. During the long limo ride home, Selby and Lars had sat in silence. When they'd arrived, they were met by armed guards who'd taken a visible presence at the front door. Exhausted, she'd checked her programs, but didn't have the energy to dig any further into Emerson's files. She'd already made the decision to first tell Garrett about how she'd met Evan, and let the chips fall where they may.

She'd hurried to take a shower, washing away the putrid smell of the hospital. As she dried her body, she caught a glimpse of her scar in the mirror and thought about how she hadn't revealed the insidious cause of it to

Garrett. Doing so would leave her completely vulnerable, she knew. Yet there was a small part of her that yearned to tell him, aware of the intimacy that would come with sharing her secret.

Selby brushed her hair, and considered that it was worth the risk. She suspected that Garrett wouldn't judge her. He'd been compassionate and forthright every step of the way, and he deserved to know everything about her. For once in her life, she wanted to let someone inside her heart.

A noise from the bedroom drew her attention. *Garrett.* No longer would she hide from herself or him. She'd tell him the truth and fight with everything she had to keep him in her life.

Selby padded out into the room without donning her robe. As Garrett came into view, her heart broke for him. Her strong, dominant lover sat on the side of the bed, his face in his hands. As she slowly approached and stood before him, he lifted his gaze and locked it on hers, pain emanating from his eyes.

"I'm so sorry," she said softly, aware that nothing could take away his sorrow.

Selby leaned into him as he reached for her. He wrapped his arms around her torso, pressing his cheek to her bare stomach. His warm tears bathed her skin and

Selby held onto him as he cried. No words could relieve his grief. Within their silent embrace, she offered him her heart. She'd comfort him, the way he'd done for her, not expecting anything in return.

Selby's fingers grazed down his back and tugged at his shirt. Without speaking, she removed it. Skin to skin, his chest brushed hers and she kissed the top of his hair. She brought his face into her hands and tilted his chin upward, his lips settling between her breasts.

"Selby," he began.

"Shh…let me take care of you." Selby gently pressed her palms onto his shoulders and guided him back onto the bed.

As her fingertips trailed down his chest, her eyes locked on his. She unzipped his pants and quietly undressed him. Garrett shoved up onto his elbows, moving up into the bed. Selby straddled him, her wet core sliding over his pelvis. Exhausted, he lay with his hands to his sides, allowing her to take control.

She bent to gently take his lips. Her tongue slipped into his mouth, sucking and tasting her lover until he moaned in response. Trailing soft kisses down his neck onto his chest, she lingered and licked over his flat nipple. A small nip to its hardened nub elicited a masculine hiss.

Her hair spilled over his skin like a silk waterfall as she made her way down his ripped abs. Slowly, tasting each ridge, she worshipped the man who'd stolen her heart. Selby's face brushed against the smooth skin of his hardened cock and she deliberately avoided taking him into her mouth. Instead, she parted her lips, nearly touching his shaft, allowing her warm breath to tease him into arousal. Selby inhaled the musky scent of her lover, and dragged her fingernails down the front of his thighs.

Garrett plowed his fingers into her hair and she bit his hip, reminding him that she was in control. He never made a move to change her course as she reached for his arms and dropped her head between his legs. Garrett accommodated by spreading wide open for her, and she smiled, pleased that he'd read her mind. Her lips skimmed along his inner thigh until she reached the apex. Wrapping her fingers around his shaft, she stroked it, taking his sac between her lips. He raised his pelvis in response, and she clawed at his chest, demanding he stay still. Selby feasted on him, rolling her tongue over his testicles. Her thumb skimmed his glistening head, spreading his seed onto the length of his cock.

"Selby." Garrett grunted her name as she teased his crinkled skin with her teeth.

"Hmm…I could eat you all day but what I really want is," she dragged her tongue from the root of his dick to its crown. Cupping his balls, her lips grazed his tip, "this."

"Selby…"

"Tell me you're mine, that you want this," she demanded, her voice husky.

"Fuck yes …yours…ahh…" Garrett's back arched up off the bed.

Pleased, Selby claimed her prize, swallowing him into her mouth. Hungry for Garrett, she meant every word. He might never speak to her again after he found out her secrets, but for tonight, he belonged to her. She sucked his cock, delighting in the salty essence emanating from its slit. Stroking his hard length, her fingers caressed the soft skin underneath his testicles. He cried for mercy, and she slowed her pace.

"No coming without me," she ordered, rising like a phoenix above him.

"God, you're going to kill me," he groaned.

"Shh. No talking. Just feel me." Selby hovered over him, giving him a sexy smile. Owning his cock, she swiped it through her drenched folds and moaned.

Selby had never been so bold, but as she dominated him, her arousal spiked. She grazed his crown over her clit, shuddering above him. As he reached for her breasts, pinching her nipples, she almost flew off the bed.

"Harder," she demanded, the sweet pain tearing through her body. On fire with desire, she screamed as he did as he was told, tightening his vise.

Giving him no warning, she impaled herself on his rigid flesh. Her core strained to take in his enormous length. She clutched at his arms and thrusting her breasts forward, she began slowly undulating her pelvis against his. Her eyes fluttered open and she met his intense gaze. Captivated, he watched her as she rode him. His hands glided down to her hips, holding onto the majestic beast she'd become. The fire in Garrett's eyes drove her into a frenzied state. She increased her pace, filling herself with every inch Garrett possessed.

Her eyes fell to his lips and she sought the connection that could only be found in his kiss. Wrapping her fingers around his wrists, she pinned his arms to the side of his head and pressed her lips to his. She tensed as she held him down, aware that any submission Garrett gave her was a gift.

Her clit brushed against him in rhythm as he penetrated her. Selby repeated his name into his mouth, over and over, her orgasm rushing over her. He'd once again mastered her as she shivered in ecstasy. She came hard and he thrusted up into her, giving her no rest.

"I need you," she heard him tell her and her heart constricted.

"Garrett...I..." Selby stopped short of exposing her true feelings, which she knew teetered on love. It was irrational to fall for someone so quickly but there was no denying the emotion that swept through her soul.

She released her control as Garrett rolled her onto her side. Her forehead pressed to his, and he gazed deep into her eyes as he plunged in and out of her. She moaned as his leg wrapped around her waist. In seconds she'd gone from owning his body to letting him devastate her with his strength.

"Don't leave me," he told her.

Selby's chest seized as his words ran through her mind.

"Never," she responded.

Garrett grunted as he exploded inside her. In the intensity of their encounter it hit her instantly; they hadn't used a condom.

"Garrett…Garrett." She froze and he kissed her protest away.

"Selby…aw fuck…we didn't. Shit, we should have talked about this."

"I'm on the pill. I'm clean," she panted. Selby wasn't sure what else to say. In the heat of the moment, she'd never felt closer to Garrett.

"We're good. It's good," he told her. "We should have talked about this. But I don't regret a second."

Garrett didn't attempt to remove himself from her as his lips touched her neck. The soft spray of his peppered kisses caused her to break out in gooseflesh. In his arms, she wished that she could stay like that forever. *Safe. Loved.* But it was all an illusion, she knew.

"We need to talk about what happened," she began.

"No, no more talking. Tomorrow. Tonight I just want to make love to you."

Make love. Selby's mind warred between confessing and embracing the love he offered. Breathing out the worry that sat on her tongue like a bitter pill, she caved to the magic surrounding her. Tomorrow would come soon enough. One more night, and she'd leave.

Chapter Twenty-Two

Garrett took a final glance at Selby as she lay in his bed. No one had rocked his world like she had. He recalled the last time he thought he'd been in love; he'd been in his twenties. Ironically when he'd found his girlfriend cheating, he hadn't cared. With his life replete with adventure and plans, her infidelity had been nothing more than a speedbump.

Endless dates and events had consumed his days over the past ten years, and he'd never once considered that it hadn't been enough. But Lars' words had played in his mind. *You're falling hard for Selby.* He'd tried to tell himself it was nothing, that they were just getting to know each other, but it was a lie; everything had changed.

Slammed by Evan and Cormac's deaths, he'd spiraled into grief. As he'd mourned, Selby had come to him, his beautiful angel, comforting him within her wings. He could hardly believe he'd made love to her without protection. Captivated with letting her dominate him, he hadn't given a thought to a condom. Selby was the only person he'd ever granted control to, embracing the way she'd turned the tables on him.

Having a child wasn't something he'd ever considered. But in the split second he'd come inside her, he'd imagined her pregnant. He wasn't sure whether it was good or bad that the image of her with his baby didn't bother him. If he were honest, he'd admit to the soul-piercing awareness, that maybe there was something more to life than making money or jumping out of planes.

Regardless of his deepening feelings for the woman in his bed, the reality of the day had set in. Both Evan and Cormac had been murdered. He'd have to wake Selby soon so she could resume her work. Of all the projects they currently had in the works, there were at least a half dozen that Evan had direct supervision over, ones that he was certain someone would be willing to kill to obtain.

As he made his way into the dining room, he spied the bag that Lars had brought over from Selby's house. He wrapped his hand around the handles of the tote bag and lifted it. He reasoned he might as well take her things into the bedroom. Soon Dean would arrive, so they could strategize how best to proceed. He'd called Laura, his chef and housekeeper, to return to his home to straighten up and begin cooking meals. His short lived stint as a cook had been amusing, but he didn't have the energy to deal with making meals. His priority was identifying the exact venture that all the victims had touched. There had to be a common denominator that tied the murders together.

Lars called his name, startling him. He'd forgotten that

he'd asked him to stay the night while he'd been at the hospital. He set the bag down and the contents spilled onto the floor.

"Shit."

"You okay?" Lars asked. "Need help?"

"No, I got it." Garrett began collecting and folding the clothes, placing them into the tote. He lifted a shirt, revealing the spilled contents of the plastic baggie that had contained her jewelry. Small baubles and rings clanged onto the hardwood floor as he shook out the fabric.

"I can't believe Cormac's gone." Lars scrubbed his hand over his head.

"As much as I hate to do this, I've gotta tell Dean what Selby found. Today, I need to review all the projects that Evan, Cormac and Selby have worked on. Some of it's going to overlap, but I have to try and figure out what the killer is after."

"Whatever it is, it's not like you can just hand it over."

"Yeah, but if I know *what* it is, then I can better figure out the *who*. If they want it bad enough, we'll trap them." Garrett knelt down, slowly gathering the shiny metal pieces into the bag. He fingered a dove-shaped crystal pin and noticed that it appeared cracked. "Shit."

"What is it?"

"I think I broke one of Selby's things. I'll send it out to get fixed." Garrett placed the rest of the jewelry into the pouch and palmed the metal bird in his fist. "Can you make some coffee? I'll be right back."

Instead of bringing her things to the bedroom, he set

them in the hallway and walked to his office. Remembering that he had the number of his favorite jeweler on a card in his desk, he sat down onto his black leather chair and opened the drawer. As he did so, the crystal wiggled in his fingers, drawing his attention. Although he'd initially thought it broken, the gold metal had come loose. He gave it a small tug, and a thumb drive protruded outward.

"What the?" Garrett held it to the sun, and wondered why Selby would have a data storage device that transformed into fine jewelry. Although pretty, it seemed impractical, especially for a no-nonsense person like her.

Recalling the day he'd found her in Evan's office, he racked his brain, and couldn't remember her wearing a brooch. It still didn't make sense what she'd been doing there in the first place, but at the time, she'd convinced him that she was looking for Evan's laptop. The more his thoughts swirled in doubt, the more his stomach clenched with the realization that Selby might have had an involvement with the murders.

She certainly possessed the intellectual capability to steal data. She'd already demonstrated her par none hacking skills, tunneling a path into Emerson. He shoved the suspicion to the back of his mind, but his instincts warned him to look at the disc. *Don't do it. It's probably nothing more than family pictures*, he told himself. He couldn't believe, after everything they'd been through, that she'd betray him. Snooping through her personal files demonstrated a complete lack of faith in her, but given the murders and the compromised laptop, he was obsessed with discovering what was on the drive.

Quietly he got up and shut the door, locking it. He slid in front of his computer and took a deep breath. If there was nothing on it, he'd never tell her he'd seen the files. In good conscience, he'd have done the right thing, knowing that someone in his company had been trying to steal secrets.

He typed in his password and inserted the drive into the USB port. Searching in the finder, he clicked open the folders. Garrett swore as the files flashed across the screen. *PFx Prototype. Detailed records of sample discoveries. Recent experiment logs. Chemical breakdowns.* All highly confidential.

Evan and Chase had discovered the PFx Prototype during a recent deep sea dive. A highly classified project, the organic compound had been discovered deep within a hole, a shelf in the Caribbean. At the time they'd mailed the samples home, Chase and Evan had had no idea how important they'd be. It had only been after several months of chemical testing and brainstorming that they'd begun to develop practical applications for its use.

Evan had been analyzing and testing compositions in the hope of strengthening military fabrics, perhaps creating more lightweight protective skydiving gear, but more importantly, exoskeleton-like fabrics that could be worn on the battlefield. They were in the early stages of testing, getting ready to file for patents.

How Selby Reynolds could have gotten her hands on

the information was beyond his comprehension. His heart pounded in his chest and he took a deep breath, attempting to calm his rage. Although he'd set up security for all his top level executives, his thoughts immediately went to Chase and he sent him a text, enforcing his order to stay home. Because of the circumstances surrounding Cormac's death, he and Dean had instructed all key staff to telecommute until they'd reinforced security at Emerson.

Garrett slammed his laptop shut and removed the flash drive. He considered calling Dean, but he planned to confront Selby first. Storming out of his office, he found Lars and Selby in the living room, sitting on the sofa drinking coffee.

"What the hell is this?" he yelled at her, interrupting their conversation. "How could you do this?"

"Do what?" Selby asked. She set her mug on the table, her eyes darting to Lars.

"Calm down," Lars told him. "What's wrong with you?"

"This." He held up the thumb drive and threw its crystal shell onto the table.

"What's that?" Lars reached for it.

"Ask Selby. It belongs to her," he said accusingly.

"I've never seen that before," Selby began. She jumped to her feet. "What's going on?"

"Lars got that from your apartment yesterday."

"That's not mine."

"It's just a pin." Lars fingered the crystals.

"No, it's a storage device. And do you know what was on it? Emerson files, that's what."

"I…no, that can't be," she stammered.

"You're a liar," he charged. "Evan's data. It's one of our projects. A top secret one, by the way. It's all here."

"No…you don't understand. I got that from Evan. I mean Patrick. Oh my God." Selby began to pace, holding her hand to her forehead. "He didn't want me to steal. He was planting data on me."

Chapter Twenty-Three

Selby cringed as Garrett screamed at her. She'd never seen someone so angry. When Evan had taken her on a date, he'd come to her home. He'd offered her the gift but she'd turned it down. It had been her first clue that something had been off. Selby rubbed her forehead, trying to think of how he'd planted it in her apartment. Recalling his visit, she surmised that when he'd used the restroom, he must have hidden it in her armoire.

"Garrett. Please, listen to me. That night in Evan's office. The reason I was holding the photograph. I knew him." Selby's stomach churned as she said the words. Garrett would never forgive her.

"You knew Evan?" Garrett slammed his fist down onto the granite countertop. Lars went to him but he held up his hands in a defensive posture. "Stay away. No. You're lying. This can't be true." Garrett shook his head.

"I had no idea. I met him at the club. He told me his name was Patrick. We talked all night and then the next day he came and picked me up at my place. It was only one date. I swear it."

"You went on a date?" Garrett's voice boomed.

"Jesus Christ, why didn't you say something?" Lars asked.

"Because it made no sense. I didn't know where he worked. I literally met him twice," Selby explained. "You're the one who told me to go work for Emerson. I never once asked for that account."

"Yeah, right," Garrett commented.

"No, that part is true. I mean, I only had her come work for you because Evan died. Selby's the best I've got."

"Oh she's the best all right. She stole top secret information. Do you realize that you can go to jail for this?"

"Now hold on a second," Lars interrupted.

"No, Lars. I didn't do anything wrong. This is the exact reason why I didn't tell you." Selby faced Garrett and pulled her robe protectively around her. "That night in his office. The picture. I recognized him, all right. But you have to look at this from my perspective. The reason I didn't tell you is because he was asking me things…things that someone asks when they are trying to get me to hack for them. It's not the first time. I know how this works."

"I bet you do."

"Would you shut the hell up and give her a chance to explain?" Lars yelled.

"Lars knows. He doesn't hack as much but he knows. You're at a party. People start asking you this or that…how you can get into things. It's always something small. They have a parking ticket they want to go away. They joke about changing a grade. It's never funny, though, because what they are asking for…indirectly, is for me to do something illegal. This was what Patrick was doing that night. I got up and left the table and never saw him again. It was over a month ago."

"Okay, let's assume any of this fantasy you have going is true. Why didn't you say something? Two people have been murdered and you said nothing."

"I tried to tell you last night. You didn't want to talk about it."

"You could have told me before then. Besides, I'm not buyin' what you're sellin'."

"You know what? If you don't believe me, go ahead and pull the security video. Where's my cell phone?" Selby scanned the room and went over to where she'd laid it next to the refrigerator. "Just wait." She ran her finger across its screen and flashed it to them. "March eleventh. That's the night we met at the club. March twelfth. That's the night we went out to dinner. Carlinos Café. Go ahead, check the security footage."

"What are you talking about?"

"My building records everything. They store them up for a year. At least they were supposed to, before they got disabled. As for the restaurant, I'm sure you can track down city cameras, maybe the restaurant even has them. He paid for dinner. He paid at the club. Check his bank records." As Selby said the words, she remembered that he'd charged the expense. "But why?"

"Why what?"

"If he was trying to hide, to conceal his identity, why pay with credit cards that could be traced? Maybe he used a stolen identity. I can search his laptop," she suggested.

"No fucking way. You aren't touching another damn thing in this house." Garrett blew out a breath and crossed his arms. "I don't want you anywhere near my data."

"Garrett. Please. I'm telling you the truth. I had no idea he planted that drive at my place. I don't know why he would give it to me, of all people. It doesn't make sense," she insisted. Selby went to reach for him, and Garrett backed away. As he glared at her, her heart shattered. He didn't believe a word she'd said. No matter what they'd shared, none of it had meant a thing.

"Selby, I'm sorry. I just can't be with someone who lies to me. You've got no fucking idea how much I want to believe you. What's been happening between us, I thought we had something, but this?" He held up the drive. "I can't believe you'd keep all this from me. I think maybe you and Lars need to move to the other wing of the house while I follow up on everything you've told me."

"You don't believe me," she whispered. Tears brimmed in her eyes as she looked to him and then Lars. "I want you to know that I would never do this to you, do you hear me? This thing we have…it's not just a thing. I care about you. Obviously a helluva a lot more than you do about me. You ask me to trust you…"

"But…" Garrett attempted to interrupt but she continued.

"No, you asked me to trust you. How many tests did I pass, Garrett? How many more tests do I need to pass before I'm worthy? I'll never be good enough for you. I'm done. Go ahead and fucking tell Dean. Have him arrest me. But I did not do this. That little trinket you have there. Somewhere on it is Evan's DNA. He did this. Not me," Selby cried. She could feel her anxiety rising, her chest tightening as she realized the implications of what she was saying. Walking toward the bedroom, she grabbed her tote bag and then paused to add, "You know, it's pretty ironic, isn't it? You demand my trust. I give it to you, but when I ask for it in return, you don't trust me."

"Where do you think you're going?" he yelled as she disappeared into the hallway.

Selby heard him call for her but she didn't care. She darted into a guest bathroom. After dressing in a pair of jeans and t-shirt, she slipped on her sneakers and dug through the bag, praying she'd find her keys. At the very bottom, she fingered the tog. Relieved, she slung the tote over her shoulder and strode out toward the foyer.

"You can't just go." Lars rushed after her, grabbing her by the arm.

"Really? Says who? Are you going to call the police?" Selby scanned the room but Garrett was nowhere to be found.

"Of course not. Listen, Garrett's just upset…everything that's happened. You have to give him some time."

"No, Lars. I don't. You know…you were right about

one thing. You said he was going to hurt me." She swiped the back of her hand against her weeping eyes. "You were right. Just let me go."

Selby tugged out of his grip and ran out the door. She struggled for breath as her anxiety attack mounted. Spotting her car, she ran to it and opened the door. She put her foot on the brake and pushed the on button, starting up the engine. As Lars approached, she locked the doors. He jiggled the handle, attempting to open it, but she put the car in gear. Holding up her hand to him, she slammed her foot on the gas and tore down the driveway.

Selby's vision blurred as the panic set in, her heart palpitations beating out of control. Her hands began to shake, and she knew she could no longer drive. Her car veered off into a gully. She should move the vehicle, she knew, but it'd lodged deep into the earth. Chills broke across her skin and she began to gasp for air.

She unbuckled her seatbelt and opened the car door, stumbling out into the grass. As the cars whizzed by, she fell onto the stones. As she lay on her back, she heaved for breath. The sweet tunnel of darkness claimed her and she surrendered to its will.

Chapter Twenty-Four

"I don't want to see him," Selby told Lars.

It had been a week since he'd found and rescued her on the side of the road. Reluctantly she'd agreed to go to the emergency room, once again reminded of her weakness. Afterward, they'd returned to Lars' home and she'd readily agreed to stay with him. Dean had warned that until the killer was caught, they were all in danger. Lars had suggested that she take on new clients to help her redirect her thoughts away from Garrett. She'd told him she'd consider it after the murderer was apprehended, suspecting that time was the only cure for her broken heart.

When Lars told her that her apartment had been restored, she thanked him, knowing that Garrett had been responsible. Within a day of the incident, Garrett and Lars had obtained security footage verifying Evan's presence at the club and her apartment. Credit cards had been traced back to him, and she suspected Garrett would run DNA tests on the drive as well. Lars had believed in her innocence long before the evidence was presented, however, demonstrating what she'd always known about him; he was loyal. Her best friend, he'd stand by her side.

Garrett, on the other hand, hadn't trusted her. He'd called several times, but she'd let it go to voicemail, the sound of his voice like a sledgehammer to her heart. Selby knew it had been a mistake to fall for him. She wished that it was just the sex that fueled her attraction, but she knew it was his heart, the person inside she'd grown to love.

As she sat on the chaise longue sunning herself, she sighed. She could hardly believe that she'd let herself be hurt by Garrett Emerson. She should have known it wouldn't turn out well. She began to doubt what he'd told her about not dating many women, that perhaps all of it had been a ruse so he could sleep with her.

Having cried every day for a nearly a week, her eyes burned from the tears. Forcing her emotions away, she dragged her fingertip underneath her bottom lid and swiped away the moisture. She sat up straight and inhaled the sea air. Her attention went to the ocean. In the distance she caught the distinctive sight of dolphin fins curving through the waves. A couple of surfers sat on their boards, patiently waiting on waves. Reminded of her time with Seth and Garrett, she sighed and looked away.

Selby set her iPad on the table, shoved out of her chair and approached the pool. She gingerly stepped into the water. Its icy sting momentarily broke her thoughts about Garrett and she dove in head first, hoping to rinse away thoughts of him. She surfaced and swam to the far side of the infinity pool. As she gripped its edge, she contemplated her action, aware it was something she'd never have done before Garrett. In the past, her fear of heights and falling would have surpassed any logic that told her she was safe. But since meeting Garrett and pushing some of her own boundaries, she'd grown braver. If there was a silver lining to this whole experience it had been that she'd developed the courage to start living again.

Selby relaxed into the aquatic paradise, floating on her back. She closed her eyes, taking deep breaths, meditating to the sound of the breakers. The unmistakable sound of Garrett's voice drew her attention and her eyes flew open. As she flipped over, treading water, she caught sight of him in the foyer. Her heart caught as he approached. Wearing a suit and tie, his commanding presence took her breath away. With his sunglasses on, she couldn't see his eyes but felt the warmth of his stare as surely as she knew she was alive. Recalling how he'd treated her, anger surfaced. She swam to the perimeter, attempting to put as much distance between them as she could.

"You planning on jumping off that cliff?" he asked, a small crook in his smile.

"Maybe I'm planning on pushing you," she said. "You seem to enjoy hurling yourself off of high places."

"We need to talk." Garrett pushed his shades up onto his head, and she caught the flicker of sunlight in his brown eyes.

Selby's stomach flipped as he came closer. Handsome and sophisticated, his charisma permeated through every pore of his body. Selby averted her gaze, praying that if she didn't look at him, she wouldn't cave to her desire to run into his arms. *He's hurt me. Called me a liar.* There was no going back.

"Would you like to come over here, or would you like me to come to you?" he asked. "Because one way or another, this is happening."

"There's nothing to talk about. You have the flash drive. Lars told me you verified my story. And I quit."

"There's a murderer out there."

"Yes, but I'm safe here. Again, we have nothing to talk about."

"I guess I'm coming to you," he said, walking toward the pool.

Selby watched in amazement as he removed his jacket and hung it over a chair.

"What are you doing?" she asked.

"What does it look like I'm doing?" Garrett unbuttoned his shirt, exposing his tanned muscular physique.

"It's over. If you have questions about the data or how Evan used the laptop to get into Emerson and save it, Lars can explain it. I'm done."

"Lars told me all about it. The data had been removed, hidden really. It had all been saved on the disc. We're thinking he brought it to you because you were a friend of Lars. He'd investigated you. Knew you'd be able to help. It has to be an inside job." Garrett kicked off his shoes and tugged off his socks.

"Why are you here, then?" Selby's pulse raced as he

took off his clothes. He was coming for her, she knew. Her heart couldn't take another second of being broken. If he touched her…she'd lose it. "What are you doing?"

Garrett stood tall, wearing only his pants. She cupped her hand over her eyes, straining to see where Lars had gone. Why had he let him in the house? She'd told him she didn't want to see Garrett.

"We're not finished."

"Yes we are. I quit. It's over. I have nothing more to say."

"This is far from over," he countered.

"What? No. Garrett. Look, I'm sorry that I didn't tell you about Evan, but I'm done apologizing. You wanted me to trust you and I did. You wanted everything from me." Her voice cracked as fresh tears came. "And I gave it to you."

"Selby…please…"

"It wasn't enough." She licked her lips and shook her head, embarrassed that she'd begun crying again.

Selby startled as he stepped into the pool with his pants on and swam toward her. She backed up against the side but there was nowhere to go. He surfaced, caging her with his hands. Dripping wet, he pinned his eyes on hers.

"I'm sorry, Selby. Please. I know this isn't exactly how things should go. I should have trusted you."

"You didn't believe me." Both furious and exhilarated, she struggled with her warring emotions.

"I know I should have, but you have to see this from my perspective. It's not like I didn't have any evidence."

"But I told you the truth and you didn't believe me. I know I should have told you sooner but you didn't trust me." Her palms pressed flat against his slippery chest. As she'd expected, touching his skin ignited her desire.

"I made a mistake." He brought his lips to her ear. "Please. We all make mistakes."

"You hurt me," she whispered.

"I'm sorry. I'm so fucking sorry." His eyes teemed with remorse. "Please, Selby. I need you in my life. This isn't just some passing thing between us. You know it."

"I need you to trust me, too."

"I do, Selby. I swear it. Forgive me," he pleaded.

"Garrett…" His abdomen brushed up against hers and the explosive heat she remembered flared to life. She'd dreamed he'd come for her, that they'd be able to somehow right an impossible situation.

"I'm sorry. I was wrong. So wrong. Please say you forgive me."

Selby's lip trembled as she lost herself in his eyes. His apology filled the cracks in her heart, and she could no longer resist. Garrett was a risk worth taking. If he could give her a second chance, she'd damn well give him one.

"I forgive you." As the words left her lips, any remaining doubts disappeared. She rubbed her face into his shoulder, accepting his embrace.

"Oh God, thank you, yes." His cool lips pressed to her skin. "I missed you so much, sweetheart."

"I missed you, too. I was so upset." She raised her gaze to meet his, their lips inches apart. "What I feel for you…I know we haven't known each other very long. But I...I don't want to be with anyone else."

"No, no, no. You're all mine now."

Selby smiled into their kiss as their lips touched, elated he'd come for her. She wrapped her legs around his waist, clinging to him. Her heart exploded as he swept his tongue against hers, gently taking her mouth.

"I need you with me," he told her. "Always."

"Don't leave me," she responded.

"You left me." He laughed.

"This is complicated." Selby shuddered in anticipation as he untied the back of her suit. A strong hand cupped her breast and she moaned as his thumb strummed over her nipple, jolting her body alive with arousal.

"Not really. I like you." His lips left hers for a second, their foreheads touching. "I more than like you, Miss Reynolds."

"I like you, too." She smiled.

"In or out of the pool?" he asked.

"Hmm? What?"

Garrett reached between her legs, and slid his fingers through her slit. She gasped as he drove his finger up into her core.

"I think in the pool. Yes?" He raised an eyebrow at her, giving her a sexy grin.

"Yes." She nodded, breathless from his intrusion. "I, ah....can't wait."

"I need to be inside you," he growled.

He tugged at the strings on her hips and her bikini

bottom drifted away. As he fucked her with his hand, she pumped her pelvis to meet him. Selby tore at his pants, dragging them down his legs. She reached for his rock-hard shaft, swiping the cold water over him as she thumbed its head.

"Now," he demanded.

She spread her thighs as he lifted her up onto him and slammed inside her.

"Holy shit...oh my God." His slippery cock plunged inside her. A sensation of hot and cold tingled through her core, and she screamed his name.

"That's right, baby. Say my name because I'm the one who's going to own your heart."

"You do," she admitted. More than he knew.

Selby clutched Garrett as he rocked inside her. She wrapped her arms around his neck, gripping his muscled back. With his hands on the ledge, he held them afloat as he made love to her. He kissed her with a devastating passion that annihilated any last apprehension she'd held. All she could do was feel the desire and love that she'd been afraid to concede.

Thrusting into her, he forcefully grazed his pelvis against her mound, tantalizing her clit with each stroke. With her bikini top half off, she clung to him, her body on fire, her swollen breasts crushed to his chest. No longer aware of space or time, she accepted him inside her. Tasting his lips, she returned his savage kiss, marking him as her lover, her future.

"I'm coming, I'm coming." Selby's orgasm rocketed

forth and she moaned into his mouth.

"Fuck, yeah, you are. That's it, sweetheart." He slowly retreated and deliberately thrust himself into her.

"Garrett...yes, yes, yes."

"Never leave me again," he told her.

"Never...just...ah...that's it...that's it. Garrett," she cried as she came. Her pussy fisted him as she submitted to her release.

"Holy...ah yeah," Garrett grunted as he spilled himself inside her.

Selby's hips jarred against his, milking every last spasm from his cock. His forehead fell to her shoulder and she smiled, her lips pressing to his neck. Joy swept through her as she breathed in his scent. Although the cool water surrounded her, she wore the sultry heat of her lover, enveloped in his arms.

A brush of his lips to her temple brought her focus to his eyes. He gazed upon her. His intense stare reached into her soul and her heart flipped. She resisted saying the words, but fantasized about what it would be like to tell him she loved him, to break down that final emotional boundary.

Garrett removed himself from Selby, but never released her from his embrace. Cradling her, he crossed the pool, lifting her out of the water. Nude, he carried her to the round open-aired cabana bed. Its mosquito netting loosely flapped in the breeze. He laid her down gently, reached for a warm pile of folded towels and covered her body. Spooning her, he rested his head onto his hand, glancing to the ocean.

She shimmied backward until her bottom brushed his half-hard dick. A warm hand glided over her belly, resting beneath her breasts. Relaxation set in but she stilled as his lips touched her scar.

"What happened to you?"

"What do you mean?" she asked, pretending not to understand.

"This." Garrett removed his arm from around her and trailed his forefinger down the long pale track.

"I was a kid." Selby's muscles tensed as he caged her with his words. Ironically, though, she knew it would set her free to tell him. The shame she'd carried. *Your fault. You should have known*, her mother had told her.

"We've all got scars, sweetheart. I don't know what happened, but you can tell me."

"It was my fault," she said, continuing to gaze at the horizon.

"How old were you?"

"Seven."

"Whatever happened can hardly be your fault. You were just a kid." He kissed her scar, peppering her marred skin.

"I'm tired."

"Rest, but tell me first."

She met his request with silence and closed her eyes. She vacillated between telling him everything and running to the house. Carrying the guilt for such a long time had been a nearly impossible burden to carry.

"You're safe with me. You can tell me. You're one of the strongest women I know."

"No, I'm not. I'm just determined. I'm good at some things, but you've seen me. I'm not like your friends. I'm afraid." Selby's eyes teared as she spoke. The childhood trauma never left her mind. It had mutated, coexisting with her reality as an adult.

"We all have fears, Selby. But that doesn't mean you're any less strong than anyone else. The pain that cracks us open, the kind that tears your soul apart; it's sewn back together by friends and family supporting you. Time can be like a steel suture holding the wound together. Maybe it never goes away. But we survive. I see the fire in you. I love that about you."

Selby's chest constricted at the word 'love' on his lips. It was as if he could see inside her, discovering her innermost secrets.

"This thing between us...there is no one else for me. I will always be here for you. You're safe," he assured her.

His lips brushed the back of her hair, the warmth of his breath teased her skin. *Safe.* She took a deep breath and opened her eyes. Selby couldn't look at him, as she let the memory spill from her lips.

"I was playing with friends. My mom, she was home but I don't remember what she was doing. We lived near the woods. I was with a group, but somehow, there was this boy...no, he was a teenager. But I didn't know him...they told me later that he was from the neighborhood. My memory is blurry in spots."

"You were only seven."

"We were playing in the trees. Somehow I got separated. He took my hand and led me further into the brush. I didn't know where everyone was. I was alone. Why do you think that happened?" she asked thoughtfully. "I still feel like I should have known better."

"Selby, I don't know who blamed you but whoever it was…was it a relative? Look, it doesn't matter. It wasn't your fault. There were plenty of times I was out by myself as a kid. Hell, I could have killed myself with some of the dumbass things I did. That's what kids do. And when adults aren't around…you know…it can be like Lord of the Flies. This world. There's predators everywhere. They don't all look evil either, so this boy, he may have seemed like a friend."

"He wasn't mean. He just…he, um, he tried to…you know. I knew there was something wrong. Just that feeling you know it's wrong. He pushed me down. He was on top of me."

"Did he…?"

"No, he didn't rape me. I think he wanted to. It happened so fast. He crushed me to the ground and then I fought. I fought and ran. But he chased me. He was so fast, so much faster than me. He shoved me down again. And we were near this creek. The mud and broken glass was everywhere. I don't know how it got there. I guess maybe the bottles had been there from teenagers who'd been partying. I'm not sure. I didn't see them until I went down. The blood was everywhere. I was screaming. He ran away but other kids heard me. They got their parents."

"Selby..." Garrett wrapped his arm around her protectively.

"But it was at the hospital...I couldn't get it out of my head. I know they were trying to help me but it was traumatic for me. You know, I was young. They had to hold me down. I couldn't move. I think that was the first time I had an anxiety attack, and then in college it started again. But then in my twenties, I thought I had it under control. I guess you can't really control it when it's happening, but you know, I meditate and exercise. Sometimes it just goes away, they say. I don't know. I'd been doing well...until last week."

"I'm so sorry, sweetheart. What happened wasn't your fault."

"I know. I was just so upset about not telling you, and when I saw that thumb drive and you told me about what was on it...it was too much. You have no idea. I couldn't believe it."

"I'm not talking about that. I'm talking about what you just told me. Have you ever told anyone?"

"No. My mom knew. The entire neighborhood found out. The kid went to juvie or whatever. I had to go through the whole police thing. I can remember them taking me into the courtroom...you know, to prepare me for the trial. But they must have done a plea deal. Anyway, it's embarrassing. I don't want people to know."

"You survived."

"Maybe, but still...you're the only one who I've told as

an adult. Even Lars doesn't know."

"I won't tell him."

"There's something about you, Garrett." Selby paused, noting that after all the years of hiding, concealing the dirtiness that plagued her soul, the humiliation had been eased. Perhaps not erased, but lessened. Garrett's acceptance and acknowledgement soothed her. Intellectually, she'd known that she'd been a child, hadn't been the cause of her ordeal, yet the validation had been a refreshing gift. Selby took a deep breath and released it. She took his hand, holding it to her chest. "You're special to me."

"Baby, there's something special about you too. You have no idea. I never thought I'd find someone. Hell, I wasn't looking." Garrett laughed and kissed her hair. "This thing that's going on with the data, the killer. Dean and I are going to fix this."

"Someone on the inside…" Selby's words trailed off as exhaustion claimed her. She yawned. "Someone knows."

"Yes." Garrett went quiet, in thought. He hugged her tightly. "I won't let anything happen to you again."

As she drifted in and out of sleep, Selby floated in paradise, her passion for Garrett fresh in her mind. She dreamed of a future with him and smiled. In the sanctuary of her imagination, she was free to express her private, inner thoughts.

"I love you," she whispered, her true feelings exposed.

Chapter Twenty-Five

Garrett celebrated Selby's drowsy words, aware she hadn't meant to say them. *I love you.* It should have terrified him, he knew. Instead, a rush of adrenaline surged through him, and he celebrated the disclosure. When he'd thought she'd betrayed him, he'd been crushed, wondering how he could have been so wrong. After he'd verified her story, he'd felt like shit for suspecting that she could have deceived him. While it was true that she hadn't told him about Evan, she'd been correct; he wouldn't have believed her story so soon after his death.

Jumping into the pool had been an impulse, and he laughed to himself, thinking about the crazy things he'd done since meeting Selby. When he'd come to her, Lars had refused to let him in the house. It wasn't until he'd sworn up and down that he'd beg on his knees if he had to in order to set things right with Selby, that Lars had agreed to allow him to see her. The spectacular sight of her, like a mermaid in the blue, set his heart afire. When he realized she wouldn't come to him, there was no other choice but to go to her.

He thanked God she'd forgiven him. Making love to her rocked his world, solidifying what he'd known; he was falling in love with her. When she'd told him how she'd suffered, had been assaulted, he'd wished he could find the asshole who'd hurt her and beat the ever-living shit out of him. The etiology of her cautious nature was driven by a deep-seated trauma, but in the short time she'd spent with him, she was slowly breaking free of the binds from her past.

Garrett knew he shouldn't let himself fall for a woman he'd only known for weeks. Hell, he was shocked that he could fall in love, period. It had been the most intense time of his life; two deaths had brought his perfect life crashing to the ground. Everything he'd thought was important had been rearranged like a complex puzzle. And now that the pieces were set anew, the image remaining was of Selby Reynolds in his home, in his life.

Garrett snuggled into Selby's small form, wrapping his arms and legs around her as if creating an impenetrable shield around his lover. The coming week would present more challenges. Although a killer was on the loose, Cormac's memorial had been planned. As he closed his eyes and submitted to the darkness, he prayed that he'd be able to keep his promise to keep her safe.

"You don't have to do this," Garrett told Selby. He glanced to the armed guards he'd hired to watch over the proceedings. "I can stay here with you on the ground."

"No, that's not fair to you. I can do this. It's just a plane ride. It's not like I'm jumping or anything," she said.

"I'm worried about you."

"It's okay. I've flown in a plane before. It's not my favorite thing but I certainly can do it," she insisted.

"You sure?"

"Positive. We already discussed this. I'll sit with you and after you jump, I'll go sit in the front with Seth," she said without hesitation.

The King Air's engines roared to life, and Garrett reluctantly nodded. As much as he wanted to participate in the ceremonial jump, he didn't want to risk upsetting Selby. She'd moved back into his house, and for the first time in fifteen years, he'd taken off work for a couple of days, staying at home. Despite Chase's involvement in the initial sample collection, there hadn't been any further attacks. To no avail, he and Selby had pored through the files and laptop, searching for clues to identify the killer.

During the past two days together, they'd made love and talked for hours. He'd been surprised when she'd admitted how much she enjoyed their sexual play, but he hadn't pushed her any further since the day of her panic attack. Despite their conversations, she never mentioned having told him that she loved him, confirming that she'd said it in her sleep. He hadn't broached the topic, but couldn't go much longer without telling her the emotions that lay hidden in his heart.

Like in everything he did in business and pleasure, Garrett knew exactly what he wanted. When this all was over, he planned to ask Selby to live with him permanently. The only reason he hadn't proposed the idea already was because he didn't want her thinking his decision had anything to do with the murders. The discussion would come soon enough, though, and when it did, he'd do it with a clear conscience, no blurred situations marring the moment.

Lars called to him from the plane to board, breaking his racing thoughts. Garrett put his arm around Selby, and they scurried over to the aircraft. Once seated inside, he called up to Seth, who piloted the craft. Before their flight, Garrett had triple checked all the equipment, having the mechanics thoroughly inspect the engine. The very last thing he needed was to have a repeat of Evan's accident. As the plane sped down the runway, he reached for Selby's hand and brought it to his lips. She'd gone silent, giving him a small smile.

When they lifted into the air, he deliberately slowed his breath in preparation. He'd jumped hundreds of times, but ever since Evan's accident, the insidious fear of splattering onto the ground had crept into his psyche. It wouldn't deter him, but it took the joy out of something he'd always loved.

Seth signaled they'd reached the correct altitude, and Garrett stood to slide open the door. A rush of air poured through the cabin, and Beckett held up the urn, drawing everyone's attention. As planned, he opened it, shaking the ashes of his brother over the Pacific Ocean. When he finished, he opened a small cabinet and placed the vessel inside. Garrett reached over and patted his shoulder, in a gesture of condolence. No words were needed to impart the sympathy felt by everyone in attendance.

As they approached their target field, Garrett pointed to Beckett, who was the first to jump. Chase, Nate and Ryder followed next. One by one the divers gracefully tumbled forward into the blue sky. Garrett was holding the railing, waiting his turn when he heard the sound of the sputtering engines. He mouthed the word 'stay' to Selby, whose face had gone white.

"What the fuck is happening?" Garrett asked, inspecting the instruments.

"Engine's gone. I swear to God. You know it was working. We both checked things before we took off."

"Keep the nose down. We gotta keep her gliding until we jump."

"No," Selby said from behind him.

"Get your gear on," Garrett told him. "Move over."

Seth quickly jumped out of the captain's chair, allowing Garrett room to replace him. He began prepping his gear, which he always kept on hand. Slipping on his rig, he prepared to jump.

"Hurry it up. She's going down fast. I think we can dump in the woods over there. Maybe in the lake. We've gotta get down in the field." Garrett turned his head back toward Selby, who shook her head. "Get her rigged up with the harness. She's coming with me."

"No," she protested. "Can't we just land this thing?"

"Sweetheart, if we could do that, I wouldn't be asking you to jump."

"Don't you sweetheart me. I can't. No," Selby ranted while Seth slipped the harness around her legs. Within seconds she was tightly secured into the straps, a helmet tightened over her head. "No, no, no."

"Seth. A little help here. Hold the controls. As soon as we go, you're on, you hear me. Don't worry about the plane. She won't hit any live targets. Call Mayday and jump, you hear me?"

"Got ya." Seth nodded.

Garrett strapped on the tandem gear that Seth had retrieved and connected her to his body. As much as he hated the fact that he had to take her out against her will, he enjoyed living and refused to crash in a fiery ball of flames. While he suspected foul play, it wasn't the first time jumpers had been forced to bail a plane during engine trouble.

"Garrett, no," Selby began.

"You can do this," he told her. *She has no choice.*

"I can't. No, I'm not going. There has to be something you can do."

"Sorry, sweetheart but you're jumping with me. Believe me, if there were any other way…"

"Please…oh dear God," she said as their feet edged the door.

"It's a beautiful day, baby. Look at those blue skies.

You're going to do this, understand?" he asked, his tone commanding. "All you have to do is relax."

"Relax? Are you kidding me?"

"This harness, here. You're connected to me. You aren't going anywhere. You don't need to do a thing, okay?"

"Oh my God, no."

"You can do this," he repeated.

Selby nodded, finally acquiescing to his demand.

"Trust me." His lips pressed to her temple.

"I trust you," she responded.

"That's a girl. You ready? One. Two. Three."

As if they were gymnasts Garrett gracefully rolled them out of the plane. He brought her arms outward until she'd spread them wide. Although he hated to have to force her to jump under duress, the joy of the flight never ceased to amaze him. He glanced upward, relieved to see Seth's body fall out of the aircraft.

Garrett slowly released her fingers, testing her willingness to trust him. Her palms opened freely and he knew she'd be fine. The freefall lasted nearly sixty seconds. He wished he could talk to Selby but knew that with the rush of wind, she wouldn't hear him. Garrett checked his altimeter and deployed the chute. The canopy released, jarring them into a slower descent.

As they drifted down, he caught sight of the plane crashing into the lake. A fire truck rushed toward the scene, but whatever had happened, it would take the NTSB several days to investigate. Despite the murders, he had a hard time wrapping his head around the fact that someone could have tampered with the engine. Not only had the mechanic given the go ahead, Garrett had inspected it as well. If it was any other time in his life, he would have accepted the crash as unavoidable risk. But in his gut, he knew someone had just tried to murder them.

A clean landing target came into view and he guided them toward it. As their feet touched the ground, they slid onto their bottoms, and he quickly checked Selby. She rolled onto her back, her eyes blinking toward the sky.

"Selby, you okay?" he asked. He pulled off his gloves and palmed her cheek.

"Garrett," she panted.

"Are you hurt?" Garrett scanned her body, checking for scrapes or burns. He inspected her ankles, moving them back and forth. When she didn't wince, he crawled upward. Removing her helmet, he cradled her head in his lap. "Sweetheart. Say something."

"I'm alive." A shaken smile broke across her face as she continued. "It was so noisy. I think I screamed the whole time but I couldn't even hear myself."

"Jesus, you scared the shit out of me." Garrett laughed and kissed her forehead.

"Mr. Emerson is not afraid of anything." She blinked and giggled.

"You're wrong." He exhaled a loud sigh. "I would have given anything for you to do this with me, but not this way. Goddammit, this has to stop."

"It was amazing. I see why you do this," she continued

as if she hadn't heard a word he'd said.

"Maybe next time…"

"I'm not sure about a next time."

He raised an eyebrow at her, aware that his little adrenaline junkie in training would most definitely want to jump again.

"Okay, maybe one more time. But I want a cool suit like you have." She winked. "Maybe in pink. No wait…baby blue. That way I'll blend in with the sky."

"I'll buy you one in every color of the rainbow." Garrett gently pressed his lips to hers, thankful she'd taken it in stride. Three little words danced on the tip of his tongue but he couldn't bring himself to say them.

"Is Seth okay?" she asked.

"Yeah, he's fine. We're all fine." *As fine as we can be with a murderer trying to kill us all.*

Dean approached and Garrett straightened his back, steeling himself for the conversation.

"I think we need to cancel tonight's event," Dean told him.

"Look, normally I'd agree, but we can't stop living because some asshole is trying to terrorize us. We need to draw him out and catch him. You need to check out the video from the hangar and see if anyone messed with the plane."

"But the NTSB…"

"Break the fucking rules, Dean. Get a copy and let them have the original. I don't give a shit. We need to stop this now. Two people are dead. You know we have what they want. They know it. They're not going to stop."

"Even if there is evidence of something suspicious, we might not see it before tonight."

"Look, we have armed guards. Undercover security. Everyone at Altura is a suspect. Double check the short list of staff who worked on the PFx Prototype," Garrett suggested.

"I already checked it. There weren't many people on it, and none of them have a motive. I think we need to consider that maybe Evan was working with an outsider. Maybe he changed his mind and that's why he took the data. And before you start defending him, I know you keep saying he didn't do anything, but he stole data. What you've got there, and of course you won't let me see it, which is an entirely different story, it's the only data. Emerson has been wiped clean of the project."

"But Evan is the one who's dead." Garrett shook his head.

"Which gets us back to thinking it's someone inside," Selby said.

"Whoever killed Evan knew his habits, how he packed his rig. Was close enough to poison him. Granted, he's jumped with lots of people who aren't tied to Emerson, but still," Garrett scrubbed his fingers over his hair, "if this is someone close it's exactly why we need to trap them. We need to lay the bait. Let them know I have the laptop and all the things that he owned. Tonight is a huge event. Most of the people Evan knew will be there. Someone who's going to this party tonight is in on this and the only way to find out who, is to root them out. Drop some crumbs about the location of the drive and they'll go looking for it."

"What are you going to say?" Dean asked.

"Not much. I'll just mention that we think I have what the perp was looking for. I'll say I have Evan's laptop and found something. When people ask what, we say it's confidential. I make it clear that because of recent security issues, I'm moving downtown. I keep a penthouse in the Gas Lamp district." Garrett glanced to Selby. "You're going to stay with Lars, and we'll keep eyes on both properties. If so much as a snake slithers onto either place, Dean's people will grab them."

"As much as I hate this plan, we have nothing. As long as you and Selby stay with Lars, it should be fine," Dean agreed.

"No. I'm going to stay in the city. I don't want anyone going after Selby. If anyone finds out I'm with Lars, they'll come for me there. No, it needs to be clear that we've found what they were looking for, and I have it. Far away from Selby. Can you pull this off, Dean?"

"I think we need to give it a shot before someone else gets killed. I certainly think keeping Selby away from you is a good idea if you're planning on telling people that you have the data."

"I think we need to keep the data somewhere else," Selby said, pushing up onto her knees. "Right now, we've got it on that drive. Talk about a shit plan for backup. I'm concerned, though, that until we clean Emerson of whatever Evan might have done, we don't want to put it up on their systems. If you trust Lars and me, we can take care of it."

"I trust you." Garrett shoved to his feet and extended his hand. He considered that he hadn't thought twice about his response. He'd already doubted her once; never again.

Selby smiled up at him, her eyes darting to Lars, who approached from the field. Garrett couldn't be sure who had betrayed him, but after everything they'd been through, they were the only two people he was certain wouldn't divulge his plans. Even though he'd shared some information with Dean, he still hadn't divulged what was on the disc, or other key factors.

He considered that Seth had had access to the engine, and the curious fact that Chase hadn't suffered any ill effects from discovering the PFx Prototype. At least a dozen people in his company all had clearance to work on the project. On face value, not one of them had ever given him reason to doubt them. Regardless, he'd called in his own personal detectives, and had begun running exhaustive security scans on their current activities. Not only was the PFx Prototype worth millions of dollars, it could potentially be utilized to protect soldiers. In the hands of the enemy, its organic composition and myriad uses would steal advantages from their country.

As he and Selby walked toward and joined up with the tight-knit group of friends, their weary faces spoke volumes about the situation. While they'd celebrated

Cormac's life in the way he would have wanted, they all knew the plane crash wasn't an accident. With friends as potential foes, a loss of trust, their spirits were beginning to falter. Garrett wondered as he scanned his inner circle, who had become an enemy. Within days, he'd find out the answer that eluded him. In the meantime, his priority was to keep Selby alive.

Chapter Twenty-Six

Selby fidgeted with her evening dress, and recalled her appointment with Garrett's personal shopper. He'd brought several dresses and studied her as she diligently tried them on, modeling his selections. Standing before the mirror in the bedroom, she'd promptly undressed in front of him when she caught sight of the fifteen thousand dollar price tag on the sheer lace, floor length gown.

Shoving her arms into a worn cotton robe Lars had brought from her apartment, she'd protested. Unless the gown converted into a small-sized car, she'd told Garrett, there was no way she'd let him spend that amount of money on a dress. He'd simply laughed, ignoring her argument. As if he were buying a box of paperclips, he'd selected the entire lot and ordered the assistant to leave.

At times Garrett was exceedingly practical, yet she often forgot the opulent lifestyle in which he lived. She wondered how she could ever fit into it, aware that there was nothing he couldn't buy. Despite his wealth, he was never pretentious, his generosity abounding with a down-to-earth benevolence. With the strength of a true leader, he led with both conviction and compassion.

After they'd dressed, the sight of Garrett in his tuxedo had taken her breath away. She'd forced herself to remain calm, as he took her hand and led her to the car. A driver held the door open and she'd gingerly sat down, careful not to damage her dress. She'd been relieved when she realized an armed guard had been assigned to sit up front with the driver. After everything that had happened, she trusted no one.

Despite Garrett's confidence in his employees, he and Lars were the only two people she knew for certain weren't the murderers. Everyone else was a suspect as far as she was concerned. If the killer could take down a plane, a car would be child's play. He'd assured her they'd take the most secure route, traveling inside the bulletproofed stretch limo. Altura had been well secured. A lingering doubt bored a hole in her stomach, but she concealed her fear with a forced smile as the car lurched forward.

"You look beautiful," Garrett told her, shaking her contemplation.

"Thank you. It's amazing what a fifteen thousand dollar dress can do for a girl," she teased. "You shouldn't have bought this for me."

"Yes, I should have. You look spectacular in it." He smiled and reached into his jacket, retrieving a black box.

"Garrett..." her words faltered as he opened it. A string of diamonds rested atop a bed of black velvet.

"I haven't bought you flowers yet," he mused, giving a

mischievous smile.

"You don't have to buy me flowers," Selby replied, her voice shaky. "You don't have to buy me anything."

"No, that's where you're wrong, sweetheart. What kind of boyfriend would I be if I didn't bring you flowers for our date?" he asked.

"Boyfriend?"

"You sound so surprised."

"I just…" she stuttered. The implication of commitment startled her despite their words at the pool.

"Unless there's some other guy I don't know about. Is there?" He laughed.

"No."

"If you're planning on dating other guys, well, I'm afraid that's not going to work out so well. Are you?"

"No." She gave him a shy grin, aware he was teasing her.

"Would you like me to date other girls? I don't want to, but I suppose if that's what you'd like…"

"No." Her lips pursed and she crossed her arms. Jealousy rose at the thought of him touching any other woman.

"All right then. I think we've got ourselves a date. And I think," he laughed and glanced out the window, as if he'd just realized it himself, "that you are my girlfriend. What do you say?"

"I say," she paused and met his gaze, "I think you are correct once again, Mr. Emerson."

"So…flowers. It got me thinking. As much as I wanted

to bring you flowers tonight, they're not very permanent. But these," he held up the choker, its tiny petals sparkling in the ambient lighting, "they're much more permanent."

"Garrett."

"Hold up your hair." He fastened it around her neck, sliding his finger under the delicate gems. Grazing his fingers over her skin, he gently adjusted it into place. "Ah…you're lovely."

Selby brought her hand to his, tears in her eyes.

"Thank you…you didn't have to do this," she said.

"No tears, baby. These flowers here are strong like you." Garrett softly pressed his lips to hers, lingering for only a second. "Unlike real ones, these won't fade or wilt. They're enduring…like we're going to be."

Selby closed her eyes, her pulse whizzing the blood so fast through her veins she thought she'd faint. She lifted her lids, her chest filled with emotion. His hand trailed over her bare knee through the slit in her dress, and her cells lit on fire with desire. Warmth rushed to her cheeks and she tilted her head, aware he'd seen her blush.

Garrett reached for a button and the privacy divider slid upward. Selby smiled at him, confused as to what he was doing. Her anticipation rose as he reached into the other side of his jacket and retrieved a tiny square box. Her eyes widened as he moved to kneel in front of her.

"What are you doing? You're going to wrinkle your pants," she told him.

"Speaking of flowers," Garrett said, ignoring her protest. He dragged the fabric of her dress upward and spread open its slit, exposing her panties.

"Garrett..." Selby's eyes flew up to the front where she eyed the partition. A small nervous laugh escaped as he slid his thumbs underneath the strings on the sides of her thong.

"I much prefer you without underwear." He tugged them down, gently sliding them around her ankles. Garrett tucked them into his pocket and grinned.

"They're very restrictive," she agreed.

"Indeed. Unnecessary." He opened the container, displaying a shiny bauble. "I'm going to need your help, I'm afraid."

"Is that an earring?" Dear God, she hoped it was an earring.

"What do you know about pearls?"

"Is this a test?"

"This is a rare natural pearl. Stunning. Unique. Again, like you." Garrett fingered the small item, its creamy stone glittering against the gold. His palms grazed up over her thighs until he reached her hips. "This is a very special type of jewelry that I think we'll both enjoy."

"Garrett...what are you...ah," she cried as he swept his thumb through her folds. Opening her lips, he revealed her pink nub. Selby clutched the soft leather seat as he blew warm air onto her wet skin.

"I love your pussy. So beautiful. I thought you might enjoy this."

"What is that...no, no, no...ah...oh my God." Selby sucked a breath as he slid the clip under her hood and tightened it down. She gripped the leather seat. The sensation of the cool metal against her throbbing clit sent her reeling.

"Easy, don't move, sweetheart," he told her, his tone firm. Garrett thrummed his thumb over the pearl and Selby raised her pelvis to meet his touch.

"I can't wear this. Oh shit...please," she breathed. "You're going to make me...ah."

As Garrett swiped his tongue over the bead, she stabbed her fingers into his hair. His raspy lash wasn't enough to push her over the edge. Her orgasm building, she needed more. But instead of continuing, he pressed his lips to her mound and withdrew.

"No, no...wait, where are you going?" she protested. A mist beaded over her forehead and she groaned. Bringing her hands to her breasts, she squeezed them, but it did nothing to assuage the ache between her legs.

"I'm afraid we've arrived at our destination." A broad smile broke across Garrett's face. Carefully setting her dress back in place, he returned to his seat.

Selby leaned her head back against the leather and blew out a frustrated breath. He'd done this to her on purpose. *Holy shit, I'll never make it through the night*, she thought.

"You're evil." She glared at him, and he laughed in response.

"Ah now, that's not very nice. Would it help to know that I have something special to show you later?"

"Bastard," she growled, not willing to concede that their interlude had come to an end. "You drive me crazy, you know that, right? I need to come."

"And come you will. But not now. Here's the driver." The door opened and he leaned toward her, brushing his lips to her ear. Taking her hand, he slid it onto his erection. "Believe me, this is hurting me just as much as you. But waiting makes it all the more sweet."

Selby palmed his cock through his trousers. "This is mine later, do you hear me?"

"All yours, baby. You ready?"

"An hour. I give you one hour." She squeezed his shaft hard, owning it. "No longer. If I have to fuck you right out on the dance floor, this is happening."

"You're on," he promised.

Selby sucked in the night air, attempting to quell her desire. She smiled as Garrett put a possessive arm around her, leading her into Altura. As the orchestra played in the distance, she optimistically dreamed of a world without danger and liars. Soon enough, it would come to an end. Later tonight, she'd go with Lars, and Garrett would become bait for a killer.

Chapter Twenty-Seven

As they stepped into the walls of Altura, Selby took in the sight of its dramatic transformation. No longer veiled in the dimness of candlelight, the elegant mansion flared to life with its crystal chandeliers and eclectic architecture. To her left in the ballroom, a grand soirée had commenced. An orchestra played upon its stage while partygoers danced.

As she followed Garrett to the right, they entered an enormous parlor, where white-gloved waiters passed epicurean delights on trays. Spectacular paintings graced the walls, and she hesitated, to confirm if the impressionist work was real. A grand piano sat majestically in the corner, its delicate keys in pristine condition.

Selby glanced out the window to the pool. Once again it was lit up, this time with floating candles set into wreaths of white flowers. In the courtyard, life-sized bronze statues of magnificent animals stood proud, illuminated under the glare of red spotlights. There was so much to look at that Selby barely registered Garrett calling her name as he handed her a glass of champagne.

"Sorry," she managed, overwhelmed. "This place...I couldn't see the last time. It's unbelievable."

"Thank you. Altura is like a chameleon. She can go backyard barbeque as easily as she does black tie. Tonight is one of the rare times outsiders are allowed within her walls. Many are employees or close personal friends, but they aren't members."

"I thought you didn't bring people here...outsiders."

"That night I brought you, that was a members only event, which is typical. I only allow these kinds of charity galas a few times a year. We're raising money for some of the local rescues that I told you about, which is another reason I was hesitant to cancel. We're talking about millions of dollars that people are depending on receiving." Garrett leaned in to whisper to her. "And many of these folks are undercover."

"Really?"

"There was no way this was happening without it."

"You're certain we're safe?"

"Yes, in the context that there's security. But don't forget that it's likely the killer is among us. Stay in the main rooms. And whatever happens, do not leave the building, understand?"

"No, of course not," Selby agreed.

"I need to talk to a few key players tonight, make sure the crumbs are sprinkled about. Lars should be here soon." Garrett scanned the room and waved him over. "Ah, there he is. Why don't you stay with him while I take care of things? But don't get too comfortable."

His seductive tone rolled over her like an erotic wave, her core tightening in anticipation. As she turned to greet Lars, the fabric of her dress brushed the pearl, causing her clit to quiver in arousal. She gave a soft gasp, her eyes meeting Garrett's. He gave her a knowing smile.

"Everything okay?" Lars asked, taking her off guard.

"Yes, thanks." Selby stumbled over her words, still focused on Garrett.

"We got business, remember, you two? You got time for that later," Lars scolded playfully. "You mind if I take your girl for a dance?"

"Not at all." Garrett raised an eyebrow at her. "Selby?"

"Sure, thanks." She extended her hand to Lars, but accepted a small kiss from Garrett.

As he gave her a small embrace, his lips skimmed her ear. "Don't come without me, sweetheart?"

"You have," she glanced up to the grandfather clock, "exactly forty-five minutes."

"It's a date." He winked at her and walked off into the crowd.

"You guys are on a date. Nice," Lars commented.

"He tortures me," she laughed.

"I don't want to know, do I?"

"Maybe, but I'm not telling. Shall we?"

"Fred Astaire, baby. Get ready." Lars winked.

Selby laughed as she and Lars danced to a waltz. They'd chatted for nearly thirty minutes straight about her jump, and shared stories from past assignments. She realized how long it had been since they'd talked, and found that she was actually beginning to relax. She saw Beckett approach and gave him a sympathetic smile. Lars slowed, and turned to him.

"Can I cut in?" he asked, a bloom of pink brushing over his pale cheeks.

Lars gave Selby a shrug and she nodded. "Of course."

"I'll be right over there," he told her.

Selby smiled as Beckett awkwardly put his arm around her. She guessed from his stiff posture that perhaps he'd taken dance lessons, but hadn't quite gotten the hang of it. His tall stature compared to her small frame made it difficult for her to see his eyes. She held her arms firm, praying he wouldn't make an attempt to pull her in close.

"You're Garrett's girlfriend, aren't you?"

"Yes," she replied, without hesitation this time.

"I knew it. I never lost an argument."

"I'm so sorry about your brother. I didn't know him well but he seemed incredibly nice."

"Yeah, he was the best."

"Do you have family?"

"We do but we've kind of been out of touch with my mom and dad for a long time."

An awkward silence hung between them as Selby let the conversation die. Aware that sometimes strained family relationships existed, her curiosity was piqued, but she resisted the urge to delve further. Her own background had been dicey at best. If she fell off the face of the Earth, her dad wouldn't even know.

As the song ended, they both clapped their hands. Selby was grateful when she caught sight of Garrett approaching.

"How are you, man?" he asked Beckett. Garrett gently set his palm onto his shoulder.

"I'm hangin' in there. It's quiet at home."

"Take all the time you need. We're all going to miss him."

"Thanks." Beckett gave a tight smile that didn't reach his eyes. He wiped his mouth with the back of his hand and pointed toward the bar. "I'm goin' to go get a drink."

Garrett nodded in understanding and turned to Selby, taking her hand in his.

"You ready?"

"More than you know."

Selby had no idea what he had planned but that was what she loved about him. The tease of anticipation drove her wild, and as she fell into his arms, she forgot about everyone else in the room.

Garrett led Selby up the grand staircase, never mentioning where he planned to take her. In silence, they turned the corner and reached their destination. She waited patiently while he unlocked the closed double doors. He gave her a sexy grin and turned the handle.

"Welcome to my secret conservatory," he said with pride.

Selby's eyes widened as she entered the glass-encased solarium. She gazed around the room, entranced at the sight of the twenty-foot trees and various ferns inside the spacious room. The masculine décor, in rich tones of brown and tan, extended to the mahogany beams that framed the enormous structure. A black wrought iron staircase led up to a balcony that circled its octagonal turret.

"This is incredible. What is this? Is this for your group?"

"I built Altura for us, but this room is mine. I don't get to spend much time here, but it's special. No one is allowed inside except maybe Lars every now and then."

"It's hardly a man cave," she noted, scanning her surroundings.

As he closed and locked the door, the din of the party was silenced.

"I do have some of my office things in that armoire over there, but this place is mostly for play, not work. It's where I come when I need to create. I know it probably doesn't seem that way, but at Emerson…all the different facets, products and services…over the years, there are just times when I need to think with no distractions."

"Like your own personal slice of heaven?" Selby trailed her finger over the chemise daybed.

"Yep. You like it?" he asked, seeking her approval. "I've got a telescope over there. We're far enough away from the city. The light pollution isn't too bad. On a clear night, you wouldn't believe what you can see."

"It's amazing."

"I installed these last month...wait for it." Garrett pecked at a panel on the wall and the lights dimmed, leaving the room illuminated by small lanterns that dangled from the ceiling. "They're solar."

Selby smiled at him, aware that once again he was sharing something incredibly important to him. The intimacy flourishing between them was palpable, so much more than a passing sexual affair. She'd never imagined falling in love could be so incredible, leaving her terrified that he'd disappear if she said the words that resounded in her heart.

As he approached, she held her breath. Everything stood still as he commanded her attention. She had an urge to spear her hands into his perfectly coiffed hair and kiss him, but she resisted, allowing him to control the situation. Within his own private paradise, she'd submit to whatever carnal pleasures he wanted.

He brushed the back of his knuckles against her cheek and her eyes lit up. Seconds seemed like hours as she waited for him to take her. A strong hand slid around her waist, and she released a sigh, her eyes never leaving his.

"I think it's been just about an hour."

Selby's heart flipped as he leaned to kiss her. Tasting champagne on his tongue, she opened to him. She returned his passionate kiss, tasting her lover. As his hand slipped through the slit of her dress and cupped her bare mound, she moaned.

"I want everything tonight, Selby." He spoke into her mouth, caressing her lips with his own. "Your body. Your heart."

Breathless, she could only give a small moan in acknowledgement. Selby's knees faltered as he fingered her tiny pearl, her swollen clit tingling in arousal.

"Hmm....you like your jewelry, don't you?"

"Oh my God..."

"I love how responsive you are, my sweet girl."

Selby cried his name as he pumped his middle finger into her pussy, his thumb continuing its erotic assault on her clitoris. She dug her fingers into his forearm, and her forehead fell to his chest, as she heaved for breath.

"Do you have any idea what you've done to me?" Garrett moved behind her and ground his erection up into her ass. "How important you are to me?"

"Please, Garrett."

"That's right, sweetheart. Beg me, because tonight you're all mine."

"I'm so...there..." Selby choked out.

She tensed in desire as he slid another digit into her, curling it inside her sensitive channel. As his other hand glided underneath the fabric and cupped her bare breast, she came undone. With his fingers deep inside her, she clenched around him, spasming in pleasure.

"Garrett...please, yes...I'm coming..." She sucked for

air as she came down, surprised as he withdrew his fingers and inserted them into her lips.

"Sofa," he ordered.

Disoriented, she allowed him to bend her over its soft fluffy arm rest. He settled a pillow underneath her head and promptly lifted the back of her gown. A rush of cold air brushed over her exposed pussy and she spread her legs wider to accept him. His palm lifted and she went to lift upward. Her effort was met with a firm slap on her ass.

"Stay. No moving."

His commanding voice wrapped around her, and she did as she was told. The sound of running water and a drawer opening drew her attention and her heart raced. A warm hand caressed her bottom and she breathed in delight. She turned her head, her eyes meeting his.

"Do you know how much you mean to me?" he asked, unzipping his pants. "Everything has changed because of you."

"Garrett... I need you." It was all she could manage without revealing her love.

His palm brushed over both her cheeks, his crown prodding her entrance. Selby thought she'd go insane from the lingering anticipation.

"Please..."

"I need you, too," he told her, sheathing himself inside her. "More than you know."

"Yes..." Selby gasped as he entered her.

Her toes came off the floor as she accepted him, but he held her in place as he plunged inside. She shivered as her core fisted him. She'd come within minutes, she knew.

"Move in with me," she heard him ask. He went still, fully seated inside her, waiting on her answer. His fingers trailed up into the back of her dress, stroking over her spine.

"What?"

"Move in with me," he repeated.

"I...are you sure?" Tears pricked her eyes as he leaned over her and brought his lips to her flushed cheek.

"Yes, I'm sure. I love you, Selby." He gently kissed her face. "I heard you...the other day. I wanted to wait until all this was over to tell you how I feel, but I can't. I need you to know how important you are to me...now...tonight."

Selby's eyes flew open on hearing his words. She'd remembered saying the words but thought it a dream.

"I love you, too," she whispered.

"Live with me. Please say yes." His lips gently took hers as he swept his tongue into her mouth.

The whirlwind romance was a force she couldn't fight, she knew. Selby was already lost to Garrett Emerson. For years, she'd followed her head, but in the heat of the night, with the love of her life, she'd follow her heart.

"Yes." Selby nodded.

"Yes," he repeated.

"Garrett, make love to me," she breathed. "Please. I need to feel you."

"All night, sweetheart."

"Yes," Selby breathed as he rose, slowly increasing his

pace.

She reached a hand back toward him, clutching his thigh.

"All of you," he growled.

Selby startled as the cool gel hit her bottom and she recalled his pledge to know every part of her body. Her arousal flared as his thumb spread the fluid over her puckered flesh. She knew what he wanted, and she yearned to explore her darkest fantasy. As he pumped in and out of her, his finger teased her anus as if testing her willingness. Although the request would come as a command, her submission to the experience was in her control.

"So tell me, Selby." He pressed into her back hole, sliding in up to his knuckle. "How far do you want to go with me tonight?"

As he filled her from behind, Selby's channel clenched around his cock. Her mind whirled, giving in to her forbidden desires, letting go of her apprehensions. He slowly added another finger, stretching her open, and her body shuddered in response.

"It feels so… yes, oh my, yes…do it," she told him. Overwhelmed by the foreign sensation, she clawed at the sofa.

"I love being with you…everything about you," he told her. "Easy now."

Selby cried in protest as he removed himself from inside her, leaving her empty.

"It's okay, baby. I'm not going anywhere. Just wait a

second."

Selby mewled as he poured more lubrication down her crevice. His firm tip pressed to her back entrance and she wiggled against it.

"Slowly. This isn't something you rush, now. Just breathe and push back onto me." Garrett gently guided himself into her. His crown pressed through the tight ring an inch and he stalled, giving her time to adjust.

"Oh my God," Selby sighed as she breathed into his invasion. The twinge of pain subsided as she expanded to accommodate him. He caressed her bottom, encouraging her. She did as he'd instructed, concentrating on relaxing her muscles.

"That's it, Selby, let me inside."

"Garrett, please…wait…go slow…yes…"

"You're so tight…aw, fuck," he hissed, filling her to the hilt.

Selby's channel tightened down and she moaned, his fingers flittering over her clit. Catapulted into ecstasy, she splintered apart as he made love to her. No matter what she'd dreamed the experience would have felt like, nothing had prepared her for the exquisite pleasure he'd given her. She heard him call her name, and her orgasm crested. He slammed into her and she climaxed, exploding in a thousand shards of rapture. As she embraced his possession, she mumbled his name over and over, lost in the moment.

"I love you so fucking much," he cried, coming hard.

"I love you, too," Selby breathed. Her body shivered as

the last spasms rolled through her. Exhausted, she went limp onto the sofa, relaxing as he removed himself from her. She smiled as he gently cleaned her, the cloth warm on her skin.

Before she knew what was happening, he'd lifted her into his embrace, cradling her against his chest. They lay on the sofa. Selby cuddled against Garrett, placing small kisses to his chest. As the party roared below, they'd made love in the moonlight, affirming their future. Happiness bloomed in her chest, and for the first time in her life, she knew she was truly loved.

Chapter Twenty-Eight

Insurmountable emotion plowed through Garrett; there was no greater risk than the one he'd just taken. Falling in love with Selby Reynolds was the pinnacle of his existence, one that would far surpass anything he'd ever do again with Altura. He pressed his lips into her hair, astonished that he'd told her he loved her and she'd returned his feelings. Perfectly content with her in his arms, he didn't want to return to the event. Her fingers ran across his bare chest, and he reveled in the peace he'd made with being in love. His only regret was knowing he'd have to leave her with Lars, so he could go alone to lure a killer.

She adjusted her small form against his, and he decided that they'd stay upstairs for a few minutes more. The party would go on without him, and he was in no rush to end his time with her.

"Garrett," she called softly.

"Hmm...what, baby?"

"Why didn't you tell me I talked in my sleep?"

"Because I wanted to tell you myself that I was falling

for you." He wound a finger into her silky hair and played with a strand. "I don't think I've ever felt like this before."

"Do you think it's real? We haven't known each other very long. It seems so crazy. But I just...that day I left you, I knew for sure. I couldn't believe it, but I kept thinking, how could this happen?"

"I think sometimes in life we like things neat and tidy. We like predictability. People like to say with certainty that they did all the right things in the right order. But that's not how life works. It's the complete opposite. Life is messy. It's unpredictable. And like with us..."

"Hmm..."

"There's this chemistry. You can't fight it. You try. But it's so strong. And you want to explain it away. You want to say that for it to be real, you must absolutely know a person for so long. Or maybe do certain things. But again, life is not full of absolutes. Life is flawed, indefinite. Who are we to say our chemistry isn't worthy of our love? That day when you walked out...no, even before then, I knew I needed you in my life. Maybe I couldn't put the words to it, but you were in my heart."

"Do you really want me to come live with you?"

"I don't say things I don't mean."

"I just thought maybe because we were...you know..."

"Selby, I love you. There is no in between with me. If there is one thing this past week has taught me, it's that we need to live each day like it's our last. You think when Evan woke up the day he died, he thought that would be his last? No way. So why wait to be with each other? Yeah, it's soon, but you've already been in my home."

"I don't live the kind of life you do."

"If you're talking about the money, I'm not going to let you use that as an excuse. I'll give it all away before that happens. Besides, you've seen how I live. Does it bother you?"

"No, I just want to make sure you know who I am."

"I know you better than you think I do. And I'm looking forward to spending lots of days and nights finding out all of your secrets." Garrett squeezed her tightly to him, pleased when she snuggled closer.

A pregnant pause followed and Garrett closed his eyes, relaxing into the embrace of his lover. Within minutes, however, Selby stirred, pressing herself upward, with her hand to his chest.

"Garrett."

"Hmm?" he responded, drifting into sleep.

"Garrett, wake up. Do you smell smoke? I smell smoke," she said, her voice laden with panic.

His eyes flew open and although he didn't see any evidence of her concern, the familiar burning scent teased his nostrils. He quickly sat up, reached for his phone, and dialed 911.

Garrett put his hand to the door, its wooden surface still cool to the touch. But as he opened it, smoke billowed throughout the hallway. Instructing Selby to crawl on her hands and knees, he guided them down the hallway and stairs. When they reached the bottom, some of the smoke had cleared. Panicked guests poured through the foyer out the front of the building. As they went to exit the patio, they bumped into Beckett, who called for their help.

"What's wrong?"

"It's Lars," he said, panicked. I've looked for him everywhere. We were all in the ballroom when the fire started. He said he was going to the wine cellar to get some champagne and he wasn't there. I can't find him."

"Why the hell would he go down there? The caterer is supposed to be handling all of this."

"I don't know. He said something about a special bottle for Cormac."

"Selby, I need you to go with Beckett. Beckett, find Seth and stay with him, do you hear me?"

"No, Garrett, don't go back in. Let the firemen handle it." Selby clutched at his arm.

"The firemen aren't here yet. I've already lost two friends in the past month, I'll be damned if I lose another one." Garrett's voice went cold. Lars was as close to a best friend as he had and there was no way he was letting him die.

"Please don't do this," she cried.

"It'll be okay…I promise you. I can't leave him," he told her. His eyes softened and he pressed his palm to her cheek. "I love you. I'll be right back. Don't come in after me. Got it?"

Garrett quickly pressed his lips to Selby's and gave Beckett a nod. The smoke thickened as he ran back into Altura, and he was certain that if he didn't find Lars within minutes, they'd both be dead.

By the time Garrett reached the basement door, the fire was raging from the east end of the house, where the small parlor rooms were located. On the west side, near the kitchen, smoke poured into the air, but nothing was ablaze. He rounded into the small hallway, and opened the basement door. His heart caught when he saw Lars lying at the bottom of the steps. Broken glass and a mixture of red wine and blood spattered the floor around his body. Under any other circumstances, he wouldn't have moved him, and would have waited for paramedics. But with the fire raging throughout the building, he had no choice but to get him out of the house first and hope he didn't injure him further. Hoisting Lars over his shoulder, Garrett noted a significant gash to the back of his head.

As Garrett bounded up the steps, his thoughts raced. The realization that someone had attacked Lars sent him reeling. By the time he'd reached the first floor, the fire had progressed. Opening the basement door, his vision was hampered. Thick with black clouds, the kitchen had begun to burn. Sirens blared through the crackle of the flames.

Garrett fell to his knees and coughed, attempting to orient himself. He crouched low to the floor to avoid the toxic air as he dragged Lars' body across the tiles. Feeling his way through the darkness, he located the back door, and forced it open, exiting into the yard. Garrett screamed for help and heaved for breath. Within seconds, Nate arrived and lifted Lars into his arms. Garrett shoved to his feet and hunched over, still choking for air. Paramedics arrived at his side and his vision blurred as a mask was forced onto his face. He sucked in oxygen and the haze cleared, bringing clarity to the situation.

Lars coughed and his eyes fluttered open, and Garrett knew that whoever had done this to him had created the ultimate diversion. This time, however, the killer hadn't killed Lars. No, whoever had done this had quietly subdued him without making a noise. Although Lars was covered in blood, the perpetrator had walked away unmarked, easily slipping into the party unnoticed.

Adrenaline surged through his veins as things came together in Garrett's mind. He tore around the front of the mansion, looking for Selby. Dazed guests sat on the lawn, and first responders attended to the injured. Screaming her name, he searched frantically, to no avail. It hit him like a ton of bricks raining from the sky, and he doubled over in despair. Selby was gone.

Chapter Twenty-Nine

Selby stared at the concrete block walls, her vision adjusting to the dark. Left alone with her thoughts, she took deep breaths, determined not to allow her anxiety to become a greater monster than the one who'd kidnapped her. A computer screen flickered in the corner, illuminating the dirty laminate floor. She stifled the urge to scream as a roach scurried across her foot. Selby tugged again on the twine he'd used to tie her arms to the chair, but was unable to loosen it. As her thoughts drifted to Garrett, she prayed he'd made it out safely.

Her legs had weakened, watching him run into the burning building. She'd wanted to go after him but she'd have only put them both in danger by doing so. Within minutes, the firemen and policemen arrived on the scene, and the guests were cordoned off on the lawn. When Beckett had suggested she leave, she'd steadfastly refused, staring mindlessly at the billowing smoke that spewed from the windows. Tears fell as minutes passed and Garrett didn't return.

When Beckett had put his arm around her, she'd gone still, uncomfortable with the intimacy. As she attempted to shove away, her eyes flew to his. A sharp metal implement pressed into her back, causing her to freeze. He dug his fingers into her shoulder, nearly bringing her to her knees, and instructed her not to say a word or he'd shoot others at the scene. Separating her from the crowd, he'd managed to get her into his BMW, forcing her at gunpoint to drive to his home in the desert.

When Selby had resisted getting out of the car, he'd dragged her by the hair. She'd fallen onto the dusty gravel, scraping her arms and legs. But she'd refused to cry as he led her down into the cellar. She wouldn't give him the satisfaction of her tears.

The door creaked open and Selby steeled her nerves, awaiting his presence. The movement of his feet stomping down the stairs gave her warning that he'd grown more agitated.

"Where's the data?" Beckett rushed toward her and grabbed her shoulders.

"I don't know what you're talking about," she lied.

As the back of his hand hit her cheek, she saw stars. The chair tumbled to the ground and her head smacked onto the hard surface. Disoriented, she coughed as she inhaled dust. Selby tasted the coppery tang of blood on her tongue, and her eyes teared in pain. As he righted her chair, her head bobbed as if she were a ragdoll.

"Listen, you fucking bitch. I know Evan took the data."

"I told you…" Selby lifted her mascara-stained lids and glared at him. "I don't have it."

"Where's he keeping it?" He whipped a gun from behind his back and tapped her under her chin. "Yeah, that's right. I heard the boss man talking about it tonight."

"Why would you do this? Your brother…" Selby gasped as he wrapped his fingers around her neck. Her lips tightened, and she was unable to speak another word.

"Shut your mouth, you stupid cunt. My brother was a weak piece of shit. He could have been a millionaire like that asshole you're fucking. But no, no, no."

Selby sucked breath as he released her throat and began to pace.

"What a fucking idiot. He wasn't ruining this for me. And you're not stopping me either. No way. I have a buyer. I'm going to be rich. Emerson will bring the files and then I'm out of here."

"Where can you possibly run? He'll find you."

"There's a couple dozen countries I can name off the top of my head that don't have extradition treaties, but it doesn't matter really. The people who want this data, they've got deep pockets. He'll never find me. None of them will."

"Evan…"

"Evan suspected someone had been in the files. I just knew that asshole would figure out how to wipe it all. But I also knew he had it somewhere in his possession. The day before his jump, when I asked him why the project was stalled…" Beckett huffed, kicking a storage box. "The dick was such a braggart. I knew he couldn't keep it a secret. He took the damn files. Had them safe with him, he said."

"But why kill him?" Selby tried to keep him talking. If Garrett didn't bring the drive soon, she'd be dead. There was no reason to keep her alive.

"It was impulsive on my part, but I needed more time to search his apartment. I didn't even know if he'd actually die. I was hoping to land him in the hospital, so I had more time to search his office, all his damn properties. When he died…well, that was an unfortunate accident." Beckett came behind Selby and knelt, grabbing her breast. "Oh yeah…I could have fucked you so good. When Garrett hired you, well," he scoffed. "I knew it would be more difficult to get what I needed. You see, I went through Evan's home office. I found all his credit card statements. I knew everywhere he'd been for over a month. That's right, Selby. I know."

Selby went silent, aware that he'd discovered that Evan had come to her club.

"I knew when you came on board that you were involved. You and Evan. How long were you fucking? You spread your legs for all the guys, huh? Garrett must love having a little whore like you." He pinched at her nipple, and she screamed. "Evan gave it to you, didn't he? I mean who else would know how to access the systems? He used you and you didn't even know it. Perfect really. Except now, I need that data."

"But that night in my apartment…" Selby's mind

swam, trying to figure out who had attacked her. Beckett had been at the party.

"You didn't think I'd break into your apartment when everyone expected me to be at Altura? I told you…I've got a buyer, someone with money. It was easy for me to get someone to help me out with your place."

"You paid someone to plant the cameras?"

"No, that was my doing, but I couldn't actually be there."

"You paid them to attack me?"

"No, no, no. They were only supposed to get the drive. That's the only reason you're alive right now. The asshole I hired didn't have the balls to take you out."

Selby blew out a breath as he released her, and circled her chair. He reached into his back pocket and pulled out his cell phone. As he tapped at the glass, her stomach dropped.

"Shouldn't be long now. Garrett will bring the data, and once he does, you both can die together."

Selby remained silent, allowing him to think he'd won. He stomped up the steps, and she defiantly scanned the room for a way to free herself. In the corner, she spied a pile of boxes. Lifting onto her toes, she attempted to hop to them. But as she hoisted upward, the chair teetered. She screamed as it toppled onto its side, her shoulder slamming into the cement. Throbbing pain stabbed throughout her body, her eyes filling with tears as the dirt-tinged air hit her tongue. Gathering her strength, she focused her effort. If she didn't do something, she'd die.

Shoving with her feet, Selby propelled herself forward. Inch by inch, she moved, undaunted by her task. By the time she reached the boxes, exhaustion had set in, and she barely had enough energy to breathe. With her teeth, she bit at the cardboard, turning the contents out onto the floor. She closed her eyes as the items spilled around her.

A metal object clanged onto the floor and her fingertips brushed at the gritty earth. A sharp edge prodded at her fingertips and she worked it into the rope that bound her wrists, sawing at it. It released with a pop, and she cried with relief. Selby shoved herself up so she sat leaning against the wall. He'd come for her, she knew. She might die today but it would not be without a fight. Slipping the tool into the front of her dress, she waited for the beast.

Enraged, Garrett sped down the highway. He'd never killed a man, but today, with a weapon on board, the possibility that he would existed. Unable to find Selby or Beckett at the scene of the fire, Garrett suspected he'd taken her. As soon as he'd received the text demanding the data, he'd gone home, retrieved his gun and taken off in the car. Beckett had specifically told him, no police. Logic warned him to let the police handle the situation, but his heart told him that he couldn't risk having the love of his life killed.

On the way to get Selby, he'd called Lars, asking him

to notify Dean of the GPS coordinates. By the time he arrived, it would make little difference. With a dummy file in his pocket, he planned to hand over the data. Beckett would check it, he knew, but Garrett had already scrubbed the data, fabricating the PFx Prototype etiology as well as any preliminary results. As a matter of national security, he couldn't allow it to fall into enemy hands.

As he pulled into the gated property, he took note of the brown land, 'no trespassing' signs littered along its perimeter. Spirals of dust spun into the air as he rolled up the mile-long driveway. Noting the desolate surroundings, he considered how he'd never known Beckett or Cormac the way he'd imagined. Clearances were of little consequence when someone went into hiding, living off the grid.

Slowly he decelerated as the modest ranch came into view and he concentrated on the task in hand. Garrett turned off the car, leaving the keys in the ignition. He reached for his weapon and tucked it into the back of his pants. Garrett gritted his teeth as the front door swung open and Beckett shoved Selby out the door. His rage exploded as he caught sight of her stumbling forth. She limped, her lip bloodied and her face pale. Beckett waved his gun in the air, and then pointed it at her.

As if he were hanging by the ledge of a cliff, Garrett breathed in through his nose and blew out the breath, deliberately calming his nerves. Whatever was about to go down, he'd approach it with the focus and precision of a sniper. He curled his fingers under the car door handle and clicked it open. Slowly he exited, with his hands held out wide. Garrett put one foot in front of the other until he and Beckett were only twenty feet apart.

Selby's eyes teared up as they locked on his. She made a move to lunge for him, but Beckett jerked her back. Garrett resisted the urge to go to her, carefully guarding his emotions. The whirl of blades buzzed in the background, a private helicopter hovering in the distance.

"The drive," Beckett called. "Did you bring it?"

"I brought it." Garrett reached into the front pocket of his jeans, but stilled as Beckett fired off a shot into the sky.

"Easy. I said no weapons."

"Just getting what you asked for."

"Do it now." Beckett raised his line of vision to the approaching aircraft.

Garrett waved the drive in the air. "Selby first. Then you can have it."

"Wrong."

The disc dropped from Garrett's fingers as the hot slice of a bullet tore through his flesh. As he fell to the ground, he struggled to keep his hidden weapon concealed. He rolled onto his back and clutched his arm.

"Stay," Beckett screamed at Selby.

Garrett lay as bait, feigning significant injury. Beckett moved toward him, his gun extended. Garrett lurched onto his side kicking the disc to divert his attention. But instead of reaching for the drive, Beckett trained his aim onto him. A click snapped to his right before he heard the shot, and he caught sight of Selby leaping forward. As she plunged the awl deep into Beckett's shoulder, he flailed his hand around behind him, striking her in the face. The projectile whizzed aimlessly through the air, missing Garrett. He reached for his own gun, firing off a round and hitting Beckett in the lower abdomen. Beckett faltered, staggering into the dust.

Garrett's heart pounded as he ran to Selby's side. Breathless, he fell to his knees and carefully cradled her in his arms, still aiming his weapon at Beckett. Garrett's chest heaved as a fresh wave of pain rolled through his body. The helicopter rotated away from the house, and he kept his eyes on both Beckett and the aircraft, anticipating its return.

The sound of police sirens echoed in the desert, and he breathed a sigh of relief. Selby clutched at him, sobbing, and he placed his hand onto the dirt, still stunned. His vision blurred and he knew at that moment, he'd lost too much blood. A tunnel of darkness closed in on him and the last thing he heard was Selby shouting his name.

Chapter Thirty

Selby lay in bed, watching Garrett sleep. It had been two weeks since he'd been shot. The bullet had grazed an artery and he'd spent the night at the hospital. Although he'd recovered nicely, the blood loss had been significant. Selby's facial bruises had faded but the trauma of Beckett's betrayal would take far longer for them to forget.

Neither Garrett nor Dean had been able to ascertain who Beckett planned to sell the data to, the clandestine accomplice having gone underground. With the brazen efforts to steal the data, they suspected whoever had helped Beckett might step up their effort to infiltrate Emerson Industries or one of its affiliates. Determined to clear house, Garrett had ordered a complete investigation of every employee in his company, triple checking clearances.

Selby and Lars had begun the transition of internal servers and applications to a secure offsite location, ensuring that any last remnants of Evan's hidden program had been removed. Selby was implementing stringent measures to ensure the protection of Emerson's corporate and intellectual property. Despite their work, she was aware that hackers never ceased their efforts; even the most impenetrable systems were still subject to security breaches.

Selby glanced at Garrett, and considered how happy she'd been. Despite their ordeal, they'd been able to spend time together alone. Garrett had arranged to move all her things into his home, and she'd been surprised how easily they'd fallen into a comfortable routine. Since the accident, they hadn't been to the office, however, and they hadn't discussed her leaving Emerson. Soon her work would be finished, and if he agreed to a few of the candidates she'd selected, she'd be off to her next client within the month.

Garrett stirred and her heart blossomed, grateful for his love. She gently played with his soft curls, and placed a kiss onto his head. He gave a soft moan, and she smiled. Aware he needed his rest, Selby retreated, leaving him in his slumber. Scooting over, she quietly sat onto the bed's edge. A squeal escaped her lips as a strong arm wrapped around her waist, and she fell back into bed.

"Where do you think you're going?" Garrett asked with a sleepy smile.

"Nowhere," she lied.

"Did I tell you how much I loved you today?" Garrett snuggled his face into her hair and kissed her head.

"Hmm...I don't think so."

"I do love you...so much."

"I love you, too. I don't think I'll ever get tired of

hearing you say it." She pressed her lips gently to his chest.

"I've been thinking."

"Uh oh."

"Be nice, woman." He hugged her tightly against him. "I want to steal you from Lars. Now Lars said you weren't his to steal, but I'm serious in that I want you to stay at Emerson. You're the best at what you do. I know the board will agree. Even though Evan had a hand in a lot of different projects, his position was CTO. You can do it with your eyes closed."

"You sure? I won't lie, I wasn't relishing the thought of traveling, being away from you."

"I've never been more sure of anything."

"I accept." She beamed. "Lars won't be happy, though."

"We'll think of something to make it up to him."

Selby smiled. Although she'd miss working at DLar-Tech, she was thrilled at the opportunity to stay on with Garrett. "Okay, it's settled then. But you should let me go call him."

"Oh no, you don't. I need you to stay with me, Nurse Reynolds." His hand found her breast. Caressing it, he elicited a small moan from Selby.

"Hmm….you are a very naughty patient, Mr. Emerson. You should be resting."

"I've rested enough. I need therapy." Garrett's lips grazed over her neck. "The kind only you can give me."

"Is that so?" Selby rolled over onto his chest, so she could look in his eyes. They hadn't made love since his injury. Selby, on the precipice of coming from his slightest touch, had resisted, worried that he'd reinjure his arm. Selby's heart fluttered as he gave her a sexy grin.

"You know a man can't live on food and water alone?" Garrett cupped her face, dragging his thumb over her lower lip. "I'm not sure I'm going to make it."

"You sure you're up for it?" Her body sizzled with arousal, all her willpower draining away. Selby threw her leg over his and straddled him. Fisting his cock into her hand, she brushed his seeping seed over its head.

"That's right, sweetheart. You know, I've been thinking…ah…" he cried as she swiped his steely shaft through her folds. "Jesus, you're wicked."

"You were saying," she laughed, enjoying how she could master his body. Within seconds, she knew he'd turn the tables on her, his dominance rising to the surface.

"I've had a lot of time on my hands…to think."

"Have you now?"

"Indeed." Garrett flipped Selby onto her back, pinning her arms to the bed.

"Hey, watch your arm. You're going to hurt yourself," she cried. His cock prodded her belly and she tilted her pelvis up toward him. He released one of her arms. Taking his dick into his hand, he grazed its hard tip over her swollen clit. "Ahh…Garrett."

"Hmm…that's more like it." He brought her palm up to his lips and smiled. "You're right, though. I could use a little help here. You see this pussy here needs attention, and since I'm injured…"

Selby moaned as he sucked her fingers into his mouth, twirling his tongue over them.

"Mmm." He released them with a pop, and guided her hand into her folds. Intertwining his fingers with hers, he brought them up and over her swollen clitoris. "Just seeing you spread wide open for me." He sat on his heels, her thighs open to him. He stroked his cock while she pleasured herself. "This is the medicine I needed, sweetheart."

"You're teasing me." Selby shuddered as he pressed his cock to her entrance.

"Like my little feisty nurse has been doing to me all week?"

"Just making sure you're healed properly. It appears my course of treatment has been successful." Selby smiled, yearning to have him fill her. "Now I'm the one suffering."

"I've got what you need."

"Ease my pain?"

"Always." Garrett smiled as he gently rocked inside her.

Selby reached for him, alive with desire as his lips took hers. With passion, she tasted her lover. Engaged in the intimacy of their love, they moved together as one in a sensual rhythm.

"I love you," he spoke into her mouth.

"I love you...ah, I missed you so much." Selby arched into his slow thrusts, his pelvis grazing over her throbbing nub. Every inch of her skin, every cell in her body sang in harmony, she was so in love with Garrett, grateful for how he'd changed her life. He'd peeled away her confining cocoon of fear, exposing the butterfly that yearned to fly.

"My sweet Selby," she heard him whisper, his lips on her collarbone.

"You're everything to me." Selby held his head to her breast as he placed sensual kisses on her skin.

She moaned as her climax splintered through her, his deliberate thrusts demanding her surrender to ecstasy. Her palms glided down his contoured glutes and she strained to keep him inside her. Selby arched up to meet him, writhing as the last spasms of her orgasm twisted through her body. Breathless, she floated into euphoria.

Garrett surged into her, releasing the explosive orgasm that he'd held at bay. With a glorious cry, he seized against her as his fierce orgasm claimed him. Garrett rolled her over into his embrace, pleased when she wrapped herself around him, her arms and legs enveloping him in her warmth.

In the silent moment that followed, nothing and no one existed in the universe but their two hearts. Garrett considered every dangerous activity he'd engaged in in an effort to capture the elusive rush that reminded him he was alive. Not one of them came close to Selby Reynolds, and he knew at that moment, it wouldn't matter if he never jumped again. He'd fall for her a million times over, knowing that his love for her brought a completeness and happiness he'd revel in for the rest of his life.

Epilogue

Lars drove toward the beach and sighed. His brush with death had made him reconsider what he'd been doing with his life. Watching Garrett and Selby fall in love had been bittersweet. It wasn't as if he thought he and Selby would be together, but he'd be lying not to admit that she'd held a piece of his heart. Although they hadn't discussed it, he knew Garrett would want her to work for him at Emerson Industries. What his friend didn't know was that Selby had already turned in her resignation.

Lars wasn't looking for a permanent relationship. Far from it; he'd been perfectly content with his bachelor lifestyle. He was lonely, bored perhaps. If anything, he rejoiced in his eclectic sexual tastes, aware that he could indulge whenever and wherever it struck his fancy.

As Lars pulled over and parked, he caught sight of Seth floating over a wave, the sunset slowly sinking into the horizon. They maybe had an hour left of sunlight, he knew. He wasn't the greatest surfer on the face of the planet, but he loved the ocean and enjoyed hanging out with Seth. Like Garrett, they'd forged a strong friendship based on trust and their enjoyment of Altura.

Lars shoved out of his car and grabbed his board. Carefully navigating the stone steps down the cliff, he gave Seth a wave. The rolling surf swelled but didn't appear too rough. He scanned the beach, noting the yellow flag. With moderate currents, they'd expect some difficulty but not an exceptionally dangerous ride.

He plunged his arms into his suit, and zipped up before heading toward the water. A swell rushed toward him and he threw his surfboard into the waves. Paddling on his belly, he swam toward Seth.

"Hey, bro. How's the head?" Seth asked.

"I'm good. Fucking Beckett." Lars sat up, floating on the surface.

"Fucking Beckett is right. What does Dean think about the guys who helped him?"

"He's not sure. Could've been a terrorist outside the country. But who the hell knows? I just, uh..." He paused and raked his hands through his hair.

"What?"

"I have a feeling that whoever it was, maybe it was personal. Garrett, he's made a lot of enemies. Even the ones who act like friends. Even in Altura, we've met lots of people over the years where things didn't always turn out for the best. Most of us are successful because of Garrett. But jealousy? Over the money? I'm just sayin', if they had the power to get into Emerson and touch Beckett..." He shook his head and glanced back to the dropping sun.

"And who really knows about Evan? I know Garrett still has faith that he wasn't involved. I guess that I'm not so sure it's over."

"I hear ya, man. We're all pretty lucky. When you look at our companies, all that's going on, there's lots of things worth stealing."

"True that."

"I'm going," Lars called and took off as the wave swelled.

Paddling to catch it, he pressed up to his feet. The familiar rush tore through him as he propelled through the tube, his fingers skimming the face of the water.

In his peripheral vision, he caught the shadow at the top of the cliff holding the pistol. A woman stumbled down the stairs, falling onto the sand. As she shoved onto her feet and began to run, Lars pitched on his board, bailing into the ocean. Rising through water, he gasped for air as gunshots echoed in the air. The bullets spun sand up into the air as the spray missed the woman.

The shooter began to fire off rounds at Lars. As the slugs splashed into the sea, he dove to avoid them, holding his breath underneath the wave. As he broke through the surface, gasping for air, his eyes darted to the cliff, but the gunman had disappeared. His vision focused in on the beach where the victim lay injured, the beige-colored sand stained red.

Without hesitation, he swam to shore. Running toward the victim, he fell to his knees in front of her. The gorgeous stranger blinked up at him, blood streaming from her wound. Another shot sounded, and he scooped her up, tearing toward an alcove in the cliff. Cradling her in his arms, he carried her into the darkened cave. He brushed away her long brown hair, and searched for her wound. Tearing her jean jacket away, he applied pressure to her shoulder.

"Hel...help me," she stammered.

"I've got you," he told her.

Lars attention went to the breakers and he caught sight of Seth's head bobbing out of the surf in the distance. He thanked God he hadn't been hit. The silence of the moment was cut with her soft cries.

"We've got to get you to the ER." Lars stared into her piercing green eyes, wondering why the hell someone would attack her in broad daylight.

"No...he's coming for me," she coughed. "He's coming for...you."

"Stay with me now." Sirens wailed in the distance and his heart tightened as she appeared to fade away. "It's going to be okay."

"Help me...Lars..." her words trailed away as her eyes fluttered shut.

As unconsciousness claimed the beautiful stranger in his arms, Lars' pulse raced. It wasn't the first time in his life he'd been scared; the rush of skirting death drove him to do the things he did. Holding her to his chest, he wondered how she knew his name, and prayed like hell she'd survive to tell him.

Erotic Romance by Kym Grosso

Club Altura Romance

Solstice Burn
(A Club Altura Romance Novella, Prequel)

Carnal Risk
(A Club Altura Romance Novel, Book 1)

Lars' Story
(A Club Altura Romance Novel, Book 2) Coming 2016

The Immortals of New Orleans

Kade's Dark Embrace
(Immortals of New Orleans, Book 1)

Luca's Magic Embrace
(Immortals of New Orleans, Book 2)

Tristan's Lyceum Wolves
(Immortals of New Orleans, Book 3)

Logan's Acadian Wolves
(Immortals of New Orleans, Book 4)

Léopold's Wicked Embrace
(Immortals of New Orleans, Book 5)

Dimitri
(Immortals of New Orleans, Book 6)

Lost Embrace
(Immortals of New Orleans, Book 6.5)

Jax's Story
(Immortals of New Orleans, Book 7)
Coming Fall 2015

About the Author

Kym Grosso is the USA Today bestselling and award-winning author of the erotic romance series, *The Immortals of New Orleans and Club Altura.* In addition to romance, Kym has written and published several articles about autism, and is a contributing essay author in *Chicken Soup for the Soul: Raising Kids on the Spectrum.*

Kym lives with her family in Pennsylvania, and her hobbies include reading, tennis, zumba, and spending time with her husband and children. She loves traveling just about anywhere that has a beach or snow-covered mountains. New Orleans, with its rich culture, history and unique cuisine, is one of her favorite places to visit.

• • • •

Social Media/Links:

Website: http://www.KymGrosso.com
Facebook: http://www.facebook.com/KymGrossoBooks
Twitter: https://twitter.com/KymGrosso
Pinterest: http://www.pinterest.com/kymgrosso/

Sign up for Kym's Newsletter to get Updates and Information about New Releases:
http://www.kymgrosso.com/members-only

Printed in Great Britain
by Amazon